I0661684

Dead Man's Wine

A Sarah McKee Mystery, Volume 1

Parker French

Published by Lucky Publishing, 2023.

DEAD MAN'S WINE

First edition. August 3, 2023.

Copyright © 2023 Parker French.

ISBN: 978-1735082844

Written by Parker French.

Also by Parker French

A Sarah McKee Mystery
Dead Man's Wine

Table of Contents

Deceit always returns to its master.

—*French Proverb*

Chapter 1 | The Crime Scene

Wine expert Sarah McKee had never heard of a person being killed over a bottle of wine. Killed *by* a bottle, sure. She was from Glasgow, Scotland where broken bottles were used as weapons in pub brawls. A broken bottle jabbed into the throat could be deadly. But in all her forty-one years—twenty of them working in the wine industry—she'd never heard of anyone being killed *because* of a bottle. And never in Northern California wine country where she had lived for the past two years. People in Sonoma were too civilized to commit physical violence. At least, that's what she had assumed.

Until today.

Sarah drove to the Boyes Hot Springs crime scene on the northern outskirts of Sonoma, all the while wondering what had happened and why—because she had been summoned by her law enforcement friend to assist in the initial investigation of a homicide. All Sarah had been told about the murder was that the victim may have had something to do with wine.

In Sonoma, that wasn't saying much.

Sarah motored into the parking lot of an apartment building a block from the highway, parked, extricated herself from her Triumph Spitfire convertible and tossed her baseball cap onto the passenger seat. As she raked her shoulder-length hair into a semblance of its former style, she wondered if she would ever be able to get out of her tiny car like a movie star—all legs and grace. So far, she hadn't achieved such a feat. No matter how hard she tried, she always found it a struggle to rise from the sportscar, what with her generous figure and long legs. And the way her weight was headed these days, she guessed the extrication was only going to get more difficult.

She skirted three Sonoma County law enforcement vehicles parked helter-skelter near the sidewalk and then climbed the external stairway to apartment 317. The apartment was constructed like a motel, with the walkways and doors on the exterior of the building. No need for protection from the elements, as it rarely rained in wine country.

A section of the balcony had been cordoned off with yellow Do Not Cross tape. In the cordoned off section, one apartment vibrated with the base of a hip hop song so loud that it induced her to clamp her hands over her ears. Grimacing, she ducked under the tape and plowed through the noise to the next door, all the while fighting to catch her breath.

She really did have to start going to the gym.

The door opened. Detective Kelley Miller, her husband's steady customer and now her friend, waved her in. Sarah smiled at her auburn-haired pal, whose petite frame looked hippy and squat in her green uniform trousers. The pants were snug in all the wrong places for a woman and cut too short. The bulky utility belt only made things worse. In her police get-up, Kelley looked like a kid standing in a swim ring.

"Hey, that was quick, Sarah," Kelley greeted. "Just got here myself."

"Happy to oblige."

"Gotta put these on, though. Sorry." Kelley held out a white hazmat jumpsuit, complete with booties. "The crime scene investigation unit has done a preliminary walk through. But we're waiting on the warrant to do the forensics. The new boss is a stickler."

"No shirt, no shoes, no service, eh?" Sarah commented, reminded of the signs in the many restaurants her husband had worked in on his way up.

"Something like that." Kelley stepped into the legs of her jumpsuit.

Sarah pulled on her garment as well. She would do anything for her friend Kelley. Women on their own in Sonoma had to stick together. There were so few of them. She knew firsthand what a lonely, isolating existence it could be flying solo in this foodie paradise of film festivals, pool parties and fund raisers. Sarah wasn't exactly single, but she often attended events alone since her chef husband Matteo worked most nights and holidays. Over the years, she had learned to develop a social network outside her marriage to keep her sanity.

She pulled the zipper to her collarbone and held out her arms. "How do I look?" she asked. "Fetching?"

"Not without these." Kelley held out two blue latex gloves.

Sarah yanked them on and held up her hands. "Now?"

"And these." Kelley slipped what looked like a shower cap and mask out of the pocket of her jumpsuit.

Sarah did the same and plopped the bonnet on her strawberry-blond hair. She fumbled with the mask to get it over her ears. "Now?"

"Now." Grinning, Kelley waved her into the main room of the apartment and then put on her own mask.

Sarah shuffled across the rug to the center of the living room, trying not to inhale the offensive polyester aroma of her suit. She could smell it, even through the mask. To get her mind off the odor, she looked around, taking in every detail, and was shocked by the clutter in the small space.

Instead of a couch and chairs, folding tables hugged two walls, one piled with paper, a paper cutter, T-square and drawing board and equipment. Another held a printer and jars of glue, brushes, various hues of ink and what looked like dirt. A power cord to a computer lay across the table like a severed umbilical cord. The computer was nowhere to be seen. A single ladderback chair had been scooted against the table with the rulers and pencils.

An expensive turntable and speakers sitting atop a case of albums dominated the adjoining wall under a picture window. Wooden wine boxes were stuffed beneath the printer table, all stamped with logos of the finest wineries in Sonoma and Napa. Every item in the room looked as though it had been ransacked and abandoned.

"What the hell?" Sarah muttered.

"We thought it was a counterfeit money operation at first," Kelley remarked behind her. "But then the boss saw the wine bottles, and I thought of calling you."

"What wine bottles?"

"The ones in the kitchen. There are dozens of them."

Sarah followed Kelley into the kitchen, which was located on the other side of the living room wall. Cardboard boxes full of used wine bottles and corks were stacked everywhere—on the floor, the counters and the stove. Bottles floated in the sink, their labels disintegrating. Scraping tools glinted on the right side of the sink and a reeking sponge lay on the left. Bottles of Goo Gone, dishwashing liquid and acetone stood near the tools. Apparently, the task of removing labels was not easy.

Not a sign of cooking could be seen, except for a coffee maker hugging a cloudy carafe that looked as if it hadn't been washed in decades. A box of nitrile gloves sat next to it, spewing bright purple fingers. She opened the cupboards. Nothing but a few bottles of hot sauce, a bag of coffee and some packets of soy sauce.

Intrigued, Sarah pulled open the refrigerator. It was warmer than normal. She looked at the settings. The temperature had been dialed up to a red-friendly fifty-five degrees. Quart mason jars full of purple liquid sat on the shelves and were marked with strange abbreviations: SECS12, DSE80 and PVZ16.

"What the hell?" Sarah said again. She reached for a jar but stopped in midair to turn to Kelley. "May I?"

"The CSI guys said the kitchen was clear, so have at it."

Sarah picked up the jar and placed it on the counter. She lifted the glass lid and bent to the rim to take a sniff.

"Hmm."

"What do you smell?" Kelley asked, stepping closer. "What is it?"

"The fridge has chilled it way too much," Sarah took another sniff. "But I'd hazard a guess that this is a really smooth Burgundy Pinot Noir once it gets up to room temperature. Probably a 1980 Grand Cru, judging by the high notes. From the Cote d'Or region. Cotes de Nuits to be exact. I'm picking up an unmistakable mushroom bouquet."

"You can tell all that by the smell?"

"*Aye.*" She tapped her prominent nose with a gloved finger. "That's what this Scottish beak is for, *ye ken.*" Sarah tipped the jar and looked at the handwritten label. "Hmm. DSE80. Domaine St. Emile Pinot Noir, I would guess." She swirled the purple liquid. "Color is off. Although it's hard to judge in this jar."

"Man, they don't pay you the big bucks for nothing!"

"They certainly don't." Sarah winked at her friend. "And I'm worth every shilling."

"So, what do you think went on here?"

Sarah paused and thought about all that she had just seen. She was aware, murder notwithstanding, of the criminal element that could surround wine. Grapes were like precious stones. Put certain grapes in the hands of a master winemaker, keep them long enough, and some wines became as rare as gems. Just as valuable, too, and worthy of being coveted, collected and bequeathed in wills—like heirloom jewelry. But when it came to crime, there the similarities ended.

If a gem was stolen, everyone knew about it. The news hit the papers and people discussed the heist for days—the Marlborough Diamond that vanished, the Comtesse de Vendome necklace snatched from a Tokyo jewelry store, The

Blue Diamond affair that fouled international relations between Thailand and Saudi Arabia, and the half-egg mystery of the Great Mogul Diamond—to name a few.

But when a rare wine was involved in a criminal activity, the act usually went unreported. Such an incident was shut away in the dark, and with hope, soon forgotten—something to hide in the cellar. Literally. No self-respecting wine collector wanted to admit he'd been duped or robbed or discover his collection might include fakes. Or worse, that he had served a knock-off unaware, and some discerning guest might have suspected and told all her friends. A wine lover's reputation was as important as his collection. Passing counterfeits, even innocently, could be ruinous.

But of all the wine crimes Sarah knew about, none had involved murder.

Still deep in thought, Sarah replaced the lid on the jar and returned it to the fridge. Then she straightened. "Well, if I were a generous lass, I'd say someone was planning an elaborate April Fool's trick."

"And if you weren't so generous?"

"I'd say someone was making counterfeit vino."

"Jesus," Kelley exclaimed. "And someone got killed for it?"

"Looks like it," a male voice boomed behind them.

Surprised, Sarah turned to see a male police officer she didn't recognize standing in the doorway. His drugstore aftershave enveloped her, blotting out the odor of the jumpsuit she wore.

She didn't know which smell was worse.

"Sheriff Bradley," Kelley said. "This is my friend, the wine expert. Sarah McKee."

"Pleased to meet you," Sarah said, holding out her hand.

The new guy was an outstanding physical specimen, and his lean body and earnest gaze surprised her. Most senior police officers she'd met were older, paunchy men who were too jaded and out of shape to trot after suspects, much less catch them. This sheriff looked as if he ran marathons every day and won all of them. He was a head taller than she was, perhaps a few years younger, too—although it was difficult to gauge with his chiseled features and clean-shaven head.

Light played off his shining temples, alert black eyes and prominent cheekbones. She could tell in a single glance that this police officer was not a member of the good old boy network—and didn't want to be. Even the fluffy shower cap couldn't offset his intense expression.

He shook her hand and was noncommittal with the friendliness angle, like most law enforcement officers when she first met them. She'd have to work on this one.

"You're the new guy," Sarah ventured.

"Yep."

"Welcome to Sonoma."

He nodded, still not friendly.

"Come into Olive, and your meal's on us. We take care of our own here. Especially our peace officers."

"Her husband Matteo owns the Olive restaurant," Kelley put in. "It's the best place in town."

"Just might do that."

He shifted his weight, looking uncomfortable with the small-town chatter. Then another man in a crime scene suit came up and said something near his ear. The sheriff bent down to listen to what the short man said.

"The medical examiner," Kelley explained. "From Santa Rosa."

"Ah," Sarah said. Then the implication of the comment hit her. "The body is still here?"

"Yes," Kelley said. "In the bedroom."

"Can I see?" Sarah asked, stepping toward the sheriff. "I might be able to identify the person."

"Not unless you can ID him by his clothing," Bradley warned. He held out his arms and splayed his bootie-covered feet to block her exit from the kitchen.

Bradley made an imposing barricade. Something about his stance and stature caused the breath to catch in her throat. The man had presence.

Sarah remained in place. "What do you mean?"

"His face has been blown off."

"Oh, my *gawd*!"

"Plus, the medical examiner needs peace and quiet to do his job—with no interference from the public."

"Sarah isn't exactly the public," Kelley protested. When Bradley glared at her, she added, "Sir."

His dark glare raked off his junior officer to settle on Sarah. "Know any red-headed men? Say thirty-some years old? Journey fan?"

"Journey?" Her musical knowledge was not nearly as extensive as her wine expertise, but even a foreigner like her was familiar with Journey, the most popular group to come out of San Francisco in the 1970s. "Why do you assume he was a Journey fan? Is he clutching an 8-track tape?"

Bradley ignored the wisecrack. "No, he's wearing a tee-shirt."

"What thirty-year old listens to Journey?" Kelley shook her head, baffled. "You gotta wonder."

"That is not what you are supposed to be wondering about, sergeant," Bradley snapped.

Sarah leveled a dour stare at the sheriff. He might have an attractive physique, but his personality was beginning to annoy her. He had no sense of humor and was throwing his weight around. She had no patience for his particular type. She'd walked off jobs because of men like Bradley. "With all due respect, sheriff, it is what Kelley should be wondering about."

"I beg your pardon?"

"The victim must be a person who appreciates the finer things in life. A connoisseur. Like the 1980 Domaine St. Emile in the fridge."

"The Domaine Saint what?" Bradley snorted.

"A rare wine. In the fridge. I think whoever's dead in the bedroom was making counterfeit wine."

"In an apartment?"

"Yes, like an art forger paints in an attic. Fake labels, fake bottles and fake corks. But a guy with an eye and palate that's discerning enough to pull it off."

"A thirty-year old wine forger?"

"That's right."

"In an apartment? Not a factory or warehouse?"

"The forger could have made enough here to live on and more. A single bottle of a rare wine can sell for five or six figures."

Sheriff Bradley narrowed his eyes and contemplated the sink as he considered her words. His neck, the only part of his body that wasn't sequestered in polyester, looked as if it was made of steel cables from the Golden Gate Bridge. He bit his generous lower lip between his teeth and then blew out a puff of air. His stare swung back to her, evaluating her as he digested her theory. From the expression on his stern face, he didn't appreciate the taste.

"If that's what he was doing, where's the goods?" He swept the air with a bony hand. The wingspan of his fingers and palm rivaled that of a Celtic goalie. "All we have are empties."

"And no incriminating labels," Kelley mused. "Just those wine boxes in the living room."

Sarah nodded as her thoughts hummed with all that she had seen here.

"Every inch of this place will be searched," Bradley said. "We'll find something. We'll find out who he is."

"Why don't you know already?" Sarah couldn't understand why the dead man's identification was such a mystery. "Don't you have his wallet?"

"Wasn't on him."

"His car's got to be down there in the parking lot. Someone must have noticed what car the guy drives. You could check the registration."

"On it already. Officers are consulting the manager."

"Who's a real nosy bastard by the by," Kelley said. "He waylaid me on the way up. Grabbed me by the uniform."

"Lovely," Sarah snorted. "You'd think he'd do something about the music next door."

"Which probably covered up the sound of the gunshot," the sheriff put in.

"Can't the manager tell us who's renting this unit?"

"He says the victim was not the legal tenant."

"What about fingerprints?"

"Checking," Bradley said. "But from all appearances, the guy wore gloves."

"Yes, I noticed." Sarah leaned against the counter, always intrigued by a puzzle. "I'll tell you what. I can do some research. See who has sold 1980 DSE at auction recently or is selling it online. I might be able to track down his name that way. That is, if he was working alone—which he probably wasn't."

"That would be helpful." Sheriff Bradley sighed and let his arms fall to the side. "Tell Detective Miller what you find."

Sarah nodded as a third officer appeared at Bradley's elbow.

"Sir, we found something."

"Excuse me," Bradley said. He backed out of the kitchen.

When the cloud of his aftershave had dissipated, Sarah pushed away from the counter. "Thank you, Mizz McKee," she quipped, mocking the sheriff's unfriendly attitude. "Thanks so much for coming. You've been a big help. Oh, and nice to meet you. Love Sonoma, by the way. Happy to be here."

Kelley's eyebrows rose as she shrugged. "He's like that."

"Poser."

"Naw, I bet he lives in a rambler in Vallejo with artificial turf on his deck," Kelley remarked behind one hand. "And drinks White Claw."

Sarah rolled her eyes. "That has to change."

They exchanged knowing smiles. No one in Sonoma could ignore the siren call of wine for long.

"So, keep me abreast of what they find out," Sarah turned at the doorway. "Will you?"

"If I can. Sometimes it's confidential."

"I'm curious who the victim is and what he was up to. But listen, Kelley, I have to go. I've got a doctor's appointment."

"Anything wrong?"

"Just some checkup results."

Kelley walked her to the front door and waited as she peeled off the personal protection equipment. "Glass tonight?" she ventured. "Or do you want to walk or something instead?"

"A glass sounds good."

"You, me and Gloria?"

"Perfect." Sarah headed for the yellow barricade.

"See you at seven," Kelley called.

Sarah waved and ducked under the barrier.

She should have elected to walk with Kelley. She should have signed up to the gym like Matteo had when the Covid restrictions eased in March. But after the grueling week she'd endured, she decided that sitting on Kelley's patio, sipping Gloria Ferrer Royal Cuvée and watching the sun go down over Sonoma Mountain was too enticing to pass up.

She trotted down the stairs and headed for the parking lot. When she got to the sidewalk, she noticed a tall, skinny man in a silk robe and cowboy boots pushing a rickety ten-speed bicycle around her car. Pink and white streamers hung from the handlebars. He stopped at the driver's side and leaned in.

"Hey, pal!" Sarah shouted. "Get away from there!"

Chapter 2 | Bicycle Man

The tall man straightened and froze, gawking at her as she hurried across the parking lot. The closer she got, the higher he lifted his free hand to ward her off.

"Wasn't going to touch anything." His whine barely made it out from under his bushy mustache. For a tall person, he had an unexpectedly short voice. "Geeze."

She gave him a once over, wondering if the man posed a threat. She knew she should be worrying about the murderer on the loose, but at the moment, she was more concerned about vehicle defacement. The smell of an expensive botanical-based shampoo mixed with mothballs wafted through the air. Did vandals use high-end shampoo and protect their clothing from insects? Probably not. She surveyed him, from his sloping shoulders to his tousled head.

He had a huge mop of curly brown hair that matched his mustache and wore a pair of aviator-style spectacles. On her trip to Europe this week, Sarah had noticed the oversized style was making a comeback, but this guy's spectacles looked as if he'd worn them since childhood. That would make them thirty years out of date. The same could be said for his too-brief athletic shorts. He was a walking advertisement for what not to wear, circa 1980.

He didn't look even faintly dangerous. In fact, she wondered if—as her Scottish father used to say—the guy's lift went all the way to the top.

"You're in my spot," he said without blinking, one arm hanging limp from his shoulders and one hand clutching the handlebar of his bike. He poked a finger at the curb and let his arm fall back down. "This is where I park."

"I *dinnae* see a sign, pal."

"Hold the phone." He took a step back. His mouth hung open even farther. "Are you Australian?"

Sarah took a breath and tried to muster a sense of humor. After twenty years of the same question from people she first met, she was a bit weary of the game about to be played. Sheriff Bradley had been an exception. He'd made no comment about her accent. But then again, she suspected the man's curiosity about other people was restricted to criminal investigations.

She started to answer Bicycle Man, but he held up his hand again.

"No, wait. Don't tell me. Let me guess." He tilted his curly head and regarded her, delighted with the quiz. His beady brown eyes flashed behind their lenses. "Irish?"

"Close but no cigar."

"English then. You've got to be English. Are you from London? That is so cool."

"English?" She rolled her eyes, disgusted at being tagged once again as a citizen of a country that her people had battled for hundreds of years. "For that, *ye dinnae* deserve an answer."

Sarah pushed past him to her car. He made way for her, his bike clicking as it rolled backward. She wondered how he maneuvered a bike while wearing a voluminous silk robe. Come to think of it, she wondered where he had acquired such a robe. She'd never seen a size that large in all the lingerie departments she shopped in. Over the years, she'd been in plenty of lingerie stores—in an effort to persuade Matteo to quit pursuing a Michelin star and chase her for a change.

"C'mon. I can't think of any other country." He hovered behind her. "Tell me."

"I'm a Glaswegian. Used to be, anyway."

"Ah." He grinned and shook a finger at her. "I knew it! Norway, right? Scandinavia."

Sarah pulled open the car door. "Something like that."

"You're still in my spot, though."

She frowned at him over her shoulder. "You park your bike here?"

"Like I said. It's my spot."

"And like I said, there's no sign."

"Still. It's my spot."

"That's ridiculous. You're riding a bike."

He shoved his glasses up on his nose. "I'm *not* ridiculous."

"I didn't say *ye* were. I'm sayin' that parking a bike here is ridiculous."

He stared at her, his expression blank. She wondered if he were struggling to come up with a line of defense. Not enough came through his thick lenses to give a clue as to what he was thinking—or not thinking, as the case may be.

"It's my spot."

"Fine, pal. You can have it back once you clear out of the way."

"For your information, that's not my name."

"What's not your name?"

"Paul. You keep calling me Paul."

"What is your name?"

"It's Wesley. Wesley Leslie III."

She didn't dare smile. He was as sincere as the sheriff had been. She turned, one hand on the top of the car door.

"Okay, Wesley. *Ye* can have your space back. I was only using it for a minute, while I helped the police."

"Police?" His mouth dropped open again. "What? Are they here?"

"*Ye dinnae* see all the cars?" She swept the air, indicating the front of the building.

He jerked his bushy head around to glance at the apartment complex. She couldn't believe he hadn't noticed the squad cars and caution tape. Perhaps he was nearsighted as well as daft.

"Why are *they* here?" he gasped. "What's going on?" His jaw slackened as he rolled his stare to the third floor. "Hold the phone. That's Woody's house."

"Woody?"

"That's what I call him." He chuckled softly, as if thinking of a private joke. "It's a nickname."

He knew the victim? She observed him more closely. However daft Wesley might be, he might be useful to the case.

Because Kelley's case was now hers.

Once Sarah was presented with a case, she found it impossible to let go. Puzzles consumed her, and unsolved conundrums tormented her until she found the solution. Her mind was like a machine, working twenty-four seven, even when she slept—which could be a blessing or a curse sometimes, depending on the amount of deep REM she lost in the process.

"What's his real name?" she asked.

"Oh, I don't know. Let's see." He rolled his eyes and looked up at the sky. "Um, John. John...um...Doe. Yes, that's it."

"John Doe." She sighed. "Are *ye pullin'* my leg, Wesley?"

"No." He regarded her slacks while he scratched the back of his head, confused by the question, because he'd taken it literally. "Never."

"He told you his name was John Doe."

"That's right. But like I said, I call him Woody." He swallowed another chuckle.

Sarah shut the door of the roadster. "All right, Wesley. Why don't you park your bike? And then come with me. I have someone who would love to talk to you for a minute."

"But you're in my spot."

It was Sarah's turn to roll her eyes. "There's plenty of room, pal. Just chain it to that post."

"It's Wesley, I said."

"Just lock it up, Wesley, and have a care. *Dinnae* scratch my new car."

"I never would." He shook his head at her admonishment and bent to concentrate on guiding his bike past her car. "What do you think I am? Some kind of idiot?"

Sarah didn't say a word. She texted Kelley instead. "Bringing up possible witness," she typed. Over the course of her career, she had been involved in many investigations and had learned one basic tenet: innocent bystanders were often integral to solving a crime.

As Wesley fumbled with his bike cable and lock, she texted her physician. "Hi, Doctor Dena. An emergency came up. I have to cancel. Sorry for the last minute."

Wesley shuffled up behind her. "Are you taking me to the police?"

"Yes. They will want to ask you a few questions about Woody."

"Has he done something bad?"

Sarah thought for a moment to make sure she wouldn't reveal too much. "Nothing has been confirmed."

Wesley squinted at the caution tape and then back at her face. Worry had replaced his blank expression. "Did he get robbed? Is he okay?"

"You can ask the officers that. Come with me."

****

Sheriff Bradley and Detective Miller met them on the third-floor balcony outside the apartment. They had removed their protective equipment. Sarah couldn't help but notice that Sheriff Bradley's trousers fit snugly in all the *right* places and were a flattering length. Although now that she saw him out of the jumpsuit, she realized that pretty much anything he wore would look good on his tall, well-built figure. He had a body like an action movie film star. A face like one, too.

"Sheriff Bradley," he said, showing his badge to Wesley. "Sonoma County. And this is Detective Miller."

"Wesley Leslie," Sarah put in.

"The III," Wesley added.

"There have been three of you?" Bradley's generous mouth quirked to the side in wry amusement.

"Duh."

"Wesley is an acquaintance of John Doe," Sarah said.

"John Doe?" Bradley's quirk switched sides.

"The guy who lives here." Impatient, Wesley shifted his weight to one boot as he tried to see through the crack in the curtains. "Duh."

"He told Wesley his name was John Doe," Sarah explained. "But Wesley calls him Woody."

"Why do you call him that?" Kelley inquired, holding a pen and pad in front of her chest.

Wesley flushed and shrugged. "It's just a nickname." Then he looked over his shoulder to somewhere farther down the balcony.

For the first time since Sarah had met the younger man, she observed his flat eyes blinking rapidly. Then in the next second, he swiveled his head back to face Bradley and shoved up his glasses. Sarah thought his reaction to the question was odd, but the officers didn't seem to notice how nervous he was. She kept silent. She wasn't on the investigative team in an official capacity.

"What vehicle does Woody drive?" Bradley asked.

"A green one."

"Can you be more specific?"

"Well, it's only got two seats." Wesley scanned the parking lot. "It's not here, though. He must be gone. Geeze. It figures."

Kelley scribbled notes as her senior officer continued the questioning.

"What figures?"

"We are supposed to do something in a few minutes."

"What, exactly?"

Wesley blinked again. "Uh, computer stuff."

"You fix computers?"

"Just stuff." He rocked on his feet, increasingly agitated by the questions. "Listen, I gotta go."

"Okay, but just a few more questions." Bradley looked down his nose at Bicycle Man, even though Wesley was as tall as the sheriff. "When was the last time you saw this Woody person?"

"Last Thursday. Duh."

"You haven't seen him for a week?"

"No, we hang out on Thursdays."

"Why is that?"

"'Cause we do computer stuff on Thursdays. Like I told you." Wesley backed up. "So, I have to go. Like now. It's almost two o'clock."

"What time did you last see Woody?"

"Two o'clock, last Thursday. Geeze."

"Wesley," Sarah touched his arm. "Do you do live streams with Woody?"

Wesley flushed and pulled away. "I said computer stuff. Okay?" Wesley's jaw snapped shut as he crossed his arms over his hairless chest. It was clear he wasn't going to divulge anything more. "Okay?"

"Okay. Show Detective Miller your ID and give her your phone number, and you can go." Bradley cracked open the door behind him and held up a finger. "But don't leave town for a few days. You got that?"

"No can do anyway. My mom doesn't come for another two weeks."

Sarah caught Kelley's glance and fought to keep her expression solemn. Bradley ignored them.

"Miller, you go with Mr. Leslie and confiscate his computer."

"What?" Wesley staggered backward, into the caution tape, stretching it to the breaking point. "You can't do that!"

"Yes, we can." Bradley slipped into the apartment and shut the door.

"No!" Wesley yelled. He ducked under the tape and careened down the balcony, his robe fluttering behind him and his boots clomping. He opened a door at the end and slammed it. Then he opened it, did something to the outside surface of the door and slammed it again.

When Sarah and Kelley walked up, they saw he had turned over a sign: *In Session. Do NOT Disturb.*

Sarah lifted a brow. "Do we disturb?"

"Have to. Boss said so." Kelley pounded on the door.

Sarah saw movement at the window beside the front door. Wesley pulled back the curtain, emphatically pointed at the sign on the door, jutted his jaw in exasperation and whipped the curtain shut.

Kelley pounded again. "Open up!" she demanded. She rattled the knob. He'd locked the door.

Sarah glared at the knob and sighed. "I think we'll get more out of Mr. III if we let him do his show and then come back."

"You're probably right. A search warrant will take longer than if we just hang around and wait for him. I'll see what the boss says."

"Text Wesley in an hour and tell him you loved his show, and you want to be on it," Sarah suggested. "He'll probably freak out and come to the door."

"Good idea."

They retraced their steps to the apartment at the other end of the balcony. Kelley stopped in front of the yellow barrier. "I thought you had a doctor's appointment."

"I did. I canceled."

"In that case, do you want to stay? Old Wesley might open up to you more than us hardcores."

"No, I should go. I haven't seen Matteo yet. I'd like to catch him before he leaves for work."

"You haven't seen him since you got back from Germany?"

"Not with our schedules and all." Sarah held up the tape for her friend. "Get me up to speed on the case this evening?"

"Sure thing, girlfriend."

                        ****

Sarah motored into the parking space in front of the Glen Ellen house she and Matteo had purchased a year ago. It was a modest mid-century modern home built above the spate line of Sonoma Creek and a few miles north of Sonoma. She glanced at the dark brown one-story building with the orange door, and once again questioned the wisdom of buying a place while keeping the old one on the island of Alameda near San Francisco.

Granted, the farther from San Francisco a person moved, the cheaper the homes were. But even so, this three-bedroom house had set them back a million dollars. Still, the location couldn't be beat. It had been updated a year ago, too. So, no extra work for her and Matteo. This house and the quaint little village of Glen Ellen had convinced them to move off the island and start a restaurant in Sonoma.

Sarah pulled her suitcase out of the trunk of her car and lugged it to the front door. She had hoped the move to a quieter place and a simpler lifestyle would improve her marriage. But Matteo's drive to excel had followed them north. If anything, he was busier than ever, trying to start a business and keep it going during the pandemic.

She punched the numbers into the keypad on the door. Fortunately for them, her business had supported them for the first few months while the restaurant struggled. People drank more wine than ever when they couldn't eat out or go to bars. Online auctions had become popular, and her expertise was always in demand before a major investment. Even though some of the restaurants she advised had fallen victim to the pandemic, she had retained most of her clients.

They'd done okay. She had been able to mask up and make house calls while Matteo provided takeout. Now that the restaurants were allowed to offer indoor seating again, Matteo was on the way to his star. So, they had survived. As always. Their love life might be lost on the moors somewhere, but they made a great team in every other regard.

Sarah pushed open the door and stepped into the small foyer. Down the main hall, she could hear the shower running. Matteo was getting ready for work. He would be naked. He might be in the mood. She would surprise him by stripping in the bedroom and joining him in the shower. They hadn't fooled around for months.

Quietly, she closed the front door and then turned for the master bedroom. Halfway down the hall, she encountered the sound of her husband reaching an escalating—and unbelievably exhilarating—sexual climax.

Chapter 3 | The Shower

Sarah froze at the bedroom door, uncertain how to proceed. Matteo must be wanking off in the shower. Would he be embarrassed if she walked in on him, or would he like it? She wasn't sure. In the past, she had read him wrong when it came to sex. Her misreads had happened enough times that now she second guessed everything and always let him initiate lovemaking. In the first months of their marriage, she had made light of her missteps, but she had stopped joking long ago, because Matteo didn't find her sense of humor funny or her female aggression beguiling.

This time it would be different. She wouldn't be the one to suffer humiliation or disappointment. This time he was primed and ready. Sarah plowed forward, letting her clothing fall, determined to get what she wanted: some flaming hot monkey sex. In two more strides, she burst into the bathroom as Matteo moaned like he'd never moaned with her. His groan reverberated in the tiled room, like the roar of a rutting lion.

Beyond the fog of the shower glass, she could see her husband's back and someone in front of him pressed to the wall. The lovers panted, braced against the tile, still caught up in mutual ecstasy. Through a cloud of steam and tumescence, Sarah counted four hands spread over the tile.

Four male hands.

Sarah paused, struck to the heart at the sight before her. She felt as if someone had cut her in half with a claymore. Her husband had just had sex in the shower, but not with her. With someone else. With a man. She stuffed a knuckle into her mouth to muffle a cry and staggered away, unable to think for a moment. No way would she interrupt this scenario while her head reeled.

With her heart pounding and her stomach flipping, she stumbled backward, collecting her discarded blouse and slacks, until her calves collided with the end of the bed. She had to think. She had to decide what to do, what to say. She should get out. That's what she should do. Just run out of the house. But her body had unhooked from her brain and was about to collapse on the end of the bed, like a drone completely out of juice.

Something clicked in her head. Old memories shifted into new slots. Data on her marriage to Matteo jiggled and spun and landed in different columns. Twenty years of history swirled around her, in utter chaos, until suddenly, sickeningly, the chaos coalesced into a stark, new order.

All the nights Matteo had been too tired, too stressed, or not in the mood, no matter what frilly teddy she had put on—it all made sense to her now. The rejections she'd endured hadn't been because of her imperfect body or the kind of lingerie she had selected or her bad sense of timing. It was because of *him*.

The bastard.

His rejections had humiliated her so often, she'd started questioning her desirability as a woman. How many times had she made a fool of herself in front of him, twirling around in a frothy little lace number only to be met with a tepid smile? *Gawd*, she hated that weary smile of his. Worse, she hated the heavy silence that always came after.

Now it made sense why she went to bed alone each night. Why Matteo worked late.

Sarah clenched her teeth. Her ears rang, but through the high-pitched whine, she heard the shower turn off and the shower door click open. She shoved her legs in her slacks and yanked them on. She pulled on her blouse.

"Sarah?" Matteo called. His voice cracked.

She looked up as Matteo hurried out of the bathroom, tying a towel around his lithe hips. She stared at him. Even his navel was sexy. He stopped in the doorway, blocking the view behind him.

"I thought you had a doctor's appointment," he blurted, wiping his sopping hair off his forehead. His face was flushed, and his eyes still glowed with the inner fire of his release.

The bastard.

She didn't want to talk about doctor's appointments. She wanted to kill him. At the very least, she wanted to shout strings of profanity at him. He had just cut through their marriage with a rusty razor blade dipped in dog shit. He had gouged out her heart with a rough-edged spoon, the kind that had been caught in a garbage disposal.

But at the sight of him, as always, words fell back into her throat, choking her.

Wet or dry—gay, straight or bi—Matteo DiSanti took her breath away. That's how attractive the man was. Dress him up, dress him down, put a spatula in his hand or a hammer—or even a flyswatter—and the guy could make her heart flutter. She had fallen in love with him the moment she had first laid eyes on him twenty years ago in a North Beach dive they'd worked at.

He had such grace, such style, and the most wonderful voice. She could listen to stories of his childhood for hours—or used to listen, when he had the time and inclination to linger in bed, chatting. Then, there were his eyes, the most beautiful melting blue eyes she'd ever encountered. When they focused on her, there was nothing like their warm shimmer. But she couldn't remember the last time they had enjoyed an intimate conversation.

His beauty might have taken her words away and shock might have taken her breath away. But nothing could take away her good sense. Within seconds, her brain chugged into gear. She buttoned her blouse, her fingers marching swiftly upward. No matter what violence she wished to perpetrate on her cheating husband, she could hear her father's advice ringing in her head.

Take the high road, lass. Always take the high road.

She focused her attention on the small gold crucifix Matteo wore around his neck and never took off. It was a gift from his revered Italian mother, who had passed away two years ago. He still went to mass every day to pray for her soul—probably his, as well, seeing how his physical activities transgressed the bounds of his faith and marriage vows.

Big time.

Looking at the crucifix—and remembering how Matteo's mother had disdained her manners, her swearing and her pitiful lack of religious affiliation—helped get her mind off his body. She stared at the cross, calming herself down as she kept buttoning. She had to think carefully, because whatever she said now would direct the course of her life.

Nothing positive would come of lashing out at Matteo. She wished he had trusted her enough to confide in her about his obvious unhappiness and sexual preference. But she knew his sense of duty to his mother's memory and his Catholic faith had probably muzzled him. He'd been living such a lie. All these years, he must have thought of marriage to her as a job. Jesus.

She felt like vomiting.

"I canceled," she said at last. She fought to keep her voice steady.

"Caught me by surprise, *amoré.*"

"I'll say. Who's your bosom buddy in there?"

"It's not important."

"You're saying your relationship with him is not important? Lovely, Matteo. Casual sex. Admirable."

Matteo's pale face flushed even more, which turned up the volume of his blazing eyes. "I'm saying it's not important to you, Sarah. To us."

"I *dinnae ken what ye mean*—us." Distress always broadened her accent. She fought to swallow it back and maintain her place on the high road. But she could feel herself losing control. "There's no us. Not now."

Matteo took a step toward her. "Sarah..."

"There *hasna* been for a long time. And now I know why."

"There will always be an us."

"Not the kind of us I want."

"Come on, *amoré*. We're good. We're solid. *Cara*. This was a one-time thing."

"A one-time thing."

"Yes." He took a step forward, obviously assuming she was considering granting him an exception.

Sarah planted her hands on her hips, stopping him in his tracks. "Well, Matteo my love, even a one-time thing is a big thing to me."

"I never intended for you to find out like this. I've been so careful. So, you wouldn't get hurt."

"Spare me. And I'm not bothered about the gay angle." Sarah retorted. "I'm fucking pissed off about the unfaithful angle."

His flush deepened, all the way to the tips of his ears. He put up his hands and started to say something but broke off. His shoulders slumped.

"I want you out of here." Sarah said. "Tonight."

"What? But I'm working..."

"You're always working." She pushed past him into the bathroom. "And you," she pointed at the slender young man with long blond hair standing in the doorway to the toilet and listening in on their conversation. He looked vaguely familiar, but she couldn't place where she'd seen him. If anything, he looked like a surfer who worked in the local food industry to support his habit. He grabbed a towel and clamped it to his groin. With a quick swipe, she whipped away the terrycloth. His brown eyes went huge with alarm as he stood there, naked and exposed.

"Get your things and fuck off," Sarah demanded. "And don't touch anything else in here, or I will yank off your balls with my bare hands."

"Okay. Sorry! He didn't tell me he was married!"

"Didn't see the ring, pal?" Sarah held up her hand and shoved it close to his nose. "It looks exactly like this one."

"Sorry. Sorry."

She raked him up and down and showed her teeth in a mirthless smile. "I hope your asshole hurts like hell."

So much for taking the high road. She knew she had lost all control. Waves of anger rolled off her like fireballs. But she didn't care.

Sarah stormed out of the bathroom and glared at Matteo. "Tonight, lover boy. By nine o'clock. I don't want to see you, much less smell you, in this house."

"Sarah." Matteo held out a hand.

She brushed past him and barreled down the hall. Furious and heartbroken, she grabbed her purse from the hall tree and stomped out to her car. There was only one place to go when her world fell apart.

The Wolf House.

****

Sarah took the long way to the Wolf House Bar and sped through the backroads in her tiny sportscar. Her inner world blurred as much as the sweltering scenery whizzing by. Swamped by Matteo's betrayal, she felt unhinged and fragmented, as if pieces of her life were breaking off and flying away in the breeze. Memories of her married life littered the road behind her like discarded fast food wrappers.

When she thought she was capable of mingling with other human beings without swearing or sobbing, she proceeded to the Wolf House Bar.

The present incarnation of the Wolf House Bar was named after Jack London's doomed Wolf House Lodge, which the famous author had begun building at the turn of the century. But long before Jack London had come to town, the bar had been a saloon, inn, post office and brothel—all called various names, long since forgotten. The two-story brick saloon had been built at the end of a bridge that spanned Sonoma Creek, so it saw a lot of traffic, both local and tourist. In fact, for the last two hundred years, the building had been the center of the little village.

Jack London's Wolf House Lodge, on the other hand, had not enjoyed such longevity. The giant residence had burned to the ground mere days before Jack and his wife could move in, leaving only a hulking stone skeleton surrounded by stately oaks and rattlesnake grass. The estate was now a historic landmark and part of the park system, but Sarah had yet to visit it. Kelley claimed the place was spooky and creepy and definitely haunted.

Some said the Wolf House fire had started under suspicious circumstances. Some people claimed that Jack's wife Charmian had vowed that he would never live in the mansion—but no one was certain why she had said such a thing. Had her words been a premonition or a threat? No one could say for sure, only that he had died soon after. But longtime citizens of Glen Ellen grumbled that Jack London was a drunkard and a womanizer and deserved to die young.

Sarah parked her car and scowled. She wondered if Jack had been a manizer, too. You couldn't be sure of anyone anymore. That's all she knew.

She struggled out of her little roadster and locked it. She could have walked from her house to the Wolf House Bar, had she been thinking straight, but then again, roaring around on the back roads had cleared her head.

Sarah walked through the dappled sunshine of the parking lot toward the front door of the pub. The bar was the heart of the village like the pubs in the UK, with the market across the street, the hotel next door and the laundromat nearby. The Gourmet Ghetto of Glen Ellen, a string of award-winning eateries, lined the winding road on the other side of the bridge, along with a vet and a mechanic who seemed to work solely on vintage pickups. She often walked the few blocks from her house to the village center to grab dinner if Matteo hadn't made her anything before he left for work.

That was going to change. Everything was going to change. She'd have to start cooking her own meals from now on. Beans on toast loomed large in her future. Canned peas. Spaghetti-hoops. All the old standbys from her university days. Well, not the canned peas. Her tastes had been elevated after her move to San Francisco.

Along with her dinner trips, Sarah often walked to the Wolf House to enjoy a game of "guess what wine this is" at the bar with her and Matteo's friend, Zach Sullivan.

The thought of Zach made her pause at the corner of the pub. She flipped through flashes of Zach and Matteo together. She analyzed old memories, examining them with a new lens. No, not Zach. Dear lord, not Zach.

Never Zach.

With their shared love of wine and dark senses of humor, she thought of Zach as her friend first, not Matteo's. If Zach had betrayed their friendship by messing around with her husband, she would be shattered.

She could feel the ground beneath her feet shifting and swaying like the aftershocks of an earthquake. Today, she had lost all terroir in her personal life. The entire history of her and Matteo's marriage had gone up in smoke, just like the Wolf House. She would have to start over. At forty-one years old, she would have to decide where to go and what to do with the rest of her life. And she would have to do it alone.

At least she'd been prepping for a solitary life for the last fifteen years. She could manage. In fact, it would be an adventure. She'd love being free. It was going to be great.

Damn that Matteo.

Sarah clumped across the ancient—and rickety—plank porch of the Wolf House and pushed through the door. Only Zach and a couple playing pool were in the place. The rest of the pub was filled with shafts of afternoon sun angling through a sea of dust motes. The lack of patrons made sense, though. Tastings and tours went on until four-thirty in wine country. Only after that time did the bar and restaurant business pick up.

Sarah plopped down on a stool at the bar. "A Macallan, Zach. Make it a double."

"What, I can't tempt you with a mystery wine?" Her black-haired friend stooped down to peer at her face. "You not feeling okay?"

She stared at the two-hundred-year-old wooden bar, still smooth and shining after endless abuse of sweaty elbows and spilled beers. She kept her eyes averted. She didn't want anyone to see how distraught she was. Especially Zach.

"I'm fine."

"You don't sound fine."

"I said I'm fine."

"You don't look fine."

She tilted her head to glare at him. "What's not fine about how I look?"

"Whoa. Who let Miss Cranky come to town?"

"Give me an Advil with that whiskey. Make it three."

"Coming right up."

Her eyes followed his slender waist and broad shoulders as he pulled down the bottle of whiskey and poured her drink. The narrow blue and white stripes of his shirt blurred as he moved. She blinked back tears and tamped down her emotions. One thing she never allowed herself to do was cry in public. And she refused to cry about Matteo.

The bastard. The prick. He didn't deserve her tears.

"Big Mac with an Advil chaser," Zach announced. "Just what the doctor ordered."

He pushed a tumbler and three pills on a napkin across the bar. Then he stood there and observed her with his hands shoved in the front pockets of his jeans.

She popped the pills in her mouth and took a sip. "Sorry, Zach. I *didna* mean to snap at you."

"No worries." He gave her a lop-sided smile. "Seeing you drinking scotch is, well—should I mark the calendar?"

"Screw the calendar. I need something salty, Zach. What do you got?"

"Peanuts, popcorn, truffle fries."

"Sounds like a flight. I'll have them."

Still grinning a bemused lop-sided smile, Zach scooped popcorn out of the old-fashioned machine at the end of the bar. Then he placed two bowls in front of her, one with shelled peanuts and the larger one with popcorn. "You have to finish these two before you can have dessert, though."

"Okay, dad."

Zach pulled up a stool behind the bar and sat down.

"So, what's going on, Sarah?" His baritone resonated with kindness. She appreciated the genuine concern that tempered his words. "It's four-thirty in the afternoon and you're having a whiskey. That's just plain unnatural."

Sarah swirled her drink and considered her options. She could pour out her troubles to Zach, only to discover at some future point that he and Matteo had shared body fluids—or worse, an emotional connection. Or she could ask Zach point-blank whose side he was on. Because lines were going to be drawn. And soon.

Why not start drawing those lines today? Like her father always said, "*Better the noo, lass. Better the noo.*"

Better now than never. Her mantra. Sarah put down the heavy-bottomed glass and looked up at Zach.

Chapter 4 | Wolf House

Zach's family had lived in Sonoma Valley long before California had been wrested from Mexico in the mid 1880s. He was like royalty here. Landed gentry for sure, what with his father's gambling addiction. But Zach was nothing like his feckless sandy-haired dad had been. His dark rugged looks and diligent work ethic were the finest fruit of the Sullivan family's rootstock. Not everyone could survive the heat, heartache and grueling work of a successful vineyard. Not everyone wanted to try.

But Zach loved the valley and fought to remain, even after the wildfires. She guessed that Miwok and Mexican blood ran in his veins, as well as Scotch Irish like herself. Looking at the man, she had to admit the combination was an excellent blend.

Everyone liked Zach Sullivan. Even she liked Zach, and she was as discerning about people as she was with the tannins of a pinot noir future. She had enjoyed his sense of humor from the night she'd met him at Olive, the restaurant she and her husband owned in downtown Sonoma. Whenever Zach and his wife made reservations for dinner, she made a point to stop in and spend time at their table. She enjoyed an ongoing banter with the man.

But tonight was a night for a more sober conversation.

"I've read that twenty-five percent of males in the Bay Area are gay," she began. "Do you believe that?"

"So, I've heard."

She gauged his reaction, trying not to be obvious that her interrogation was aimed at him. "That's such a high percentage. Think it's accurate?"

Zach shrugged a muscular shoulder. He'd spent his youth toiling in the family vineyard, wine cellar and tasting room, expecting to inherit the business instead of taking a salary. All he got for his years of hard work was part of a college education, a fine set of shoulders and an exceptional palate. Two years ago, he had come back from vacation to discover Paradise Valley Winery had been sold and his father had gambled away Zach's future seconds before dying of a heart attack at a blackjack table in Petaluma. Now Zach worked two jobs and coaxed cabernet berries off a sunny slope on Moon Mountain, hoping to restore the family's place in the valley.

"How many gay men do you meet?" she prodded.

He shrugged a shoulder. "Don't usually ask."

"You never get propositioned?"

Zach's regard swept over her face, obviously curious now about her line of questioning. But he didn't blush. He didn't blink. He didn't run a hand over his hair. All tells. He smiled his slow, confident smile.

"Well, now, Goldilocks, look at me. I'm not exactly the San Francisco type."

She looked. She liked looking at Zach. There was something solid about him. No nonsense. She liked the way he folded his shirt cuffs up over his sinewy forearms. She liked the way he wore his grandfather's silver watch on his right wrist. She liked the fringe of black hair that hung over his forehead. He wasn't particularly handsome. He wasn't particularly tall. She wasn't sure what color his eyes were. But he had a quiet confidence about him that she'd found reassuring from the moment she'd run into him at the restaurant. Best of all, he smelled good, in a natural way, like fresh laundry.

Gambling father. Lost inheritance. Drought. Wildfires. Pandemic. Zach was still here. Persevering. Working the land. Everything was going to be okay if a Sullivan still lived in the valley.

"Is there a San Francisco type?" Sarah finally asked.

"If there is, I'm not it." He chuckled. "What are you getting at?"

It was her turn to shrug. "I don't know. Something I've been thinking about."

"Something that's upset you enough to drink whiskey?"

"*Aye.*" She encircled the tumbler with her hands.

"Does this have anything to do with Matteo?"

Sarah masked her surprise. Did Zach know something she didn't? She wondered if Zach could see through her odd line of questioning. "Why do you ask?"

"Just wondering." He stood up. "Now, Matteo. There's one good-looking guy. Really takes care of himself."

"He does."

"I expect he would get propositioned a lot. You should ask him your questions."

"*Aye.*" She ground the word through her teeth. She picked up the tumbler and swirled the dying ice cube at the bottom. "I certainly have questions, that I do."

He touched her wrist. "What aren't you telling me?"

Zach held her gaze. His dark eyes bore into hers, drilling down, auguring into thoughts she couldn't say out loud. Not yet. She didn't know how to frame the situation, because anything she might say about Matteo would reflect on her as well as their marriage. People would see how blind she had been. How stupid. How naïve.

She trusted Zach to be understanding if she confided in him. She had to talk to someone before she exploded. But would talking to Zach betray her relationship with Matteo? Did she *have* a relationship with Matteo? What would their future relationship look like? At this point, she couldn't see staying married, not with visions of the shower scene still scalding the backs of her eyes. Still, she longed to tell Zach everything.

Before she could decide how to answer Zach's question, the door creaked open.

"Hi honey!" a bright voice called.

Without looking around, Sarah knew who had walked in: Zach's schoolteacher wife. Small, vivacious Courtney Sullivan could talk forever about absolutely nothing in a coma-inducing monotone voice. But for once, Sarah was glad to be interrupted by the woman.

"Hi, Sarah."

"Hi, Courtney."

Courtney walked up to the bar in a cloud of vanilla perfume, plopped her large bag on the counter and pointed at Sarah's tumbler. "You're drinking whiskey?"

"That I am."

"She's had a rough day," Zach put in. He leaned over the counter. Courtney pecked him on the lips, leaving bright pink gloss on his mouth. He picked up Sarah's napkin to wipe it away.

"Want to talk about it?" Courtney asked, sliding on the seat next to her and putting an arm around her shoulders.

"Not really."

"It couldn't have been as bad as my day." Courtney rolled her eyes. She gave Sarah's shoulder a squeeze and released her. "You wouldn't believe how nasty some kids can be. After being cooped up at home for a year and stuff? But I'm glad the pandemic is over. Online teaching was such a pain. Perfect for some kids, but for the others—I'm not sure what their parents are teaching kids these days. If anything. Like for instance, this kid I have…"

Sarah tuned out Courtney's voice. Judging by the glazed expression in Zach's eyes, she guessed he did the same. He slid a glass of pinot grigio toward his wife, slanted an apologetic smile at Sarah and turned to help the pool-playing couple at the cash register.

A few minutes later, Sarah's phone rang. She excused herself and took the call outside, happy to have a reason to break away.

"Sarah? It's Arthur. Arthur Chen."

"Arthur, how are you?" Arthur was a Chinese buyer whom she had bumped into at auctions and conferences over the years. They shared a love of Zinfandel and Impressionist art. She couldn't afford originals, but he'd filled an apartment in Hong Kong with Monets and Morisots.

"Fine, thank you. Great. Say, are you in town?"

"If you mean Sonoma, yes. I'll be here until after the Flight of Fancy Auction. It's going to be a big deal this year, being live and all."

"That is why I am here, too," he said. "My clients are eager to buy."

"From what I've heard, it's going to be a mob scene."

"That's why I'm calling." He sighed. "Listen, I have a huge favor to ask."

"*Aye*?"

"It involves your old boss."

"Which one?"

"Bill Friske."

Managing Bill Friske's wine collection in San Francisco had been one of the jobs Sarah had walked away from. Within months of being hired, she'd come to detest the man's imperious attitude, his lack of confidence in her expertise and his condescending remarks about women in the industry. That Bill had bought Paradise Valley Winery for pennies on the dollar and had fired all the longstanding employees made her dislike him even more. That he couldn't bother to live in the old Sullivan mansion and was letting the estate fall into disrepair vaulted her dislike into out and out hatred.

"What's going on with Bill?" she asked.

"He's got some items coming up at the auction that I'm interested in. But last time I bought from him..." Arthur's voice trailed off.

"What?" Sarah propped her elbow on her wrist and watched two joggers slog by in the heat. "What happened last time?"

"I don't know." Arthur let out a burst of air. "I don't think the wine was all that it should be. One of my clients voiced...um...concerns."

Client concerns were disastrous. Sarah clutched the phone closer to her ear.

"About something from Bill's collection? Are you certain?"

"Deadly certain," Arthur replied. "Wine is big business in China. As you are aware. A lot of money involved. People can lose their lives if they aren't careful. Including myself."

"Do you think your life could be in jeopardy?"

"If I broker fakes to certain clients? Yes, I do."

Sarah stared at the Wolf House logo on the large front window of the pub, while her thoughts raced. "Which wine are we talking about? I hope it wasn't something I bought for him years ago."

"A Domaine St. Emile pinot. Was that one of yours?"

Sarah's pulse quickened. DSE was also the same wine she had identified in the fridge of the dead man in Boyes Hot Springs. "No, thankfully. He wouldn't listen to my advice."

"I have an appointment to view the lots at the auction warehouse, and I was hoping you would accompany me. Perhaps you can spot something off. I will compensate you for your time, of course."

"If I can, I will. When?"

"Tomorrow? One pm?"

"Okay, Arthur. That's the Oakville Wines warehouse, right?"

"In Oakville, yes. I really appreciate this, Sarah. I will see you then."

When Sarah asked Siri to add the appointment alert to her calendar, she remembered her date with Kelley that evening. After everything that had happened, she *needed* a sit down with her best friend.

Sarah went into the bar to pay her tab and say good-bye. After two whiskies, she knew better than to drink wine with Kelley on an empty stomach. She couldn't go home for a snack or change of clothes, though, not until the nine o'clock deadline she'd given Matteo. She'd have to drive into town and grab a couple of fish tacos.

Damn that Matteo.

****

At seven-fifteen, she rapped on Kelley's front door. Kelley rented a tiny one-bedroom cottage off Sonoma Square, tucked in the back yard of a massive Victorian home. Kelley didn't have any privacy in the front, but her back yard bordered a vineyard and a gorgeous view of Sonoma Mountain to the west. She and Kelley had spent many a night on her wisteria-draped patio, drinking wine by candlelight.

"Hey," Kelley greeted, pulling open the door. "I was just going to text you. See if you were on the way."

Sarah held out her contribution to the evening, a bottle of Benziger chardonnay that she particularly liked: limited oak and lots of pineapple.

Kelley took the bottle and motioned her in. "Shall we repair to the patio?"

"Is the pope Catholic?"

Once outside, Kelley poured two flutes of bubbly while Sarah settled into her usual cushioned patio chair. She sank back gratefully. It had been a humdinger of a day from the moment she'd got off the plane from Germany and driven north to Sonoma. Not until she collapsed into the familiar chair, did she realize how exhausted she was.

That could happen to a person when they flew across the Atlantic and drank whiskey at 4:30 in the afternoon, after being awake and in transit for twenty-four hours. Not to mention experiencing a life-altering drama in her own home.

Kelley sat down beside her and propped her feet on the remaining chair. They toasted.

"To Gloria," Kelley said.

"The best." Sarah sipped her Gloria Ferrer sparkling wine, certain it would do wonders to revive her body and her spirit.

"So, anything new on the case?" Sarah asked. "Did you talk to Wesley?"

"We couldn't get anything out of him. The sheriff is getting a warrant for Wesley Leslie's computer. But I was hoping you'd stop by with me. You know, 'cause you have that way about you. People talk to you."

"It's the accent. They think I'm friendly."

"You are." Kelley gave her upper arm a gentle shove and chuckled.

"No, I'm an over-analyzing bitch from Glasgow."

"You're not a bitch," Kelley retorted. "But the over-analyzing part? Sure. That's why I want you to talk to Mr. Leslie. Like tomorrow morning?"

"I suppose I could." Sarah gazed at the sun melting behind the oak-covered mountain. "Did you find out who the victim was?"

"Not yet."

"Who discovered the body?"

"The manager. He saw two people moving stuff out of the apartment and thought they were suspicious—like they were skipping out without paying or burglarizing the place. When he challenged them, they drove off in a hurry and left the door open. So, he went in."

"He didn't recognize the people?"

"No. All he could tell us was that it was a man and a woman. He didn't get their license numbers, either. But this is the weird thing. I took a picture for you." Kelley pulled out her phone and swiped through an album until a photo filled the screen.

"We found this in the victim's pocket."

Sarah took possession of the phone and enlarged the image. Kelley had snapped a photo of a sheet of paper marked with a series of numbers. The numbers were grouped together, with a space between each group, and each group marked by another number. Some of the numbers had tiny checkmarks by them. Some were circled.

Sarah frowned, mystified. "What is this? A new kind of Sudoku puzzle?"

"We don't know."

"Do you think it's significant?"

"We don't know one way or the other. Plus, the boss doesn't know I'm showing this to you."

"Okay." Sarah gave back the phone and held up her glass in salute, "Mum's the word."

"Did you have time to look up that wine in your database? The wine from the fridge?"

"Not yet." Sarah took a sip, wondering how much she wanted to tell Kelley about her day. "I got distracted."

"Good distraction, I take it?" Kelley wiggled her eyebrows, knowing Sarah had gone home from the crime scene to see her husband. "Did Matteo come to the door, naked, with homemade chocolate mousse spread all over his six pack?"

"Not exactly." Sarah refilled their drinks and shoved the bottle into the slurry of slush swimming in the ice bucket. "But I have to say, he did surprise me."

"Do tell."

Sarah told her. Every shattering detail. When she finished, Kelley tilted her head and gazed at her, her brown eyes full of sadness.

"Oh, Sarah," Kelley stroked her arm. "I'm so sorry."

"I should have seen it coming. I'm an absolute *thickee*."

"No, you're not. You and Matteo were such a cute couple. I would have never guessed he was a big, fat cheater."

"The prick." Sarah sighed and put down her empty flute with a clink.

Kelley got up. "Another?" she asked, hands on her hips.

"Glass or bottle?" Sarah grimaced. "Or case?"

"You choose."

"I really shouldn't have any more. I have to drive back to Glen Ellen."

"Oh, no. You're not going home tonight, sis. You're staying here."

"I am?" Sarah glanced up at her friend.

"Yep. We are having more bubbly. We're going to sit here until we think of every synonym for dickhead, and that might take all night."

Sarah smiled and sank back. Thank goodness for Kelley. "Bastard," she muttered.

"Asshole," Kelley added, reaching for the empty bottle. "I'll be right back."

As Kelley retrieved more Gloria, Sarah looked up at the moon, which rode full and bright in the April sky. Human beings were prone to crazy behavior during a full moon. In a day or two, when the moon waned enough, this would all blow over and her life would reassemble, like a car crash video played in reverse.

But in her heart, she knew the pieces of her marriage would never reassemble. Stills from the shower scene were etched in her memory and would stay there forever. Those four hands on the tiled wall. Matteo in his towel and his navel. Blondie in his altogether. The sated pleasure melting in Matteo's eyes. *The prick.*

For Sarah, betrayal was a one-way street. As far as she was concerned, Matteo had just driven a flashy Italian Ferrari down their tunnel of love in the absolute wrong direction.

Sarah clutched the arms of her chair and stared up at the moon, choking back tears. She would not cry. She would never think of Matteo DiSanti again. She would move back to the house in Alameda and never return to Sonoma. There was nothing for her here now.

But that wasn't true.

She had made friends here. She liked it here. Sonoma wasn't just any small town. It was a community of people who cared about the land and its history and the art of fine wine. She loved the cultivated hills and valleys striped with vines that turned from brown to green to gold and then to red, marking the progression of the seasons. She liked driving up Broadway and seeing the stately stone courthouse waiting for her at the center of the sleepy plaza, the barrel palms, the pomegranate trees and the smell of bread baking at the tiny French patisserie. Her heart twisted at the prospect of leaving it all behind.

She would have to find a way to stay.

Chapter 5 | Puppets

The next morning, after four cups of coffee and a greasy but satisfying breakfast at the Palms Restaurant on the edge of town, Sarah felt capable of talking. Thinking, on the other hand, would take a bit more time. But she had twenty minutes before she and Kelley were due to knock on Wesley Leslie III's door.

She let her gaze wander over the comfortable old-fashioned restaurant, with its burgundy vinyl booths, carpeted floor and long eating bar trimmed in metal. The upholstered stools at the bar had supported patrons since WWII and could still swivel without squeaking. Even the waitresses looked as if they were from another era, with their paper order pads stuffed in their aprons and glass coffee pots in each hand.

The Palms was not a flashy restaurant for tourists. It was a place the residents protected as their own and never recommended to outsiders. In fact, you couldn't order a latte here, much less *kale*—only down home, inexpensive grub, with senior Thursdays, two-for-one steaks on Fridays and a buffet dinner every Saturday night.

Matteo refused to step foot in the place.

Kelley put down her phone and looked across the table at her.

"Ready to go?"

"As I'll ever be."

"And afterward, you'll go home and talk to Matteo?"

"He's probably not there. I told him to clear out."

"Then go to the restaurant?"

"I'm not sure I'm ready to talk to him."

"You can't let it fester, Sarah." Kelley rose. "Are you going to work things out or give him the heave ho? You have to decide."

"I know. I know."

Kelley paid the bill and drove Sarah to the apartment complex in Boyes Hot Springs. By the time Kelley rapped on Wesley's door five minutes later, Sarah's jet-lagged brain had joined the real world.

Wesley's door opened a crack. Through the opening, Sarah could see a glint of his glasses and the fuzz of a fluffy blue slipper. A cartoon played in the background.

"What do you guys want?" he whined.

"To talk," Kelley said. "Just to talk."

Sarah stabbed a thumb in Kelley's direction. "Before her boss arrives with a warrant and makes a mess."

"A mess?"

"You know how it is, pal. When the police search a place, they pull out drawers, toss stuff around..."

"I've seen that on TV," Wesley said. The door opened a couple more inches.

"We'll only take a few minutes of your time." Kelley wedged a clunky police shoe into the crack to prevent him from closing the door on them.

"If you tell us about your friend Woody," Sarah added, "we might be able to prevent a search altogether."

"Promise?" He glanced from Kelley to Sarah, his mouth open.

"Promise." Kelley smiled for effect, but Sarah knew Kelley couldn't promise anything.

"Well, if you promise." Wesley opened the door. He sported a silk robe again, this time a raucous number covered in parrots and palm leaves and trimmed in peacock blue. His shorts were orange, his socks black. In one hand, he held a white bowl with a spoon sticking out.

"I was having my Cap'n Crunch." He looked down at the bowl. "But now it's all soggy."

"Sorry," Kelley grimaced.

Sarah followed her into the apartment and looked around. Wesley was remarkably neat. Not a dirty dish could be seen, not a towel or shirt had been tossed on the furniture. Three pairs of colorful cowboy boots hugged the wall by the door, their heels aligned against the baseboard. The coffee table in front of the beige couch held only what appeared to be a sewing kit and yesterday's Sonoma Post-Intelligencer. But what caught her attention was a black and glass bookcase on the far wall. It was stuffed with small cloth figures, like dolls of some kind, displayed on narrow glass jars, the type olives were sold in.

She strolled across the room for a better look. "What are these, Wesley?"

"My puppets." He put his cereal bowl on a placemat at the end of the dining room table.

Sarah estimated there were fifty figures on the shelves. His puppets ranged from dirt bike racers to drag queens to deli counter workers, all created in tiny, incredible miniature.

"Finger puppets?" she asked.

"You could say so." He came up behind her. "I mean, that's how it started."

"And now?"

He didn't answer. A flush spread down his slack cheeks, starting at the frame of his glasses and shooting down to his jaw.

"Why aren't they finger puppets now, Wesley?"

Wesley's eyelashes fluttered behind his huge spectacles. "I really can't say."

"Why not?" Kelley inquired.

"Because Woody told me not to talk about them. So did my mom. She doesn't want me to show these to people."

"Why not?" Sarah asked. "They're fantastic. Did you make them?"

"Yeah. I sew them. I used to put on little plays with them. Make movies. You know. Stuff."

"But your mom doesn't like that?"

"She thinks they're stupid. She wants me to work at Office Max or something. Get a real job."

"And Woody?" Kelley put in. "He thought they were stupid, too?"

"No, he likes them." Wesley hid a titter behind his hand. The hem of his robe shook as he choked back a giggle.

Sarah watched him. "What's so funny?"

He swallowed and gawked at her, his expression suddenly slack. "Nothing."

"You always think it's funny when you talk about Woody."

"Because it is. Woody, I mean. The word." He clamped a hand over his mouth to stifle another laugh.

Suddenly his behavior made sense to Sarah. "Ah," she said. "This is about hard-ons, isn't it?"

His jaw dropped as he gaped at her.

"Stiffies, boners, *stauners*," she goaded, resorting to Glasgow slang.

"I believe the proper term is erection?" he chided in a whisper. "You don't have to swear."

"*Aye*, erection. So, your friend got an erection sometimes. That's why you call him Woody."

Kelley pointed at the couch. "He had erections here?"

"He wouldn't want me to tell. He would be mad."

"Well, Mr. Leslie, you don't have to worry about that," Kelley continued. "Because I'm sorry to say, your friend is dead."

"What?" Wesley's head swiveled in her direction.

"Someone killed him. Yesterday."

"That's why the police were here," Sarah put in.

"Someone killed Woody?" Wesley clutched the sides of his bushy hair in both fists and turned away from them, bent over, as if someone had punched him in the gut. "No!"

"I'm sorry," Sarah said, staring at his skinny back. "But that's why you have to tell us everything you can think of. So we can catch the killer."

"I don't know anything about killers."

"But you do know about Woody."

Wesley shuffled to the couch and collapsed into it, his head in his hands. "Someone killed Woody?" he murmured. "No way. No way."

Kelley sat beside him. "Did he have any enemies? Did you see anyone visit him?"

"Could it have something to do with your live show?" Sarah added.

"Our show? What? I mean...crud, I don't think so." He pushed his fingers through his hair, as if trying to tug the answer out of his skull.

"What do you do on your show?"

"Stuff."

"Like what?" Kelley urged.

"Let me guess." Sarah walked to the nearest bookshelf and studied the puppets. "Woody puts this cowboy on his dick," She caught herself choosing profanity again and substituted the textbook word instead. "I mean phallus and..."

"No, he hated the cowboy," Wesley whined. "He always made me be the cowboy."

"So, you put the cowboy on..."

"No, he put it on."

Kelley scowled, confused. "But he didn't like the cowboy, you said."

"*He* put the cowboy on *me*. Duh." Wesley glared at her.

"And you put a puppet on him?" Sarah ventured. "Right?"

"Yeah. Different ones. Whatever our viewers paid for. But Woody liked the astronaut the best."

"Which made him get a woody."

Wesley nodded but didn't look up.

"You did, too."

Wesley shrugged a shoulder. "I guess."

"That was your show?" Kelley asked. Her eyebrows shot up in disbelief. "Getting woodies from puppets?"

"No." He shot her another disgusted glare. "The puppets did things. Talked mostly. Woody was funny. At the end of the show, he made his puppet's hat fly off. People liked that."

"Oh?" Sarah kept a straight face. "And what would you do?"

"I would make new puppets for each show. On request sometimes. People paid us to watch. A lot."

"To show your dicks on the web."

"No. For the puppet show. It's against the law to show your private parts to people. You ought to know that." He studied Kelley, his eyes grave. "You're the police."

She nodded and glanced at Sarah for assistance.

Sarah ambled closer to the coffee table. "So, people paid you for special puppets. How?"

"PayPal."

"Can we have a look at the account?" Kelley asked. "If you show us, we may not have to take your computer."

"I can't. Woody did all the technical stuff."

"He took care of the money?"

"Yeah."

"How did he pay you?" Sarah inquired. "No, let me guess. Cash?"

"What's wrong with cash?"

"Nothing." Kelley rose. "So is your mom's name Gladys?"

"Yes. What of it?"

"A Gladys Leslie pays for Woody's apartment. Does your mom know Woody?"

"Of course not."

"Then why would she pay for his apartment?"

"She doesn't. Not really."

As Sarah listened to Kelley's new line of questioning, she knew what the answer was.

"You switched apartments," she mused. "Why?"

"Woody said this one was quieter. For our show. 'Cause it's on the end."

"Right." Sarah met Kelley's calculating gaze. The counterfeiter was a man who knew how to hide his tracks. Now all they had to do was find out who had leased Wesley's apartment, and they might learn the identity of the victim. Once they traced the PayPal account to a bank account, they could get more proof of whom John Doe had been dealing with.

"What's the name of your show?" Kelley asked. "It sounds intriguing."

"Puppets..." Wesley jutted out his chin. "Puppets on a Thing."

Sarah suppressed a snort and nodded. "I like it. Can't wait to see it."

Kelley held out her hand. "You have been very helpful, Mr. Leslie. Thank you."

He stared at her fingers as if her hand was covered with spiders. "So that means the other policemen won't come and wreck my apartment?"

"I'll do my best to prevent that from happening."

Sarah followed Kelley to the door.

"Wait a sec," Wesley sputtered.

Kelley turned to look at him.

"How will I get paid now? I was gonna buy a new camera today."

"That's for Woody's estate lawyer to figure out. If Woody's the only one on the account, you're out of luck."

"But that's not fair!"

"Well, it's the law, I'm sorry to say."

"I need hot dogs. I'm out of hot dogs. Chocolate milk, too."

"We'll do what we can for you," Sarah put in. "But for now, can't you call your mom?"

"No. Jeeze." His shoulders slumped. "She'll be mad."

"I'll tell you what." Sarah slipped a money clip out of her front pocket. Whenever she traveled, she always carried money on her person, not just in her purse—in case of theft or accident. "I'd like to buy one of your puppets—that is, if you don't mind parting with one." She flipped through the American twenties and pulled out five.

"A hundred dollars?" he gasped.

"Not enough?"

"No. Jeeze. Which one? I mean, which puppet?"

"You pick, Wesley."

****

Later, in Kelley's SUV police vehicle, Sarah slipped on the pink ballerina puppet that Wesley claimed had never been used on the show. She tipped the dancer's tin-foil tiara annoyingly close to Kelley's nose. Kelley batted it away.

"That ballerina has one awfully big leg," she drawled.

"Better to pirouette by," Sarah retorted. Humming the finale of the 1812 Overture, she danced the ballerina at the side of Kelley's head and then along the edge of the dashboard, leaping up at each high note. For the first time since coming back from Germany, she burst out laughing.

Kelley pulled out of the parking lot, trying not to giggle, but by the time she drove to Highway 12 a block away, she had tears running down her cheeks.

Minutes later, Kelley dropped Sarah at the Palms Restaurant, still shaking her head and chuckling. Sarah jumped out and reached for her car key with her free hand.

"You and that ballerina should go dance for Matteo now," Kelley called after her.

Sarah wiggled her puppet finger and her eyebrows at her friend. "Okay, we will."

****

But Sarah didn't have time to talk to Matteo. In one hour, she was slated to meet Arthur Chen in Oakville.

In preparation, she took a moment to check her database of wine sales. Sitting in her car, she fired up her tablet to look for all recorded sellers of older vintage DSE in recent years. Only two names came up: Bill Friske and SS Wines, LLC.

She had never heard of SS Wines, so she did a quick web search. All she found was a flashy web page boasting a high-end design and very little content. She clicked around and didn't find a shopping cart or an "About Us" or "Staff" page. It was more a blog than a shopping experience, with articles about recent wine auctions and industry news. She scrolled to the bottom for a street address and found nothing but a "contact us" link, which took her to an email address.

There were no social media links anywhere. No phone number.

Not unusual. Some wine collectors were very old school.

Then a link, almost hidden at the very top right caught her eye. Had it appeared after she had been on the front page for a while? She was certain the link had not been there when she'd first opened the site. "Ask Us," the link prompted. She clicked it. The "Ask Us" page listed three wines: Domaine St. Emile Pinot Noir, Screaming Egret Cabernet Sauvignon and Paradise Valley Zinfandel, all sought after wines by top-rated vineyards in France and Northern California.

Something about the three names seemed familiar. She realized where she had seen the list before. DSE, SECS, and PVZ had been scrawled on the labels of the jars in the fridge of the dead man. Paradise Valley Zinfandel? Were PV fakes being sold, too?

She had to let Kelley know. And Zach. She called Kelley, but her friend didn't pick up. She left a brief text for Kelley. Zach, she could tell in person. But first, she had to get to the tiny village of Oakville.

Chapter 6 | The Inspection

Sarah took the switchbacks up Moon Mountain at a breakneck speed, enjoying the sensitive handling of her little roadster and the cool darkness of the redwood forest at the higher elevation. She had to concentrate on maneuvering the hairpin turns without fishtailing over the drop-offs, as well as dodge squirrels making a run for it, which took her mind off The Shower. All good. With one hand gripping the wheel and the other clutching the gearshift, she raced toward the tiny village of Oakville on the eastern flank of the Mayacamas mountain range.

By the time she zipped into the gravel parking lot of Oakville Wine Storage, her mind was clear, ready for the appointment with Arthur Chen. She enjoyed the challenge of inspections and thought of them as a sport that she excelled at. Even better, Zach Sullivan's day job was managing this warehouse, and seeing him always improved her outlook.

Sarah smiled as she parked her Triumph in front of the large metal warehouse. She wondered if Zach would notice that she was dressed in the same clothes she had worn yesterday at the bar. In fact, she was wearing the same clothes that she had worn on the plane from Germany. After this appointment, she would have to go back to the house and take a shower. She couldn't put it off any longer. In this heat, her antiperspirant would last only so long, and the last trace of her signature scent, Versace Crystal Noir, had faded a day ago.

Like all the fine things she had learned to appreciate, Matteo had introduced her to the perfume. Every time she misted the scent on her throat, she would be reminded of him. Did that mean she had to find another cologne to call her own? It was just another item she would have to jettison.

She didn't want to think about jettisoning anything. Or Matteo. Instead, Sarah shifted her attention to her destination.

Oakville Wine Storage was a refrigerated and heavily insured building set in the center of a square gravel lot, which provided space between its valuable contents and raging wildfires. It was also situated in the coolest spot of Northern California wine country, where redwood trees still grew, and refrigeration was more economical. People stored their wines here for extra room or security or sent them here to be inspected for onsite and online auctions.

Sarah dropped her iPad into her purse in case she needed it at the inspection. At the last minute, she remembered to grab her jacket, since it would be cold where the wine lots were stored. As she lifted the jacket, she saw the ballerina puppet roll onto the seat and lodge face-down, her smaller leg sticking out behind her.

"Later, girlfriend," she said. "Time to get to work."

As she walked toward the glass door of the warehouse, she spotted Arthur Chen's slight figure in the lobby, dressed in charcoal-colored slacks and a blue shirt. She pressed the intercom, stated her name, and was buzzed in. Arthur held the door for her.

"Good afternoon, Sarah. Thank you for coming."

"Arthur." She nodded at him as she passed into the lobby. The space was not designed for public use and was sparsely decorated with a water cooler, a suffering parlor palm, two plastic chairs and a reception desk. The business end of the building was beyond the locked door near the desk—with a loading dock, forklifts, wrapping machines, shipping supplies and a counter full of inspection equipment and computers.

"It is a hot day," Arthur commented. "Very hot."

"*Aye, 'tis.*"

She was not in the mood for casual conversation. Come to think of it, she never was. But if she didn't say something more, the silence in the lobby would become awkward. To her relief, Zach opened the locked door a second later and saved her from further inanities. As usual, she was glad to see him.

Besides developing his own vineyard and working the evening shift at the Wolf House, Zach's day job was director of Oakville Wine Storage, where he managed incoming product, the inspection process, storage and transport. She marveled that he could keep up such a pace, working a day job as well as a night gig. Then again, Matteo worked similar long hours. Sarah wondered if Zach's wife felt as abandoned as she had with Matteo.

The bastard.

Sarah had to quit thinking about her husband. He didn't deserve any time in her head.

"Sarah," Zach greeted. "Long time no see." Then his dark eyes trailed down her torso. "How many of those red blouses do you actually own?"

So, he *had* noticed. She should have known he would.

"Just the one. But it's my favorite."

"It is agreeable to the eye," Arthur put in. "You do not see this hue much in America these days."

"Red's my color," Sarah said. She arched a brow and shot a hard glance at Zach to squelch any more comments about her apparel or her possible whereabouts the night before. "Zach, this is Arthur Chen. He called about Bill Friske's DSE?"

"Yes." At the mention of Friske, the twinkle in Zach's eyes faded and a dark look flitted through, like the shadow of a buzzard sweeping over a fallow field. "I've checked him in already."

Zach strolled to the reception desk and picked up the check-in log on a clipboard. Valuable wine storage required extra precautions when it came to anyone coming or going. He scribbled Sarah's name, date and time on the paper and then placed the clipboard near the phone.

"All right. Come with me." He led the way into the main warehouse.

Sarah liked the way Zach's slender hips rolled as he walked. He was obviously a man accustomed to walking: down the rows of his root stock, along the stacked stone fence lines and over the vine-striped hills of Sonoma Valley. He could take the heat, the breathless afternoon air and the foggy mornings that nurtured the finest Zinfandel and pinot noir grapes—always walking, always evaluating. She could picture him ambling along a dusty lane cobbled with acorn shells, inspecting his land before dinner, a dog at his heels.

She also noticed how his jeans fit him perfectly—not too tight and not too long. His clothes always appeared to be clean and neatly pressed. She wondered if Courtney ironed his jeans. Maybe ironing was the secret to a good marriage. She didn't even own an iron. Perhaps that's where things had gone wrong. Who knew anymore?

In the main warehouse, Zach consulted a computer for the general location of Bill Friske's DSE and then indicated them to follow him again. He punched numbers on a keypad and pushed open the door to the vault. After turning on a bank of low lights, he motioned them forward.

They walked single file into the vault, which was much colder than the main warehouse and designed very much like an underground cellar. Sturdy metal racks crowded the space, stacked with wooden crates and cardboard boxes labeled with barcodes to identify each owner and wine lot sent to the storage facility. The vault was so large and so dimly lit that Sarah couldn't see the far corners. Zach closed the door behind them and turned for the counter near the door.

While Zach pulled on latex gloves, Sarah slipped on the jacket that she had purchased in Frankfurt a few days ago. It was a military style coat with a double row of silver buttons down the front and a high collar. It fit her well and accentuated her shoulders and neck, which she considered her best features. Best of all, the soft cotton fabric was a perfect insulator against the chilly fifty-five degrees of the storage room.

Zach turned left and padded down a row, scanning the barcodes with a handheld device while Sarah and Arthur trailed behind him. When the scanner beeped, Zach looked up at a box above his head.

"Here it is." He stuffed the scanner in a back pocket. "I'll bring it over to the counter, so you two can have a better look."

"Thank you." Arthur made way for Zach to carry the wooden box to a counter at the end of the room. Zach switched on another light. The glow pooled on the Formica surface and outlined the faded initials stamped on the top of the box.

To start the inspection, Sarah ran a practiced eye across the wooden crate, taking in each detail. This was her specialty. This was why people all over the world sought her out and paid her outrageous fees. They wanted to be sure before they purchased expensive wines that they were buying the genuine article. Collectors and restauranteurs counted on her nose, her palate, her eye—and yes, although it was unsexy as hell—her meticulously curated database.

At her nod to continue, Zach carefully slid the lid out of its tracks and set it aside, taking great pains not to nick the edges. His company would be liable for any damage sustained to the product here in the warehouse. There would be proof of the slightest mishandling. Photos and documentation trailed expensive wines wherever they traveled.

Sarah moved forward to stand at Zach's elbow.

"Huh," she said, gazing down at six bottles laid flat, tops to bottoms, resting on wooden racks and surrounded by fifty-year old wood shavings that still smelled of pine. "Who would have guessed." She breathed out a low whistle.

"What?" Arthur asked, hovering close. "What is it?"

"A rare Domaine St. Emile. I encouraged Friske to buy this vintage years ago. But he only laughed at me. And now here it is...a '73. So rare. Unheard of, almost. An original box lot, too. An OBL. I wonder how much he paid for these puppies?"

"A great deal, I suspect," Arthur leaned close for a better look. "An OBL of this wine is the holy grail, is it not?"

"I wonder what this will fetch at the auction?" Sarah murmured. "Might set a record."

"All I know is my client is willing to pay handsomely. To add to his collection. To corner the market."

Sarah slipped a penlight out of her purse and swept the powerful beam over the bottles. Without touching anything, she inspected the capsules, the level of the liquid in the bottles, which in her line of business was referred to as the *ullage*, as well as the color of the wine and the labels. Behind her, she could sense the men holding their breath, watching.

After a few seconds, she snapped off the tiny flashlight. "I've seen enough. You can put the lid back on, Zach."

"So?" Arthur studied her face intently.

Sarah nodded at the crate. "Was this the same vintage your client thought was off?"

"Yes."

"He actually opened and drank a '73 DSE pinot?"

"My client can afford to."

Sarah slipped the flashlight into her purse. "Well, he's got chops, that's for sure."

"What do you mean?"

"He recognized that it wasn't a '73. Maybe not even a DSE. I don't know what he bought. Could have been a red blend from Walla Walla."

"I knew it," Upset, Arthur stepped back.

"Zach," Sarah touched Zach's arm. "Take this lot out of the catalog. They're all fakes."

It was Zach's turn to be surprised. "They are? What did we miss?"

"Something easily overlooked when you aren't that familiar with a vintner. How often do you come across a DSE?"

"Last year was the first time."

"So, you aren't aware of the nuances of the label of this particular house."

"The label gave it away?" Zach leaned in for a better view, as did Arthur.

"*Aye*," Sarah replied. "In 1974, in winter, I believe, France suffered a significant earthquake. Lots of wineries lost their futures that year. Domaine St. Emile managed to save a single barrel of their '73 pinot. Just one barrel. It was a real shame because their grapes were exceptional that year. It was a spectacular harvest. Truly remarkable."

"But what does that have to do with the label?"

"The earthquake caused damage to the chateau, not just to the cellar. One of the chimneys collapsed and was never replaced. After the earthquake, the DSE logo was changed to reflect the damage."

Zach bent over a bottle and scowled. "There is only one chimney on these labels..."

"Exactly."

"It can't be a '73 then," Arthur murmured. "When there were still two."

Sarah nodded. "Whoever is counterfeiting knows that '73 DSE is pure gold. But they don't know about the chimney. Because they have never actually seen a '73. Very few people have."

"I knew it!" Arthur exclaimed. "That thief, Friske. He must make good on the last deal or suffer the consequences."

"Hold on," Sarah advised. "Friske may not know his cellar is compromised. The man might be full of himself, but I don't think he's a counterfeiter."

"I wouldn't put it past him," Zach growled, pushing the lid back into place. "The guy's shady."

Sarah watched Zach adjust the lid until it was perfectly centered. "Before we jump to conclusions about Bill Friske," she said, "I suggest we pay him a visit and clear this up. He might have bought fakes himself. He might be a victim, too."

"Victim, my ass," Zach said.

"I don't like the poser any more than you do, Zach, but a counterfeit rumor could ruin his reputation. Oakville Wine Storage, too, if the fakes got past you last year."

"Good point." Zach sighed. "Think Friske's up here in Sonoma, though?"

"We'll soon find out." Sarah reached for her phone and called Friske, but no one answered.

Everyone knew that Friske spent most of his time in his swanky Pacific Heights mansion in San Francisco while he snapped up distressed and dying wine country properties, building his portfolio on the misfortunes of others. Worse, he sat on the properties, gambling on inflation to make a profit, while the estates produced nothing but dust bunnies, weeds took over patios and fruit rotted on the vine.

"Come on, Arthur." She headed for the door. "We'll drive up to Paradise Valley and see if he's in. We might get lucky."

"You mean go today?" Arthur's black brows rose.

"Better the *noo*, pal."

Not understanding her Scottish burr, Arthur shrugged, confused.

"No time like the present, Arthur. Let's go." Sarah grabbed the door handle. "Thanks, Zach."

"You got it, Sarah. Nice work, by the way."

She grinned. Praise coming from Zach was the best. "I need to talk to you about something, though. You working tonight?"

"Yeah. At seven."

"I'll stop by."

Arthur stood to the side, chafing his chilled biceps while he waited for the conversation to end. She turned to him. "Arthur? Follow me in your car. Let's get some answers from Mr. Big."

Chapter 7 | Friske Office

Sarah guided Arthur out of Sonoma and north to Glen Ellen, home of Paradise Valley Winery. Once they got to Glen Ellen, they were the only vehicles on the road. But she liked that. She enjoyed the slower pace of the little village.

She hoped Bill Friske was at the winery, and they could resolve Arthur's issue in a few minutes. If not, at least she would be close to her own house. She could finally go home and take a shower. That is, *if* she could bear to look at the shower. She might have to switch to baths from here on out. Really change it up.

She turned left at the Wolf House Bar and switched off her personal problems, so she could, concentrate on the road. It curved up a hill through a canopy of monstrous live oaks and messy eucalyptus, with their ribbons of bark hanging off the trunks and littering the dirt. Nothing much grew beneath the trees but brambles and burrs. The soil was too poor and the sun too hot for anything but the hardiest flora—of which grapes were king.

At two o'clock, the mid-April day was already too hot to walk more than a couple of blocks. But Sarah loved the heat. After growing up in cold, rainy Glasgow and then living in foggy San Francisco, she appreciated all the sunshine she could get. She loved the big old trees and the lazy streams. She drove with the top down and her blond hair blowing in the mentholated breeze.

At the crest of the rise, she spotted the unassuming sign for Paradise Valley Winery.

The property couldn't be seen from the entrance, and a person could easily miss the drive as well as the sign. Even using navigation, a person might think the directions were wrong and would look for a grander entrance down the hill. Sarah made sure Arthur was close behind her and then turned onto the narrow, paved lane, which seemed to be leading them into the wilderness. But that was part of the design of the place. Like its complex wines, Paradise Valley revealed itself in layers of unfolding delights.

The lane wound between two high berms covered in dried grasses, which appeared to be a wasteland. But after a few seconds, the vegetation changed. Mounds of lavender dotted the slopes, along with bright orange California poppies backed by huge clumps of pampas grass. A larger-than-life metal statue of a rearing horse rose on the left, rusting in the sun, and probably boiling hot to the touch. Sarah felt as if she were venturing into a magical world through an increasingly lush corridor—exactly what the landscape designer had intended.

The lane gradually curved to the right, and suddenly the vista opened to a wonderland of irrigated green. Sarah shifted to a slow roll, gob smacked once again, even though she had seen this place before.

Stretched out in front of her was a magnificent vista as beautiful as any Tuscan estate. Paradise Valley was comprised of a wide bowl with a lake at the bottom, fed by a year-round stream and surrounded by hills striped with leafy vines. Terraces of silvery olive trees ringed an incline on the left. A vineyard curved around the slope at the right. Cypresses stood sentinel along the drive that meandered gently downward to the winery buildings and tasting room. Far in the distance, the windows of the gigantic Victorian mansion glinted through oak leaves, while a flag sporting a rearing horse flew from the roof of one of its towers.

To the right, overlooking the lake, Bill Friske had gouged out a building site and a temporary drive, where he and his wife Hunny were erecting a modern cement and glass structure. Sarah wasn't averse to modern architecture, but such a home didn't belong here. Not in Paradise Valley. The steel and glass building ruined the Tuscan Fantasy vibe and looked more like a downed alien spacecraft than a home.

While construction dragged on, Bill and Hunny were forced to live in the old house when they came to town. Socialite Hunny probably hated every moment she had to spend in the drafty old Victorian with its intense wallpaper and dark walnut woodwork. But the times Sarah had visited the winery years ago, before it had been sold and before she knew Zach and Courtney, she had thought the tall cool rooms of the house were a welcome respite from the sun. She put her car in gear and set out for Zach's childhood home.

Conveniently for Arthur Chen, Bill Friske was indeed in residence at his wine country domicile. A housekeeper ushered them into his office to the left of the enormous foyer and told them Mr. Friske would join them momentarily. Just as she reached for the door to close it, an imperious female voice called from another room.

"Maria!" the voice scolded. "Come here at once! Look at this baseboard!"

The housekeeper shot Sarah an apologetic look and hurried back out to the foyer.

Sarah watched her skitter across the foyer to an apparently upset mistress, and then she turned her attention back to her client.

"It is a beautiful home," Arthur stated, breaking the awkward silence. He rotated slowly, taking in the room with its blue and green wallpaper and velvet furniture.

"You've never been here before?"

"No."

"The tasting room used to be in this building. I once brought lots of visitors here. It was one of my favorite wineries for a tour and tasting."

Sarah decided to give him the history of the place while they waited. For some reason, the tales of the wineries stuck in her head like no other data. Each winery had a personal story of vision, loss and triumph. And she loved them all.

Matteo could tell her an anecdote about street food in Singapore, and she would forget the details immediately. But a winery story? Never.

"Paradise Valley is one of the original wineries of Sonoma County. It was founded by Zachariah Sullivan, Zach Sullivan's great-great-grandfather, who won a fortune on a horse and decided to emigrate from Ireland. He came over by boat in the 1840s, landed in San Francisco, and walked up here. I mean, actually walked."

"One certainly gets to know the terrain that way."

"He claimed this was the most beautiful spot in Northern California. The best terroir."

Arthur was still nodding thoughtfully when Bill Friske swept through the doorway. He was a fifty-something gentleman, in excellent physical shape, with the easy grace of a guy who could spend two hundred dollars on custom made cashmere socks. At first glance, he seemed like a tall man, with his steel-gray hair, steely blue eyes and expensive slacks and polo shirt. But the height sleight of hand was due to his impeccable posture and burning confidence. He was only a couple inches taller than Sarah, making him at the most five foot ten.

Bill strode across the room, waved them toward chairs and lowered his lean frame into the large leather chair behind his equally large desk.

"Sarah McKee." His cold perusal passed over her rumpled clothes. She thought she saw his lip curl. But she could be reading into things. "What brings you here?"

"The usual. Wine."

"Of course." He smiled smugly and turned his attention to her companion.

"Bill, this is Arthur Chen, a broker from Hong Kong."

Arthur bowed his head slightly. "Mr. Friske. A pleasure to meet you."

"Likewise. Here for the auction?"

"I am."

"It's going to be a helluva party. My wife Maeve is the chairman this year. Let's hope she can handle it. Speaking of which, there she is." He indicated the door behind them. "Do come in, Hunny."

Sarah rotated in her chair, curious to see what Maeve "Hunny" Friske looked like in person. She'd only seen pictures of the woman in newspapers and magazines. She knew Maeve was a blond beauty, a former model, decades younger than her husband, with a figure only Pilates and pills could achieve. Her toned upper arms looked as if they could crack nuts against her ribcage. Her shoulder length hair, flipped over one artfully drawn eyebrow, was so perfect, it had to have been shellacked in place. She wore a light blue knit dress, spotless and perfect, with a charm bracelet that glinted with yachts and Eifel Towers—a twinkly testament to every luxurious holiday she'd taken with her millionaire husband.

Sarah watched Hunny flow across the floor in her bright red heels, walking as if she were on a stage, shoulders back, boobs leading the way, and chin held high. Did husband and wife attend posture classes together? She had to wonder. She also had to wonder at the way Hunny's eyes glittered at Bill. She didn't know what was frostier—Hunny's eyeshadow or her expression as she regarded her husband. Apparently, Bill and the housekeeper were currently out of favor with the queen.

After introductions were made, Hunny stood at the window, backlit by the afternoon sun, her arms crossed, looking like a silhouette of a paper doll, tapping an index finger on her bicep.

"I take it, this isn't a social call," Bill began.

"It isn't." Sarah leaned back in her chair. "Mr. Chen asked me to evaluate one of the lots you're offering at the auction."

"Oh?" The word was icy with curiosity and affront.

"A client of mine purchased a similar lot last year from you," Arthur said. "And it was not as it should be."

"Not as it should be?" Bill skewered Arthur with a haughty glare. "What are you talking about?"

"In a word, my client claims it was a knock-off. And my client, I must tell you, is very angry."

"Chen, is it?" Bill struggled to contain his umbrage. "I do not sell knockoffs, Mr. Chen."

"Perhaps it's a mistake or some kind of oversight." Sarah put in. "But it appears there's a problem."

Bill's head swung in her direction. "That's ridiculous. My collection is the finest around. Without a doubt, *the* finest in the whole damn country."

"I have proof, Bill."

He sat back, his eyes locked on hers, as his mind swept through his cellar, eager to prove her wrong. Just like the old days. "Which wine are we talking about?"

"A '73 Domaine St. Emile pinot noir."

"Wasn't that the wine you told me to buy?"

"Yes, it was. And you blew me off." Sarah held his stare.

"Because I never liked your tone. Not then. And certainly not now."

"Think that bothers me, pal?" She didn't drop her glare. They glowered at each other.

"I could ruin you, McKee. You and your husband's little restaurant. One word from me, and Olive is the pits." He quirked a smile. "Pardon the pun."

Sarah rose. "Are you threatening me?"

"I'm warning you. Play nice, or things could get messy."

"I'm here because I *do* play nice. If you want to lose your reputation by selling fakes at auctions, be my guest, Bill. But I suggest you find out what's going on in your cellar."

"I know what's going on in my cellar. I have the best manager in the business. Chris Girard."

"Girard?" Sarah blew out a disgusted puff of breath. "I wouldn't trust him to manage my fruit bowl."

"That's enough." Hunny released her arms and marched forward. "No one speaks to William this way."

"But Ms. McKee speaks the truth." Arthur Chen rose and slipped an envelope from the breast pocket of his suit jacket. "However difficult to hear. And I must warn you, Mr. Friske, of the gravity of the situation."

"Gravity?" Bill leaned back in his chair and huffed a snort of disbelief.

"Yes. My client, Mr. Xu, does not suffer offenses lightly. He demands restitution for the fakes you sold to him."

"Again. I do not sell fakes. In addition, Mr. Chen, I don't own a '73 Domaine St. Emile. Not a single bottle."

"I must disagree. You sold a case online to my client last year. My client opened a bottle two weeks ago on his anniversary. And as I said, he was not happy with the experience." Arthur placed the envelope on the desk blotter, restraining his frustration with studied grace. "The information is here. As well as the numbers of a bank account where you can make restitution. Within two days."

"This is outrageous!" Bill vaulted to his feet.

Arthur indicated the envelope with a graceful sweep of his hand. "It is all there. Proof of purchase. Documentation. Photographs. In them, you will see the chimneys are wrong."

"Chimneys?" Bill stared at Arthur as if the man had chimneys growing out of his head.

"I would encourage you to make amends. My client is very powerful."

"Your client can go to hell. You *and* this extortion racket." Bill rolled his eyes. "Sarah, really. I can't believe you've brought this...this person to my winery."

"I'd take him seriously, Bill," she said.

"Mr. Xu has relatives in Oakland," Arthur added. "An hour from here. Who will do whatever he asks. No questions."

"Like what?" Bill sneered. "Spit in my walnut prawns?"

"This is not a joking matter, Mr. Friske. Good day." Arthur bowed curtly and treaded to the door.

Sarah raised her eyebrows at Bill and then walked through the cloud of Hunny's dark surveillance. At least one of the Friskes was concerned. She hoped that Hunny might talk sense into her husband after they left.

Just as Sarah and Arthur reached the bottom step of the porch, she saw a man walking briskly toward the house. His bearded face looked familiar.

"Sarah?" he greeted, glancing from her to Arthur, evaluating them, and not in a friendly way. "What a pleasant surprise." His flat eyes undercut his words.

"Chris Girard, I never expected to see you so far from civilization." Sarah stuck out her hand. He still looked the same as the day he replaced her. Still thin and cocky, still smiling that know-it-all smirk, still an arse.

"Likewise. Chen." He nodded at Arthur and then his hard glance returned to rake over her. He pulled a cigarette from a pack hanging in his chest pocket and a lighter from his slacks. He lit his smoke and then wiggled the lighter in front of her face.

"Look at this beauty. Fine, isn't it?"

Sarah evaluated the small metal container, which was decorated with a rearing horse, like the statue at the winery entrance, and covered in silver filagree. A ruby or piece of red glass decorated the center. She wasn't a gem expert, so she wasn't sure. But judging by the Sullivan family history, she assumed the gem was real.

"Cool, huh?" Chris continued. "Friske gave me the entire collection. Thought they were junk. Apparently, old man Sullivan had them made every year until he popped his clogs."

"And you're using them?"

"Why not?" He took a drag. "That's what they're for. They work like a dream, too." He smirked and dropped the lighter into his pocket. "I heard you moved up here."

"*Aye*. We did."

"So did I." He blew smoke to the side. "Rents in San Francisco are insane."

She watched him take another drag on the cigarette and wondered how a person who smoked could ever keep their nose and palate sharp. "So where are you living?"

"Here, as a matter of fact."

"At Paradise Valley?" Sarah was shocked. Living with a client was totally unprofessional.

"Yeah, in the carriage house. With that maid of theirs down the hall. That's going to have to change. You know how I need my own space."

She didn't, and she didn't want to.

"Bill actually hired me to manage the entire place," Girard continued. "Not just his cellar. It's wild. It's a biodynamic winery. Lots of woo-woo stuff with the moon.

Bugs. Composting crap. What a mess. That's going to have to change, too. No doubt about it."

"Sounds like your work is cut out for you."

"No kidding."

"Sounds like you won't have much time for your other clients."

"Oh, Bill's my only one now."

"Really?"

Chris nodded. "Keeps me busy. And I have to say, the pay isn't shabby. No complaints there."

"Be careful about being sucked into the Friske world, Chris. Folks in the valley don't like him much."

"Laughing all the way to the bank." Chris reached for the banister. "All the way, McKee. So, no need for the unsolicited advice. Nice seeing you, Chen. Catch you at the auction?"

"If you can get the cow shit off your shoes," Sarah drawled.

Chris shot a glance at his footwear, realized she was toying with him and glared at her, his face red and his sense of humor MIA.

"I see you haven't lost the potty mouth," he shot back, tossing the cigarette butt into the hydrangeas that bordered the porch. "Still think you're funny, too, don't you?"

She shrugged and returned his smirk. "You can take the lass out of Scotland, but you can't take Scotland out of the lass."

"Somebody should." He glowered at her.

She motioned for Arthur to follow her out to the parking lot.

"That is some duo." Arthur trailed after her. "Bill Friske and Chris Girard."

Sarah nodded. "I'll say. Who knows what they'll get up to together."

"Perhaps counterfeiting after all?"

"I can't see it," she mused. "Bill has spent a fortune on his collection. Why turn to counterfeiting?"

"Business troubles?"

Sarah walked the rest of the way in silence. Arthur could be right. Bill might have finally overstretched his finances.

At their cars, Arthur paused. "All I know, Sarah, is I would not wish to be your Mr. Big or Mr. Girard if he does not comply."

"What would your client do if Bill doesn't pay?"

"I would not venture to guess. But as I told you, lives could be at stake. No one crosses Mr. Xu. No one."

****

Sarah drove to her house in Glen Ellen and unlocked the door. She loved the cheerful orange front entry and mid-century panel at the side and noticed them every time she entered her home. But as she walked down the hall, her appreciation faded, as she was overcome by visions of Matteo and his lover in the shower. She pushed the scene out of her mind and turned on the taps of the tub in the guest bathroom. The roar of the water helped blot out her thoughts. Then she hurried down the hall to the master bedroom to strip and put on her robe.

Damn that Matteo. This was her house. Glen Ellen was *her* village. But how could she live here now, in this place of defilement? As she unbuttoned her blouse, she looked around the bedroom. Had Matteo slept with others here? In the bed? Her bed? Hot bile rose in her throat. She trudged to the door that opened onto the deck and looked down at the creek. The deck had been one of her favorite spots on Earth. But would it ever be a place of refuge again? Had Matteo poured Prosecco for a lover out there while she traveled on business? The possibility burned in her gut.

Ghosts closed in on her, swirling around her, making her ears ring.

"I need a bath and some sleep," she said out loud. "Then we'll see who's king of this castle."

After a bath, she fell asleep in the guest bedroom and didn't awaken until a car door slammed outside.

"What the hell?" Groggy and disoriented, she rose on an elbow and picked up her phone. Dusk had settled over the glen outside. How long had she slept?

The doorbell rang.

She squinted at the time on the phone screen. 7 pm.

Who was here? Not Matteo. Not during dinner service.

The doorbell rang again.

Sarah dragged her protesting body off the bed and stumbled down the hall, fumbling with the belt of her robe with hands that hadn't awakened all the way.

Before she got to the end of the hall, someone pounded on the door.

Chapter 8 | The Sheriff

"Hold your horses," Sarah called as she paused to run her fingers through her tangled hair. Then she turned the deadbolt, pulled open the door, and was surprised to see Sheriff Bradley standing there, posed to pound again.

He paused, his fist in the air as he took in her tousled state. The intense determination in his eyes eased into simmering interest.

Sarah read each reaction as it streaked over the taut skin of his face—surprise, amusement, confusion, and something she could only define as smoldering male hunger. The female part of her, so often denied during her marriage, came to immediate and breathtaking attention, catching her off guard.

She usually didn't allow herself to entertain physical reactions to men other than Matteo. In the wine business, it was all too easy for a person to get swept away by the romance of a vineyard or the intimate ceremony of sharing a special vintage with a collector, sequestered in a dark, dimly lit cellar. Sarah made a practice of keeping her business dealings strictly business. Fooling around with a client could jeopardize her career.

Fooling around with a law enforcement officer might be just as dangerous. But there was no denying her body wanted to fool around with Sheriff Bradley.

"Am I interrupting something?" He lowered his hand, as if suddenly realizing it was still in the air and hooked the thumb in his utility belt.

"No. You're not interrupting." She flushed and swept him forward. "I was taking a nap. Jet lag."

"Ah. Kelley mentioned you had just returned from Europe."

"*Aye*. Germany. Come in."

The cloud of his aftershave enveloped her as he strode by her, into the living room. "Sorry to wake you. My apologies."

"No, it's all right. I shouldn't have slept as long as I did." She adjusted the lapels of her robe. "Can I get you something? Cup of tea? Beer? Or are you on duty?"

"No. I'm on my way home."

"Where's home?"

"Santa Rosa."

So not Vallejo after all. He might not have fake grass on his deck, either. But the aftershave was, sadly, all too real.

"Well, I need a cup of tea before I can think straight." She headed for the kitchen. "Come this way."

She doubted that tea would have any effect on her libido.

He followed close behind her, like an enormous shadow. His towering frame and wide shoulders filled up the hallway as well as her consciousness. She was exceedingly aware of his measured step behind her and knew without looking back that he was evaluating her hips and waist. His survey should have upset her. Instead, her nipples tightened to pebbles beneath her cotton robe.

"Beer for you?" She asked, struggling to overcome her primal response to the man.

"Why not? Sure."

Sarah reached into the fridge for a Peroni, Matteo's favorite beer, and popped off the cap with a wine opener.

Bradley stood at the island, too close for comfort, and casually propped one lean hip against the countertop, watching her hands as she worked. His leather utility belt creaked. She didn't dare let her gaze linger on that part of his body.

"Glass?"

"Bottle's fine." His black eyes flicked from the Peroni to her breasts and then away. Had he noticed her perky nipples? *Gawd*. She flushed. She thought she detected a similar flush on his sharp cheekbones, but it was difficult to be sure because of the rich tone of his skin.

She thrust the bottle toward him and kept her gaze trained on the drink instead of his handsome, sculpted face. But even that did nothing to steady her pulse. Why did beer bottles look so much like dicks? As he took possession of the drink, his fingertips grazed hers. Goosepimples shot up her arm.

"Thanks." The word tumbled from his lips in an intimate rasp that sent the goosepimples racing across her chest and down to a place she refused to acknowledge.

She couldn't look into his eyes. She was afraid he would discern the inexplicable hunger flaring inside her. She didn't know this man, and yet she wanted to discover what his body looked like and felt like. Tasted like even. There was something about the combination of his runner's physique paired with the uniform that was indisputably sexy. Masterful. Like he could back her against a wall and do things with her that she had never dreamed possible.

She would wager the man had amazing stamina.

She had to get a grip.

To distract herself, Sarah went through the motions of making tea, as any agitated Scottish person would do. She pivoted and switched on the electric kettle while she tamped down her racing pulse.

"What brings you here?" she asked, keeping her back to him. She fumbled in the cupboard for the cannister of Yorkshire Gold tea.

"Actually, an acquaintance of yours. Bill Friske."

"Friske?" She glanced over her shoulder at him.

"He called me this afternoon. Mad as hell. Said you and some Chinese guy threatened him."

"We did no such thing." Sarah plopped a tea bag into her favorite cup. "We warned him."

"About what?"

"About passing fakes at the auction."

"He claims the Chinese guy demanded money from him. Told him if he didn't cough up the cash, thugs from Oakland would pay him a visit."

"He was trying to make a point about how critical the situation is. The fake wine Friske passed wasn't Two Buck Chuck, you know. Far from it."

"It was still a threat, Sarah."

"Did he also mention that he threatened to ruin my husband's—my ex's—restaurant?"

She shot a challenging glare at him. He blinked and stared back as he digested the information she'd just relayed. She wondered which fact interested him more—that Bill had made a threat of his own, or that she had separated from her spouse.

"Arthur Chen's client could sue Friske," she continued. "The issue could go public and ruin Friske's reputation. That's what the visit was all about. To make it known that we were onto him. To encourage him to make good on his deal with Mr. Xu."

"Xu?"

"Arthur Chen's client."

She poured boiling water into her cup. Bradley heaved a sigh behind her.

"Regardless, McKee. If there is something illegal going on in this county, it is my job to investigate it. Not yours."

"I wasn't investigating." She turned to face him, only to discover that he had moved closer. She hitched a breath and pressed against the counter behind her. "I was just doing my job. For a client."

She sustained his probing regard and then noticed the brooding uncertainty glinting in his dark eyes. She wasn't sure if the glint pertained to Chen and Friske or the heat that had flared to life between them the moment he walked into her house. Was he daring her to make the first move? Or battling his own animal instincts?

Finally, he broke off the stare and put the empty bottle on the counter. "I told Friske I would follow up with you."

"And you have." She lifted a brow, trying to make light of the dark undertow that pulled at her. "Will that be all, sheriff?"

He stared down at her, his eyes glittering. His stare dropped to her mouth. Sarah felt her entire body flood with heat. Her nipples caught on fire. Her panties went wet with dew. She braced her hands on the counter as a tidal wave of desire swept over her. For a long moment, his commanding figure trapped her in place, and his dark eyes consumed her.

Then he backed away.

"Thanks for the beer," he rasped. "I should go."

"Right," she answered, barely able to think. It must be the aftershave that muddled her thoughts. Or jet lag.

"Don't go near Friske again." He shook a finger in the air as he walked toward the unlit front room.

Sarah's fantasy screeched to a halt. No man shook a finger at her. Or told her what to do. She stopped in the hall, suddenly clear-headed. He opened the front door.

"Just so you know," she called after him. "The fake wine Friske sold was the same wine I found in the fridge of the dead man."

He looked back at her. "The Domaine whatever?"

"The Domaine St. Emile. Yes. Different year, but same vineyard."

"Think there's a connection?"

"I couldn't say. You're the investigator." She crossed her arms over her breasts, in command of her senses at last, and determined to keep her nipples as far from Sheriff Bradley as she could get them, preferably behind a padded underwire bra. And maybe a flack vest. "You tell me."

"I plan to." He gave her a long, smoldering stare and then a quick salute and closed the door behind him.

His reply hung with a double meaning that sent the tidal wave roaring over her again. Sarah sank against the wall near the foyer, still thrumming in a way she hadn't vibrated since she was a teenager. She couldn't believe how strongly she had reacted to the man.

Nothing a steaming cup of tea wouldn't fix. She returned to the kitchen, sloughing off the last few minutes of crazy as she walked into the light.

Sarah's stomach growled as she sipped the fragrant brew. She tapped the screen on her phone. It was seven-thirty Friday night. She was wide awake and not about to mope around the house. She'd also told Zach that she would see him at the bar. She texted Kelley, asking her to meet her at the Wolf House at eight. There, she could tell Kelley about SS Wines, the seller of the DSE, and Zach about the PVZ, if he could spare a minute. Friday nights at the Wolf House were often busy, even with two people tending bar.

Sarah dressed in a pair of jeans, suede ankle boots, white shirt and a scarf covered in a riot of poppies. Then she brushed on blush and mascara. Out of habit, she reached for the Crystal Noir perfume, but changed her mind and slipped out of the bathroom, naked of fragrance. One step into the hall, she turned around, grabbed the black bottle, stormed to the deck and threw the perfume against a tree. The bottle ricocheted off the trunk and rolled down the bank toward the creek, unbroken. Mocking her.

Sarah regretted her rashness immediately. She glanced over the railing at the slope behind the house. She would have to retrieve the bottle tomorrow and put it in the trash. The trek down the steep bank would be dangerous. High water had left piles of tree limbs and debris along the spate line.

Still, tossing the perfume overboard had felt freeing. She smiled. But the smile soon faded, replaced by the ache of loss and betrayal. She needed to get out of the house and get out now.

The six-block walk to the Wolf House Bar would do her good. She stuffed her phone in the pocket of her jeans, along with a credit card and cash. The last thing she needed right now was to be saddled with a purse. She locked the door with the keypad and turned for the road.

The night air smelled of warm earth and eucalyptus trees as well as the sea, which was only forty minutes to the west. She took an appreciative breath and strode up the hill to the main road. This was the first night of the rest of her life. It was up to her to make the most of it.

Kelley's silver Subaru Outback was already parked under the sycamore trees in front of the Wolf House. Sarah clumped across the old planks of the porch and opened the door. She caught Zach's eye and raised her brows. He nodded and smiled as he topped off a beer.

Sarah looked around the saloon. The place was packed. In the next room on the right, balls clacked and thumped at the pool tables. A woman laughed. A mélange of perfume and fabric softener laced with popcorn and beer rolled toward Sarah, finishing with a low note of a cherry cigar. Someone had broken the rules and smoked in the bathroom. Zach hated that.

In the next second, Sarah spotted Kelley sitting at their usual roost at the end of the wooden bar. Kelley waved. She wore bangles on her wrist, a print dress with a faded jean jacket, and bright red lipstick. In her off-duty hours, she worked hard to present a feminine front to the world.

"Hey," Sarah greeted.

"Look what the dog dug up," Kelley replied.

Sarah held out her arms. "Do I look that bad?"

"Naw," Kelley grinned. "You look great actually. Rested."

"I just got up. In fact, your boss woke me up."

"He said he was going to stop by. Did he read you the riot act about Bill Friske?"

"*And* shook his finger at me."

"Not the finger." Kelley rolled her eyes. "He doesn't know who he's dealing with."

"Right, but for some reason—because of everything that's going on with Matteo and me, I guess—I had the weirdest reaction to him."

"What do you mean?" Kelley picked up her beer.

"Like I wanted to jump his bones."

Kelley choked on her drink and covered her mouth with her hand, as she stared at her friend, her eyes dancing.

"I know," Sarah added. "It's hard to believe, right?"

"I'll say," Kelley sputtered.

Zach interrupted to slide a wine goblet toward Sarah. He pointed at it, cocked a brow at her and then left to help a customer. Sarah pulled the glass closer and looked down at it, pensive.

"It isn't like me," she added. "That reaction."

"Well, he is your type."

"A cop?" Sarah shook her head. "No way."

"He's built, handsome, well-groomed, kind of overbearing."

"Is that my type?"

"You always perk up around attractive men with attitude."

"I do?"

"Yeah."

"Well, I was so caught off guard that I forgot to tell him what I found in my database."

"About the DSE?"

Sarah nodded. "There were only two sellers in my records. Friske and a company called SS Wines."

"SS Wines? Does that sound familiar to you?"

"Not at all. I checked out their website, which was sketchy. I think it's a front. But let Bradley know, will you?"

"I will. SS Wines." Kelley typed notes into her phone. "I'll look into it."

"Did you find out who rents the apartment that Wesley lives in?"

"Someone named Anya Sarnova."

"Another mother? Maybe Woody's mother? Or girlfriend?"

"It's hard to tell. Records are scarce. So, I'm guessing possibly an illegal immigrant."

Sarah nodded, frustrated by the dead end. "What about the PayPal account?"

"Our tech is still working on it." Kelley chuckled. "What's with the questions? Have you decided to take over Sheriff Bradley's job?"

"Just interested. You asked me to help, and I like a puzzle." She nodded at Kelley's phone. "Speaking of which, could I see that photo again? The list with the numbers on it?"

"Sure." Kelley found the image and slid her phone in front of her friend.

Sarah studied the list again, trying to make sense of it. "Why the circled items?" she mused.

"We don't know yet. The list might be nothing. Not connected to the case."

Sarah bit her lip and kept staring at the photo until Kelley pulled it away from her.

"Did you talk to Matteo?" Kelley chided, breaking into her thoughts.

"Not yet."

"You might want to let him explain?"

"What's there to explain?"

"I don't know." Kelley dropped the phone in her purse. "And yeah, I called him all kinds of names the other night, but I can't see you two splitting up."

"It's been happening a long time, little by little. I simply didn't notice."

"Well, it's a shame."

Kelley's heartfelt words churned up a wave of remorse in Sarah. For an instant she grieved her broken marriage, but a moment later snuffed the pain that shot through her. It was better for her mental health to change the subject. Immediately. "Let's see what the quiz master has given me this time."

She picked up the goblet and swirled the wine, holding it up to the light and watching the fingers cling to the curve of the glass. "Oh, Zachary," she murmured. "Think you are going to stump me?" She stuck her nose into the top of the glass, as he materialized in front of her. She could tell it was him without looking up, by the fragrance that wafted toward her. The subtle stripes of his shirt curved in the glass. She held the goblet to the light again as if to study the color of the wine but took a moment to look at him through the glass instead. He grinned at her.

"Take your time," he said.

"*Dinnae* need to, pal." She put down the goblet with a clink.

"You haven't taken a single sip."

"*Dinnae* need to." She clasped her right wrist with her left hand and realized she'd forgotten to remove her wedding band. It glinted in the low light, mocking her, reminding her that she had an important decision to make.

"So?"

"Whitehall cab. Alexander Valley. 2002. No, make that 2003."

"Dammit." Zach's eyes gleamed in admiration. He reached for a bottle under the bar, showed her the label and filled her glass. "On the house, as agreed."

"As it should be."

"You're doing a number on my bank account, woman. I have to pay for the entire bottle now."

"Then quit trying to stump me."

"Why would I ever do that?" He poured himself a few ounces and savored a sip. "It's what I live for."

"Then you need a real life, my friend." Kelley held out her empty beer glass and shook it at him.

Zach took it and reached for the Deschutes tap. "You mentioned you had something to tell me, Sarah?"

"*Aye.* I think someone is selling 2016 Paradise Valley Zin," Sarah said.

"Not possible." Zach slid the frothy new beer toward Kelley.

"Why is that?" she asked.

"I own every bottle."

"You do?" Kelley gulped her brew, as curious as Sarah was. "Why?"

"As an investment. 2016 was a crappy year with an early frost. Most of our grapes didn't make it. My dad thought the ones that did were not fit to bottle. So, he threw out the must. Or told me to throw it out."

"But you didn't." Sarah took a sip of the wonderful cabernet sauvignon. The sunshine of the wine wrapped her in a comforting embrace, warming her to her bones.

"Nope. I did a side project that year. The old man didn't know about it. I hoped the wine would mature and improve. Even become drinkable. More than drinkable. By that time, my father's gambling addiction was starting to cause problems, and I was worried about the future."

"Hedging your own bets, huh?" Kelley put in.

"Just the kind of guy I am." He winked at her. Then he turned his regard to Sarah.

"Here for dinner?"

"A burger for me, please."

"Okay. One burger with extra American cheese. And I promise not to tell Matteo you've gone rogue." He crossed the air over his left breast. "Kelley?"

"I'm fine, Zach."

Zach left to start Sarah's dinner order while Kelley leaned closer. "You haven't told Zach about you and Matteo?"

"Not yet."

"You're going to have to tell him sometime."

"I know." Sarah pulled out her phone. "I have to find a right time for these things, though, *ye ken*?" She did a quick web search, which helped her focus on a less troublesome subject. "Just as I remembered."

"What?"

"The 2016 Paradise Valley Zin won all kinds of awards."

"But it's not for sale?"

"Like Zach said, he's holding onto it as an investment. I remember tasting it once at an auction reception. It caused quite a buzz."

"Why let people taste it if they can't buy it?"

"To whet their appetites. Make them want it more. Zach knows what he's doing." Sarah sipped her wine and closed her eyes, enjoying the velvety liquid that slid down her throat. "And so does Whitehall."

Kelley chuckled. "I wonder if there's anyone in the world who loves wine more than you do."

"He's right over there." Sarah nodded at Zach, who filled a bowl with popcorn for a waiting customer. "He could become a stellar winemaker at any of the places around here, but he's too proud. If you ask me, he's wasting his talents."

"As to talent, guess what I did?"

"What?"

"I auditioned for a part in a play."

"What?" Sarah pulled back to stare at her.

"Yeah. Me."

"Why?"

"It's something I've always wanted to do." Kelley shrugged. "After burning through every dating app on the planet, I thought I'd try something else. Something more rewarding than serial first dates."

"Is dating that bad?"

Kelley patted her hand. "You'll soon find out, my friend."

Sarah couldn't fathom getting back into the dating game. Not after twenty years. "So, this audition—did you get the part?"

"I did!"

"Congratulations!" Sarah held up her goblet and clinked it against Kelley's glass. "When's opening night?"

"June sixteenth. At the Community Center. You'd better be in town, girlfriend."

"I'll put it on my calendar." Sarah added the appointment and finished her wine.

"It's Cats, by the way. Your favorite."

"*Gawd.*" Sarah rolled her eyes. She didn't care for musicals, and Cats topped her list of productions never to be seen more than once, if ever.

"The costumes'll be a hoot, though." Kelley mused.

"For you, I will go. But only for you."

****

Late that night, Sarah refused Kelley's offer of a ride and insisted on walking home. From now on, she would try to get more exercise, even if it meant traversing a few blocks of road without a sidewalk and in complete darkness. She wasn't worried, though. People rarely drove through Glen

Ellen after midnight. The most dangerous animal she might encounter would be a raccoon or opossum.

She turned the corner and started down the hill to the house, keeping her phone trained on the gravel lane ahead of her. Not until she was a block from the house did she notice the silhouette of a second vehicle parked in front of the garage. She aimed the flashlight at the house and saw a Land Rover next to her Triumph.

Matteo had come back.

Chapter 9 | Matteo

Sarah scowled as she padded through the dark house and out to the back deck, where she found Matteo sitting in a pool of light, drinking a Peroni. She would never turn the back light on when she sat out at night, but he was probably Facetiming someone or taking selfies.

He slumped back in the chair, with one shapely leg crossed over a shapely knee. The deck light accentuated the lines of his wavy black hair and highlighted his supple abdomen beneath the silk tee-shirt he wore. With his tan body and five o'clock shadow, Matteo oozed masculinity and sexuality—merely by sitting there.

His perfect body was not for her anymore. She broke off her perusal and pulled open the sliding door. At the sound, he stood up in a quick, fluid motion.

"Sarah." The light above his head threw his eye sockets, nose and lips into shadow, transforming his striking looks into a distorted mask. But it was better for her that she was unable to see his gorgeous face or be affected by the warmth of his eyes. "Where have you been?"

"What are *ye* doing here?" she countered.

"I live here."

"Not anymore, *ye* don't."

"Come on, *amoré*. I can't keep sleeping in my office. People will talk."

"You should have thought of that before boinking the blonde." She tromped into the kitchen. He followed, hovering on the threshold between the house and deck.

"How many times do I have to say I'm sorry?"

"Let's see..." Sarah paused and looked at the ceiling, thinking back. "*Have* you said sorry? Your boyfriend did. But you didn't."

She yanked open the fridge and snatched out a bottle of water. A lump blocked her throat. She doubted she would be able to drink anything. But she had to do something other than look at her cheating scumbag of a husband. Or the rack of kitchen knives glinting near the stove.

"Then I'm sorry, Sarah. I am. But like I said, it was a one-off."

"I doubt that, Matteo. Looking back at our life together, I really doubt that."

"You travel a lot."

She glared at him. "That gives you the right to cheat?"

"I have needs." He shrugged. "I'm a man. I get lonely."

She pointed the bottle at him. "Don't put this on me, Matteo. This is all on you."

"Okay." He sighed and eased forward. "All right. If I admit that I was wrong to do what I did, will you let me stay? Work things out?"

"I don't hear the slightest bit of remorse here."

"We have a partnership, Sarah. Sometimes partners screw up. But that doesn't mean the partnership has to end."

"Depends on the screw up, pal."

"I hate it when you call me that."

"Well, I hate it when you screw other people." She opened the cap with a hard twist and took a drink, hoping the cold beverage would douse the wildfire in her stomach. No chance.

"Don't go provincial on me," Matteo said. "It doesn't become you."

"Provincial?" She gagged on the water, outraged. "*Provincial*?"

"You think long-term marriages don't have bumps here and there? Grow up."

"This isn't a bump, Matteo. This is Mt. Everest."

"Maybe to you."

"That's where it counts. To me."

"So, because of something insignificant, and I admit, totally out of character for me, you are going to throw away everything we have? Just like that?"

"What do we have, Matteo? What?" She slammed the bottle down so hard that water surged out the neck. "You work all hours. We never go out. We rarely eat a meal together. And we never have sex."

"We had sex a couple of weeks ago."

"Make that a couple of months ago," she shot back. "What kind of relationship is that? I'm always alone."

"Not for long. Once the restaurant takes off, we'll have a lot more time to spend together. I won't be so distracted."

"That's what you always say. Now I know why."

"*Cara...*"

"I'm not your *cara*, Matteo." She reached for the bottle cap. If she kept her hands busy, she might keep from wringing his neck. "I'm not your *amoré*. I'm not your anything. And I'm filing for divorce."

"You aren't serious."

"I'm dead serious." She wrenched the cap so hard, she made the bottle crackle. "I picked up your towels. I cleaned your piss off the toilet seat. I washed your skivvies. I gave you the best years of my life. And what do I get? No children. No companionship. And no respect."

"I respect you. God, Sarah, I love you. In my own way, I love you. More than anyone in the world."

"Well, pal, it's not enough. I expect loyalty."

Sarah met his intense regard and was surprised at what she saw when she really looked at him. An entirely different version of her husband stood before her, one she hardly recognized. Perhaps, not being blinded by love and lust, she was seeing his true character for the first time. There was a slight uptick at the center of his brows and an uncertainty in his eyes that had never been there before—or that she had never noticed. His shoulders sloped down to one side, revealing his fundamental insecurity. She saw his weakness, his helplessness, and his sad attempt at a rueful smile.

For the first time in their marriage, she perceived him as a little kid, standing in front of her, hoping for leniency. A slap on the hand. A verbal reprimand. Nothing more.

She felt like throwing up.

She had been living with a little boy for twenty years and had never recognized the fact. Until this moment.

He misinterpreted her silence and stepped toward her, arms held out.

"*Cara*, let me make it up to you. I promise I'll be good. I can be loyal. You'll see. We can work this out. We *will* work this out. We're a team."

She stood her ground. He could usually cajole her when he wanted to, but this time she would be strong. Then in the next moment, memories flooded over her, undermining her resolve. She remembered what it felt like to be enfolded against his warm body, to hear Italian words of love murmured in her ear. To feel his lips on her breasts.

She swallowed, suddenly appalled by the vision. Her stomach churned.

Now the thought of his lips on her breasts gave her the willies. What did he imagine when he kissed her there? She didn't want to know.

"I don't want to work it out, Matteo." She rocked the wedding band off her finger.

"Why?" He lowered his arms, distraught. "Why, after twenty years?"

"Because I'm not what you really want." Sarah placed the ring on the island, next to the salt and pepper shakers.

"Excuse me?" His sexy, vulnerable mouth twisted in confusion.

"You don't want a wife, Matteo. You want a mother."

He stared at her for a moment and then let out a puff of disbelief. "Ridiculous." He held out his arms again, displaying his sculpted figure and perfectly styled hair. "Does this body look like it needs a *mamma*?" He wiggled his fingers at her, urging her to step into his embrace, confident that she couldn't resist him. "C'mon, *amoré*. It's me. Matteo."

"*Awa' n bile your head.*" She waved him off, too upset to think of anything but Scottish slang.

"What's that supposed to mean?" he shot back.

"You're a chef. Figure it out."

Go away and boil your head. Of all people, he should be able to decipher the phrase. She brushed past him. "I have work to do. Clear out."

Sarah strode down the hall to her office and slammed the door. Matteo didn't pursue her, and after a few minutes his Land Rover peeled out of the drive. Sarah clenched her jaw and set to work making updates to her database, adding information from her trip abroad and notes she had gleaned from numerous blogs and digital magazines she had scanned on the plane. The act of typing entries kept her mind as well as her fingers busy.

The nausea lingered. She shouldn't have had that extra cheese. Or maybe that third glass of cabernet. When would she learn?

Sarah worked until three o'clock in the morning, fell into bed, and didn't rouse until her phone rang.

Chapter 10 | Wesley's Show

"Sarah," Kelley greeted on the other end. "You up?"

"I am now."

"Sorry!"

"It's okay. Sarah put her on speaker and sank back to the pillow. "What's up?"

"You have to see something."

"What?"

"Wesley's show."

"Really? Now?" Not all that interested in watching anything but the inside of her eyelids, Sarah tapped the screen. "Is it really nine o'clock?"

"Yep. Time's a wastin'," Kelley retorted.

"*Gawd.* I've got severe jet lag this time around." Sarah sat up and pushed the hair out of her eyes. "Call you back?"

"How about I come over? I'll bring some doughnuts, and you make coffee? Then we can watch the show together. Look for clues. It's a hoot."

"Deal."

"See you in twenty." Kelley rang off.

Sarah dragged herself to the guest bath and took a quick shower. As she dried herself in the tub, she planned her day. Today she would reclaim this house. Starting with throwing Matteo's belongings in a pile in the garage and then buying a new set of bedding and towels. She was not a guest to be relegated to a smaller bed and bathroom. She was the lady of the manor. And she would make the master suite her own again.

****

By the time Sarah had consumed a maple bar and three cups of black coffee, she felt almost human. What really woke her up, however, was Wesley's show, *Puppets on a Thing*. Kelley cast the live stream to Sarah's TV, and they sat in the living room, tittering and shaking their heads. The show was raunchy and teetered on the edge of smuttiness, but it was definitely funny—hilarious even—with the falsetto voices of the men shouting and whooping.

"Why do I find this so funny?" Kelley sputtered. "It's guys fooling around with their thingees."

"It's the eyes of the puppets." Sarah pointed at the TV. "They always seem surprised. Oh, dear *gawd*!" She burst out laughing.

"And look, the gun belt is falling off." Kelley giggled.

"And there goes the astronaut's helmet!"

They sat back, laughing hysterically while reactions from viewers exploded up the right side of the screen.

"Want to see a third one?" Kelley asked, picking up her phone.

"*Aye*, but I wish we could see Woody's face. So, we might have a clue what he looks like."

"It would sure help to identify him."

"What if he has a wife, Kelley? Kids. And they don't know he's dead?"

"Think a married guy does stuff like this?"

"Kelley, you can never tell what married guys might do."

Kelley flushed. "Yeah. Sorry."

"Let's watch another one. I could use the laugh."

Kelley located another episode, but this time a payment notice came up.

"Shit," Kelley exclaimed. "We have to pay to watch more."

"So that's how they do it. With a few teasers like the big guys do. Woody and Wesley must be raking it in." Sarah picked up her coffee mug. "Even I want to watch more."

"Me, too. But there's no way I'm setting up an account on their site."

"Probably a good idea." Sarah sighed. "I guess the fun is over."

"Yeah," Kelley disconnected her phone.

Sarah stood up. "I'm going to the mall in Corte Madera later. Do you want to tag along?"

"Wish I could. I've got a rehearsal this afternoon. The first one."

"That's exciting."

"It is. I'm pumped. But I have to learn my lines before then. So, I have to scoot." Kelley grabbed her purse and skittered to the door. "See you later, Sarah."

Sarah never made it to the mall. Packing up Matteo's clothes, books and electronics and carrying them to the garage took her longer than she anticipated. By the time she finished at five o'clock, she was sweaty and beat and in no mood for shopping. What she was in the mood for was food. Her only nourishment that day had been one and a half doughnuts. Her stomach growled. At least it had stopped churning.

A quick search of the kitchen made it clear that she had to go to the grocery store or grab dinner out. She chose the lesser of the two evils, took another shower, and left for the plaza.

In her former life, she would have popped into Olive for a bite and a glass of house red. Now, Olive was no longer an option. She decided to go to Greens & Beans instead. After her burger last night, she intended to mitigate the American cheese by eating healthy for a change. That is, if she could find a place to park.

Downtown Sonoma was crowded, with the throng of usual visitors swelled by early arrivals for the wine auction later in the week. All the convenient parking spots were taken, forcing her to go around the block to hunt for a space. She rolled down an alley to a lot she had never used before. She spotted a small slot just right for her car and pulled in.

A breezeway, with little stores on both sides, connected the back lot to the shops on Napa Street. A blue-tiled fountain tinkled in the center of the walkway, a cool respite from the still-warm afternoon. As she passed the spray of water, something caught her eye: the dusty window of a vintage record shop.

Curious, Sarah walked closer. So, this is where Matteo had been bitten by the vinyl record bug. He had told her that vinyl was coming back in vogue, and that nothing compared to the sound of an LP. In fact, Matteo had invested in a high-end turntable, speakers and set of albums that he had yet to listen to. Old albums in good condition were the best, he claimed, like rare bottles of wine. So, he had begun to collect his favorites.

All she knew was that vinyl albums were as heavy as sin when you had to schlep them out to a garage.

Posters for classic bands covered the windows of the shop: Led Zeppelin, Yes, Foreigner, Pink Floyd and Chet Atkins. Sarah smiled at their long manes of hair, and in the case of Chet Atkins, his super short one. Then a memory hit her full force. The dead man had been wearing a Journey tee-shirt. Could he possibly be a customer of this store, too? It was a long shot, but she decided to take the chance and ask. She pulled open the door.

A bell tinkled.

"Closing," a man's voice called from the back. "Sorry."

"I'll be quick."

"That's what they all say." A large man with a belly pushing out from under his striped tee-shirt, a neck like bread dough and wearing unlaced sneakers waddled up to the counter. He tried to smile, but he appeared more pained than delighted to see a late-in-the-day customer.

"I just have a question, sir."

He rolled his eyes, impatient. "No, I don't have any Justin Bieber."

"Is he still a thing?"

"Some people think so. Listen, just so you know, I don't carry anything beyond 1983. That's when real music stopped being written. So, if you're wanting anything after that, lady, I suggest Discogs. That's online." He sighed. "Or maybe for you, Amazon."

She ignored the disdain in his voice. "What about Journey?"

"I usually have some Journey, but right now I'm out. Can't really say when I'll have more. Supply chain issues and all."

"Did someone buy them all?"

"As a matter of fact, yes. For cash. A real collector."

"A red-haired guy? Young guy?"

"Yeah." His small eyes narrowed. "And your point? Because I'm closing." He peeked at his wristwatch and put a meaty hand on the counter. "I'm closed."

"Could you possibly tell me the collector's name?"

"Like I said, I'm closed."

"Well, then I'll have a friend of mine come and see you about those cash sales when you *aren't* closed. She's a cop. Doesn't like to see the state deprived of sales tax. Never gets a raise when that happens, *ye ken*."

He wagged his head and stared at her, his eyes full of annoyed unfriendliness. He rolled the tip of his tongue over the inside edge of his puffy lips as he considered the threat. For a moment, she worried that he might pay sales tax on his cash transactions and was about to vent his indignation on her. Judging by his massive body and the expression on his puffy face, she guessed the volume of his indignation would be considerable. She stood her ground, though, determined to get an answer.

He narrowed his eyes again. "Describe the customer again?"

"Thirty-something male. Red hair. Skinny."

"Could be Joe."

"Have a last name?"

He tilted his large head. "What do I look like? A telephone directory?"

"You must have a customer database. A point-of-sale app."

"It's updating," he retorted. "Because I'm *closed*."

"Fine, pal." Sarah turned for the door. "I'll come back tomorrow when you're open. With my friend. And ask you then."

She pushed through the door. The bell tinkled a second time. The hot afternoon air blasted her skin when his voice stopped her.

"Okay. Okay. It's Salgado."

"Joe Salgado."

"Yeah. Music freak. Regular."

"Thanks, pal."

"Next time, buy something, lady," he called.

"I would have, but you're closed." She shot him a sweet smile and shut the door.

Sarah walked through the breezeway to the restaurant, pleased with herself. She had discovered the name of the dead man: Joe Salgado. She couldn't wait to tell Kelley when rehearsal was over, but that might be awhile. She would text her when she got to the restaurant.

She was almost out to Napa Street when she saw a sale sign hanging in the window of a clothing store she liked. Even though her stomach growled, she knew it was unfashionably early for eating dinner. If Matteo was aware of her dinner plans, he would tease her about becoming a senior citizen. Fashionable people—young people—ate late, especially in Europe.

Sarah decided it wouldn't kill her to spend a few minutes in the store and find a summery dress to wear to the Flight of Fancy auction. She still didn't have enough warm-weather clothes—even though she had lived in the area for two years—and had nothing appropriate for the wine auction.

Sarah flipped through a rack of dresses and found a split-neck Kate Spade cocktail dress in cobalt blue. Elegant but not too formal. She could pair it with her vintage 1920s beaded clutch and braided slings. Perfect. She checked out and walked the rest of the way to the restaurant.

The restaurant was empty except for a single customer—and the last person she expected to see frequenting a soup and salad spot. Sitting at a booth in Greens & Beans was Sheriff Bradley, appearing very unofficial and extremely attractive out of uniform. He was dressed in a black polo shirt and black jeans and held a menu in both hands as he perused the single laminated sheet. When he flipped it over to survey the items on the other side, the tendons in his powerful forearms flicked. Her mouth went dry. She forgot all about his finger shaking.

"Sheriff Bradley," she greeted, crossing the room without waiting to be seated. At the sound of his name, he looked up. His eyes glinted over her with definite interest.

"Ms. McKee."

"Have a moment, or are you meeting someone?"

"Hardly." He swept her forward. "A man in my position has to be careful about who he spends time with."

"How careful?" she teased. She couldn't help it. Bradley was so staid. And so sexy.

"Really careful. I have to be, in a small town like Sonoma."

"Am I a risk to your reputation?" She tilted her head. He regarded her, smiled quietly and gazed back down at the menu.

"Not quite sure about you, McKee."

"Call me Sarah."

"Okay." He shook his head, seemingly amused. "Have a seat."

"You don't often see men in here," she remarked, sliding into the booth. "You're a vegan?"

"Is that a surprise?"

"I guess it isn't."

"What's that supposed to mean?"

"Well, you're so...so..."

"I'm so what?"

She fought for a reply, sidetracked by his simmering gaze. "So...healthy looking."

"I make it a priority." He raised his chin. "Because good health is the most important possession a person has."

"I suppose it is."

"No question, McKee." He pushed the menu toward her. "I recommend the kale Caesar. It's packed with vitamin A. Plus pistachios for protein."

"Does it come with a little loaf of sourdough? Or truffle fries?" Or a cold shower, she added under her breath. He didn't seem to hear her. He was too busy directing her dietary choices.

"You don't want starch." He nodded at the menu. "And try the cranberry/carrot smoothie. Good for your kidneys."

Sarah smiled, but it all sounded horrible. She'd only been in this restaurant once before, for a green juice, and now she knew why.

Bradley leaned back. "Pistachios are good for you, too. They have more zeaxanthin[1] and lutein content than any other nut."

"Good to know." She perused the menu, but nothing appealed to her. "Whatever that's for."

"Eyes. I've got 10/10 vision in both eyes. You don't get that kind of vision by eating cheese curls."

"I'll be blind in no time, then." She chuckled, but he only frowned at her, humorless.

"Laugh now, but when you're sixty, you'll wish you had been more careful."

"I've got decades to change."

"Well, I don't. I'm fifty."

It was her turn to sit back in surprise. She stared at his wrinkle-free face, his defined pecs, and muscular arms. Every move he made accentuated his superb muscle tone. "You're kidding me."

"I don't kid. Not when it comes to my health."

"You look about thirty-five."

"Well, I work at it." When the waitress came to take their orders, he chose items for Sarah before she could say anything. She was too busy admiring the tight line of his jaw and the way his Adam's apple rose and fell between the cords of his neck when he talked.

1.　　https://academic.oup.com/jn/article/132/3/518S/
4687218?searchresult=1

Matteo's jaw was always in a state of perpetual five o'clock shadow. Sheriff Bradley's skin was smooth as polished stone. She swallowed back the desire to reach out and feel the tight line of that shining jaw and forced herself back to reality.

The waitress repeated the order and turned to leave.

"Actually," Sarah put in, coming to her senses, "I only came in for a smoothie. That's all I want. To go, please. Separate checks?"

"You got it," the waitress replied.

"Not eating dinner?" Bradley asked, frowning.

"I think I have a bug. Or something from the plane food. My stomach's off." What she really suffered from was a severe case of lust. In fact, she felt downright feverish.

"Sorry to hear it. That's why I don't travel."

"Not an option for me." She shifted her weight. "I came over to tell you I discovered the name of the counterfeiter."

"Oh? How? Who is he?"

"I parked in the alley out back and noticed a record store in the breezeway. So, I popped in because I remembered the counterfeiter was a Journey fan. I thought they might know him. Sure enough, he was a regular."

"So, who was he?"

"His name was Joe Salgado. The clerk remembered him."

Bradley nodded and surveyed her, obviously surprised at her resourcefulness. "Good work, McKee."

Had he just checked out her boobs? He had. Desire streaked through her. She fought it back and reached for his water, her hand unsteady. She hoped he didn't notice.

"Does the name mean anything to you, though?" he asked. "From the wine industry?"

"Not at all."

Bradley pulled out his phone and did a quick web search while she watched his capable thumbs tap dance on the screen. She could imagine those thumbs dancing up her ribcage and around her breasts.

"Lots of Salgados." He scrolled the screen with one fingertip. "My staff will take it from here. And I'll have someone interview the clerk." He looked up. "We'll find the killer. I'll get the job done."

"I don't doubt it," she replied, gulping the water.

The smoothie arrived. Sarah paid the bill and stood up.

"Drink plenty more water," Bradley advised as she turned to leave. "It'll process out the bug faster."

"Will do. Cheers." Sarah tried not to hurry out of Greens & Beans, but she couldn't get away quickly enough. She felt as if she couldn't breathe. Sexual hunger hummed through her, tangling her thoughts. As she walked back to her car, she took a sip of the smoothie, grimaced, and dropped the drink in the trashcan outside the record shop. Then she drove to Safeway, got some cheese curls and Diet Sprite and went home.

She pulled into the drive and was relieved to see it empty. She let herself into the house, all the while planning her Sunday. She would shop for new sheets in the morning. And retrieve that perfume bottle she'd tossed down the ravine. And text Matteo to get his belongings out of the garage. For now, however, she would sit on the deck in her jammies, eat junk food and listen to the frogs in the glen, and then spend one more night in the guest room.

Tonight was another first night of the rest of her life. If she wanted to eat cheese curls and drink soda for dinner, then dammit, she would.

But her doorbell had other plans. Just as she settled into her chair on the deck, she heard it buzz.

Chapter 11 | Special Delivery

"I do believe I have a habit of interrupting your sleep," Sheriff Bradley drawled, glancing down at her lounge pants and tee-shirt, while a smile swam in his eyes.

She crossed her arms over her bra-less torso. "Apparently, you do."

"Sorry," he shrugged and smiled. "But I thought you might want this." He lifted a shopping bag into view with the handles looped over one finger.

"*Gawd*, did I forget that at Greens & Beans?"

"Found it on the seat after you left."

"Where is my head?" She reached for the bag. She knew where her head had been at the restaurant. The same place it was right now: completely focused on Sheriff Bradley's gorgeous body.

She grasped the handles of the bag, but he didn't release his hold on it. Surprised, she saw the humor in his eyes morph into hunger—the same hunger that made her fight for breath again. His free hand shot out and surrounded the back of her neck. Shocked by the bold move, she tipped back her head to regard him more intently, her hand and his still clutching the bag. He bent to her lips and moved forward to push her into the wall of the foyer. His warm mouth trapped hers and his lean chest and hips pressed against every pleasure point she possessed. It was as if his tall runner's figure was designed to perfectly align with her tall womanly curves.

Sarah surrendered to his kiss, astonished but aching for everything he had to offer. His fingers left her neck to slide down her arm and grasp her free hand. He pinned her wrist against the wall, so that both hands were trapped by her ears. He splayed her against the flat surface, taking her prisoner.

"Officer," she gasped, stunned by the lust flaring inside her but still trying to make light of it. "I swear. I'm innocent."

"I doubt that." He dipped to her mouth.

"Maybe you should read me my rights," she murmured against his hot lips. He ground into her breasts and hips.

"You have the right to remain silent," he rasped.

Then he cut off all conversation by kissing her as if he had been stranded in a squad car for ten years. And she kissed him back, as if she'd been ignored by a husband for even longer. She tried to climb onto his powerful frame, using only one leg, but couldn't quite make it. Desperate, she tugged at the hand still tangled with his.

"What's in the bag?" he gasped.

"Kate Spade."

"Don't want to ruin anything," he breathed, kissing her under her jaw.

"Don't care."

He released his hold on the handles and she did the same, and the shopping bag plopped to the floor. Then he growled in her ear, shut the door with his foot, and lifted her buttocks into his powerful, vicelike hands.

"Ma'am, I'm going to have to take you in," he said, playing along with the cop and criminal game.

"I do believe that's *my* line," she replied. She ran her hands over his warm, smooth cheeks, up and over his shaved head and across the muscular wedge of his back. Desire fanned over her in a wildfire she had no intention of fighting. He felt so good. So wonderful. So male.

In a frenzy, she disrobed him as he undressed her. They staggered through the room like two dancing bears, flinging away all trappings of civilization and consuming each other with growls and groans. He took her again and again and didn't let her go until they had rolled and writhed over every surface of the living room and the house went dark. And though he had amazing stamina—as she had guessed—and she gave him hints as to what she liked, she didn't reach a climax.

But she wasn't complaining. There would be a next time. In a bed. In her master bedroom. Music. Wine. Some intimate conversation. And an entire box of rubbers. A proper lovemaking session.

Still on the floor, Sheriff Bradley rolled onto his back, breathed out a sigh and stared up at the ceiling. She propped herself up on an elbow and gazed down at him, deliciously spent and feeling much better about the world.

When she reached out to caress his shining pecs, however, he angled one elbow in the air to glance at his watch, cutting her off. He sighed again and sat up. "Gotta go," he said.

"So soon?"

"Evening shift."

"Oh."

He rose and dressed. She got up and watched him, admiring his athletic ass and thighs as he pulled on his jeans.

She grabbed her tee-shirt and held it to her chest, conscious of her nakedness once he was dressed.

"Well," Bradley looked down at her. "Um, see you around?"

She blinked, surprised. Was that all he could say after ravishing her? She felt a stab of disappointment at his lack of imagination. At the same time, she chided herself for the critical review. The man had been amazing. A fantasy. She had never done anything like the gyrations she'd experienced with him for the past two hours.

"That was..." She broke off, lost for words. Any description of the session would lessen the moment. She opted for humor again. "That was some delivery."

He scowled, confused by the double entendre.

"You know, your delivery," she winked.

He stared, still confused.

"Of the dress," she added, dismayed. "I appreciate it."

"Ah." He brushed the top of her arm. "Sure. See you, Sarah."

"*Aye.*" She walked him to the door and stood behind it, hiding the state of her undress but feeling very close to him. She didn't want him to go. It would have been pleasant to make something to eat together. Have a glass of wine or cup of tea. Talk for a while. Instead, she watched him trot out to his truck. He waved and a moment later backed his shining Toyota Tundra out of her drive and left her standing in the dark.

Sarah sighed and closed the door. She should be accustomed to being left alone by now, but this time, the solitude closed around her in a heavy curtain, smothering the buzz.

Her only recourse was to distract her mind. She set to work, straightening the pillows and throw on the couch, centering the lamp on the end table, and picking up her lounge pants. Then she padded to the shower, where she hoped to suds away all traces of Bradley's *gawd* awful cologne.

Her body still thrummed, but her mind felt strangely blank. Maybe it had been jiggled free of its moorings with all the pummeling. She did feel soundly pummeled. In fact, her knees wobbled as she walked down the hall.

She couldn't believe what had just happened and with whom. She wondered what he had thought of her curves and her forward behavior. It had been so long since she had been swept off her feet by a partner whose appetite matched hers that she had nothing to gauge the experience by. All she knew was that Bradley was little more than a stranger. And a *polis*. The profession wasn't viewed in the best light these days. She set her jaw. So, what.

Like her father had always said, quoting the Scottish poet Robert Burns, "*A man's a man, fae all that.*" It wasn't what a man did for a living or what title he held, but the man himself that counted.

She washed her hair and then her body, remembering how Bradley's hands had felt on her buttocks and breasts. He had taken from her, but she had taken just as much from him. At the time, it had felt wonderful to be the object of someone's desire. Glorious, even, with the driving quest for more urging her own body on.

She'd be ready the next time. In the zone. Or not. She stepped out of the shower and reached for a towel, refreshed by the water into a more rational state.

She was of two minds about how to handle the future where Bradley was concerned. Her body was ready for more. Much more. But her head suggested the most prudent way forward was to downplay the liaison and pretend it never happened when she saw him next. Maybe he would do the same. After all, they both had reputations to protect.

Like Matteo with his boyfriend, she might be better off classifying her session with Bradley as a "one-time thing."

She dried her tender fanny while a vision of Bradley's six-pack and shoulders flashed through her thoughts. An aftershock of desire ripped through her, splitting her mind and body into warring camps.

****

The next day at the mall, Sarah's body bought Sheriff Bradley a new cologne. All the way home, her brain warned her that she should shove the box in the back of the linen closet and forget about it. The less she encouraged him, the better.

Still, she plopped the cologne on the kitchen island in full view, where she wouldn't forget to give it to him. The box and Bradley were symbols of her emancipation. She wasn't going to mince into her new future with careful, tentative steps. That wasn't her style.

Besides, giving Bradley a new cologne would provide a public service to anyone who rode in a vehicle with him or sat near him in an enclosed space. It was her civic duty to elevate his choice of fragrance.

Sarah spent the day retrieving her old perfume bottle from the side of the creek, putting new linens on the bed, cleaning the house and looking up divorce lawyers. Overwhelmed by choice, she called a few acquaintances who had recently ended their marriages and got some recommendations.

Then, still a victim of an empty fridge, she decided to drive into Sonoma for dinner.

The Delhi Garden was one of Sarah's favorite places to eat. The restaurant was a block off the plaza, with indoor booths and a patio in the back, festooned with wisteria and lights, and a jungle of tables arranged around a gurgling fountain. No matter how hot the day, the patio could be counted on to be shady and cooled by a slight breeze.

Raj, the owner and host, greeted her at the door.

"Sarah, wonderful to see you. The usual?"

"Yes, please."

"You are lucky that you came early. We are entirely booked this evening."

"It's the wine auction, I think. Sonoma is hopping."

"Yes, but who is complaining?" He winked at her and then led her to her favorite spot in the far corner of the patio. It was the smallest table and sometimes the breeze sprinkled it with spray from the fountain, but she didn't mind. She could see all the comings and goings from here, while being secluded by trailing vines. She liked observing people. Sarah sat down.

"The usual?" Raj asked again. "Syrah and lamb vindaloo?"

"Why mess with a good thing?"

"Indeed. I'll be back with your drink." He bowed slightly and disappeared into the main restaurant.

While Sarah waited for dinner to arrive, she noticed a tall blonde rise from a nearby table and accost the new waiter, Eddie. Sarah recognized the attractive features and sleek figure of Hunny Friske.

"How long is it going to take?" Hunny demanded. "I've been here a good half hour. At least."

"My apologies," Eddie replied. "We are very busy, ma'am."

"But I called ahead."

"As did many others." The waiter motioned toward her chair. "Please, have a seat. I will bring you a beverage of choice. On the house."

"Why didn't someone tell me I would have to wait so long?"

"Please, it will only be a little while longer, ma'am. Now, what can I get for you?"

Frowning, Hunny plopped down in her chair. "Oh, a white zinfandel." Annoyed, she waved him off without another glance.

Sarah swirled the wine in her goblet. She hadn't touched white zinfandel since the 1990s. She could still recall the mineral taste in the back of her throat. To her, white zin was like drinking rusty cotton candy. Not her favorite. She sipped her much more complex red wine, thinking there was no accounting for taste. That's why there were so many different wines in the world. And that's why she loved her job.

She read the latest edition of Wine Spectator on her phone as she waited for dinner. When she was finished, she tried to pay, but Eddie said her meal was on the house. Baffled but grateful, Sarah walked through the noisy diners toward the front door. As she reached for the door handle, a voice stopped her.

"Sarah." Raj hurried up behind her. "Just a moment."

She looked over her shoulder at him. He held a bag of food in one hand.

"Are you parked at the plaza?"

"Yes, across the street."

"Could you do me a favor?" He held up the white plastic bag, which she assumed was full of food containers. "Could you take this to someone in the park?"

"Ah." She arched a brow. "There really is no such thing as a free lunch, is there?"

He grinned a toothy smile behind his black mustache. "Favor for favor?"

"For your lamb vindaloo, anything." She reached for the bag.

He nodded toward the plaza across the street. "There's a guy that hangs around the fountain over there. Bushy beard. Red sneakers. We all take care of him. Sunday's my night. Your husband does Thursday."

"Matteo feeds someone in the plaza?"

"Yes. We all do. But it's so busy here tonight. I can't get away."

"No worries, Raj."

"Many thanks. You are a lifesaver."

Sarah stared at the fountain as she crossed the street. She had always avoided that area of the plaza. Down on their luck locals hung out there as well as scruffy skateboarders and what Sarah supposed were drug dealers. In the two years she'd lived in the area, she had never used the sidewalk that skirted the fountain, but tonight, she was forced to walk it.

She shook her head at her own behavior. What was the problem? She was from Glasgow. Approaching the fountain crowd was a walk in the park compared to some neighborhoods in her hometown. She concentrated on examining the shoes of the loiterers.

Within seconds she spotted the red trainers, dusty but neatly tied, and raised her regard to the rest of the man: a pair of bare ankles, jeans, lavender polo shirt, beard, a pair of unsmiling brown eyes and a shaggy mop of curly, salt and pepper hair. She guessed the man was in his fifties and going through a midlife crisis. He must be well-known in Sonoma and well-loved to be fed by all the restauranteurs.

All eyes swung in her direction as the fragrant smell of spicy food wafted toward them.

Sarah held out the bag. "Raj at Delhi Garden asked me to give you this," she said.

The brown eyes flicked up to examine her face. "Is it Sunday?"

"*Aye, 'tis.*"

"Scottish?" He reached up for the bag.

"*Aye.*"

"Glasgow?"

"*Ye nailed it*, pal."

He nodded and settled the bag onto the lichen-covered edge of the fountain, next to him. "You and your husband have been here, what, two years now?"

"We have." She was surprised he knew who she was. "How did you know?"

"You sit here all day, you notice things." He folded his hands in his lap. Every movement he made was full of grave deliberation. She wondered what his life had been like before the fountain. Had he been a priest? A professional? The mayor? She had no idea. She didn't even know his name.

"Your husband makes excellent ravioli."

"I'll tell him."

"His gnocchi could use more salt, though."

She fought back a smile. The phrase "beggars can't be choosers" ran through her mind, as well as "beggars can't be food critics." But she held her tongue.

"I'll tell him."

"The name's Roger," he said. "Roger Larue."

"Sarah McKee."

He looked down at the bag and sighed. Two skateboarders sidled closer, their eyes full of interest as they watched him open a container of samosas. Sarah took the opportunity to leave and strolled to her car.

She started the engine and paused. For the first time since she'd returned from Germany, she felt rested and well fed. The nausea had abated. Maybe the state of her health had something to do with all the pummeling. Remembering the gymnastics of the previous night, she smiled.

Sarah took the long way home, not anxious to return to the empty house. She would have stopped in at the Wolf

House Bar and asked about Roger LaRue, but Zach didn't work on the weekends. No sense sitting at the bar alone with no one to talk to. She could do the same thing at home in a more comfortable chair.

Once at the house, she poured a second glass of wine and took her phone out to the deck. She googled the name "Roger Larue," read the first headline, and sucked in a breath.

Chapter 12 | Mr. Xu

"Family of local dentist killed in Kincaid wildfire," the article began. Sarah clicked on the story, only to be diverted to a subscription pop-up window.

"Bastards," she muttered under her breath. She tried another link, but all stories pointed to items in the Santa Rosa and Sonoma papers, to which she didn't subscribe. She would have to get the details from Zach or Kelley.

The next day, Sarah spent the morning in phone meetings with clients. Just as she took a break to make tea, she heard a vehicle pull into her driveway. She peeked through the mini-blind of her office window and saw a Sonoma County Sheriff's Office SUV lurch to a stop. Bradley jumped out. Sarah's heart skipped a beat before her brain told her to stop the skipping. The official vehicle was evidence that this was not a social call.

She hurried to the front door.

"Sheriff Bradley?" she greeted, keeping her tone and regard as formal as possible. She could tell by the look on Bradley's face that he was here on important business.

"Sarah, can you come with me?"

"Why? What's wrong?"

"There's been another murder. I'm on my way there now."

"In Glen Ellen?"

He nodded grimly. "Kelley suggested I bring you with me, since the victim is someone you know. You might have some insight."

"Who is it?" Sarah slipped on her shoes.

"Not really sure. Just have the address."

"I'll grab my purse."

Gravel flying, Bradley roared out of the driveway, raced through the little village of Glen Ellen and up the hill toward Paradise Valley Winery with his lights flashing and siren blasting. Sarah held on to the strap above the window as Bradley fishtailed into the winery's drive and sped down the slope toward the house. Sarah stared at him in surprise.

"Who is dead? One of the Friskes?"

"Don't know, I said."

Kelley's vehicle was already parked in front of the mansion, as well as that of the Santa Rosa medical examiner and forensic unit.

Sarah hopped out and followed Bradley up the steps to the porch. The housekeeper greeted them at the door, her face pinched with worry. Bradley displayed his badge and introduced Sarah. Sarah shot the older woman a small smile, but the housekeeper was too distraught to notice and wouldn't make eye contact. Kelley popped into the foyer, as Hunny Friske marched down the stairs, dressed in a sea green pantsuit with a snakeskin belt, her eyes red from crying.

"This way, boss," Kelley said. "Hi Sarah."

"Wait a moment." Hunny stabbed a fistful of tissue at Sarah. "What is *she* doing here?"

Bradley ignored the question and blocked Hunny's forward progress by holding out his badge. "Sheriff Bradley, Sonoma County. And you are?"

Hunny didn't so much as glance at his badge. She raked him with an imperious stare, incredulous that he didn't recognize her.

"This is Maeve Friske," Kelley put in. "Wife of the victim."

Bradley didn't seem fazed by the woman or her social standing. Sarah liked that. He stood in front of the socialite, unmoving, his face somber.

"Step aside," Hunny demanded, trying to push past him. "At once."

But Bradley held up a hand to stop her. "Ma'am, you need to remain clear of the crime scene."

"But that's my husband in there!"

"Yes, and his death is being investigated by professionals."

"She's not a professional," Hunny jabbed an index finger at Sarah. "In fact, she's the reason my husband is dead."

"I sincerely doubt that."

"It's true. She and her slanty-eyed friend were here threatening him. Just a couple of days ago. On Friday, in fact."

Sarah could tell from the surprise that flitted over Bradley's face that—until this moment—he hadn't put two and two together: that this was the residence of the man who had called to complain about Sarah and Arthur. Much to Bradley's credit, he masked his surprise immediately.

"Ma'am," Bradley continued in a calm tone, "Please step back while we do our jobs."

"It's not *her* job!"

"It is today. Ms. McKee is an expert we use in cases like these." Bradley kept his voice brisk. "She is here on official business. Ms. McKee?" He waved her through the doorway of the library. "And ma'am, remain in the house. We may have questions for you."

"For me?" Hunny bristled. "Why? I wasn't here when it happened."

"Still, we may have questions."

Bradley followed Kelley into the library where the medical examiner and the forensic team were packing up equipment. Numbers on red plastic cards dotted the library. Sarah stood in the middle of the room, free to observe while Bradley handled the official business behind her. His body and that of the medical examiner blocked her view of the victim, not that she was anxious to see a dead Bill Friske.

She pivoted, sniffing the air. Someone had sprayed air freshener in the room. Or perhaps what she smelled was a substance the forensic team had used during their investigation. She doubted it. The fragrance that hung like a cloud in the room reeked of lilac. Did the forensic team use floral-scented aerosols? She could hear Bradley and the medical examiner talking beside her and didn't think it was her place to interrupt them with questions.

"Coroner's on the way," the short examiner said to Bradley.

"Anything for me yet?"

"Cause of death, gunshot wound to the right temporal fossa. Splatter pattern suggests suicide, although there is somewhat of an anomaly."

"In what way?"

"The splatter indicates the victim held the gun at an unusual angle."

"What do you mean by unusual?" Bradley treaded closer.

The medical examiner pointed to the edge of the desk and floor. "You see those drops? The length is shorter than we normally see in this manner of death, and the shapes are rounder than they should be."

"Meaning the gun was held slightly above his head and not at his temple?" Sarah asked.

"Exactly." The medical examiner nodded at her. "But we'll have forensics confirm it."

"Good," Bradley commented. "And the bullet blew out the victim's face as it exited. Just like the victim in Boyes Hot Springs."

"Very similar. Yes."

"Same weapon, do you think?"

"It's quite possible."

As Sarah listened to them, she turned her attention to the dead man.

Bill Friske slumped sideways in his giant chair, like a king asleep on his throne—a faceless, bloody king with one half of his skull sitting on top of his neck and the other half splattered across the room. A red tag marked the desk as item #13. Appropriate. Bad luck had certainly found Bill Friske. She fought back a wave of nausea and turned her attention to the less grisly aspects of the library.

She could see no sign of struggle. None of the desk drawers were open. A nearby broadside, topped with tennis trophies, sat undisturbed, each racket still reaching for the sky, but smattered with blood. The chairs where she and

Arthur had sat had not been moved. The only thing different about them was the crimson spray that covered the one Arthur had sat in.

The fingers of Bill Friske's left hand splayed across a blood-splattered paper. A Mont Blanc fountain pen with its cap off lay near his thumb. Sarah inspected the grim scene, hands behind her back, careful not to touch anything or step on the splatters of blood.

Before Bill Friske had killed himself, he had scrawled the letters "XU" on the sheet of paper. Had the henchmen of Arthur's client already been here, seeking vengeance? Had they held the gun to his head, and he still wouldn't pay? That would mean Xu had given Friske only a handful of days to make restitution. Arthur had mentioned a two-day deadline, but surely that had been an empty threat. It was unlikely Xu would resort to murder. Unless Friske had lashed out at the triad chief and made a permanent enemy—which, knowing Friske, was certainly possible.

She continued to survey the scene, looking for clues. Bill's left arm was draped between his cellphone and a crystal tumbler—the kind a gentleman would drink whiskey from—that had, in fact, tumbled. She sniffed the rim of the glass. Sure enough, he'd been drinking blended whiskey. Jameson. Then she smelled something else. Something that made her touchy stomach take a turn.

Vomit. The scent was faint. She bent closer and sniffed, from the tumbler to the middle of Bill's desk, where the scent grew stronger. Her gaze traveled back to the whiskey glass. If Bill had spilled his drink or the killer had spilled it, where was the puddle of booze? It couldn't have evaporated so quickly. Or would have left a stain. There wasn't a sign of a spill. Maybe he had finished his drink before the glass had tipped over. Or maybe...her mind raced, thinking back to the day she'd been in this office before. Something was different. Her observations from the previous Friday shifted into focus, as her subconscious observations always did when she examined a bottle of wine. She stared at the desk while she let her vision race over the scene unimpeded by conscious thought. Something was different.

As she stared, she was vaguely aware of the medical examiner crew saying good-bye behind her. Only Bradley, Kelley and she remained, with Hunny hovering in the background.

"Poor guy," Kelley said, coming alongside to stare at the victim. "What a way to go."

"If it is how he died."

"What do you mean?"

"Something isn't right. I can't put my finger on it, Kelley, but something isn't right here."

"I'll tell you what isn't right," Bradley said, pushing past Kelley to stand in front of Sarah. "The fact that you were here with that friend of yours, threatening the victim. It doesn't look good." He glared at her, every shred of friendliness gone. "You should not be here."

Sarah propped her fists on her hips. "Are you serious?"

"Dead serious. This isn't a mystery. And it's not a suicide. It's a triad killing. Plain and simple. I want the name of your friend and his phone number. I'm bringing him in for questioning. And don't you do anything—and I mean anything—to interfere with this investigation. Do you hear me?"

"Loud and clear, pal."

"Kelley, escort Ms. McKee to your vehicle and take her home. And get the name of her Chinese friend."

"So, you're saying the triad also killed Joe Salgado?" Sarah countered. "With the same murder weapon? Why? What would the motive be? It doesn't make sense."

"It not your job to figure it out," Bradley snapped. "It's mine." He pointed toward the door.

Sarah bristled at his cold treatment of her. She knew he was only doing his job, but he had a complete lack of bedside manner. Especially when he had all but *been* in her bed. No doubt that was why he was lashing out at her. He was overcompensating for previous unprofessional conduct and didn't want to appear lacking in front of Hunny Friske.

Well, she didn't like it. He had no reason to treat her like a criminal. She hadn't done anything wrong. Anger flared up her neck and filled her head, turning her thoughts crystal clear. Data fell into place. A vision passed before her eyes. In an instant, she realized what was different about Bill Friske's desk.

"Ask where the blotter is then," she said over her shoulder.

"The what?"

She turned to face him and was gratified to see a glint of uncertainty in his haughty expression. "The desk blotter that was there on Friday." She pointed at the dead man. "It's gone."

Sarah left the sheriff standing at the desk, hands on his hips, surveying the body. She walked toward the door, with Kelley at her heels.

Hunny's voice stopped their exit.

"If either of you says anything about this, I will sue."

"Pardon?" Kelley turned around.

"This...this...what happened to my husband. Don't say a word. To anyone. It could ruin everything."

"You mean the auction?" Sarah asked.

"Of course I mean the auction." Hunny crushed the tissue in her fist. "If the auction doesn't go forward, we won't make any money. For the children."

"*Aye*. For the children." Sarah knew the proceeds from the popular auction supported a children's wing at a research hospital in San Francisco, but a hefty amount of the proceeds was pocketed by the organizers to pay expenses. No doubt Hunny Friske, mentored by her dear late husband, had already racked up huge expenses as chairperson of Flight of Fancy.

Bill Friske was a mastermind when it came to expenses, taxes and offshore accounts. His tight-fisted, just-shy-of-illegal business practices had been another reason Sarah had left his employ.

"Of course, for the children," Hunny retorted. "It is imperative that we move forward."

"How are you going to explain Bill's absence?" Sarah asked. "At the auction?"

"I'll think of something."

No doubt she would.

"So, nothing." Hunny warned, holding up a finger like a chastising parent. "Not a peep to anyone. Do you understand?"

"Ms. Friske, we can't make any promises," Kelley opened the door. "Whatever Sheriff Bradley decides to do about this homicide is how we move forward."

"But what about you?" Hunny glared at Sarah.

"I have no stake in this," Sarah shrugged.

"Your wine friend does. That Chen person."

"And I am not the boss of him," Sarah replied, playing the part of the child to Hunny's admonishing parent. "Am I now?"

"This isn't a joking matter," Hunny hissed.

"No, *lass, 'tisn't.* Your husband's dead. And I'm sorry."

Sarah followed Kelley out the door.

****

On the way home, Sarah relayed her observations of the crime scene to Kelley, hoping that her friend could assist in solving the murder that she was now supposed to ignore.

"You smelled vomit?" Kelley asked, turning into Sarah's drive. "I didn't."

"It was faint. I think it had been recently cleaned up. That's what the air freshener was all about."

"Well, being sick wouldn't have anything to do with being shot." Kelley turned off the engine. "Homicide victims sometimes lose control of their bladders and rectums. They don't throw up."

"True."

"But I'll mention it to the boss."

"Hunny also said she wasn't at the house last night. You should find out where she was and if that's a strange occurrence."

"I'm sure Sheriff Bradley will follow up on that."

"And ask about Chris Girard."

"Who's that?"

"Their winery manager. See what he knows. He lives on the estate. He might have seen something."

"Right." Kelley made notes on her phone.

Sarah opened the car door. "Time for a coffee?"

"Ah, I'd better get back. We'll probably take Hunny in for questioning."

"Okay. See you later this week sometime?"

"How about tonight. Drink at the Wolf House?"

"Okay." Sarah climbed out of the car and noticed the muscles in her thighs and upper arms were stiff from her romp the night before. "See you at eight."

****

An hour later, Sarah's phone rang. She picked it up.

"Sarah, it's Arthur Chen."

"Arthur, how are you?"

"I need a favor. They let me call you."

"They?"

"The police."

"*Gawd.*" Sarah rolled her eyes. Against her best advice, Bradley had apprehended Arthur. "How can I help?"

"I need an attorney."

"Yes, I'd say that you do."

"I am not answering any of their questions until an attorney is with me."

"A wise decision."

"But I don't know anyone local. Could you find a lawyer for me? Someone you trust?"

"I'm not acquainted with any criminal defense lawyers around here, but I know people who might be. I'll make some calls."

"Oh, thank you, Sarah. Thank you."

"And Arthur, I know you didn't do it."

"I appreciate it."

"What about your client, though? Mr. Xu."

"If he was responsible, we will never have proof," Arthur replied. "Which is unfortunate." He paused and then came back on the line. "Sorry, they are making me hang up now."

"Okay. Try not to worry, Arthur. I'll make some inquiries right now."

Chapter 13 | Housekeeper Spills

Monday night, after a trip to San Francisco to meet with a new client, Sarah returned to her Glen Ellen home. She was frazzled from the horrendous traffic in and out of the city, and she was starving, with less than an hour before she had to meet Kelley. She walked to the refrigerator, pulled open the door and scowled at the contents, as if magic elves might have come in while she was gone and restocked her larder.

No such luck.

The same bare shelves held the same old condiments and little else. She couldn't live on stone-ground mustard and bleu cheese dressing. Not even if she had bread. Which she didn't. She'd have to go grocery shopping or grab something at the Wolf House. She opted for eating out. And, keeping the promise to herself to get more exercise, she opted to walk there.

Ten minutes later, Sarah pushed through the Wolf House door, only to hear the bell echo through an empty house. Not one customer was in the place. Worse, Zach wasn't there. Sarah ambled to her usual spot at the end of the bar and sat down. It was then she spotted Zach kneeling on the floor, loading shining bottles onto a lower shelf.

She had so much to tell him. About Matteo. About Bill Friske. But she couldn't yet, not about Friske, not when Sheriff Bradley's admonishing words still rang in her ears. To distract herself from those burning topics, she would see what Zach knew about Roger Larue.

Sarah leaned over the bar. "I like a man who knows how to clean," she said, humor warming her voice.

Zach sat back on his haunches. "Why do you think I do?"

"Look at those bottles. All sparkly. Like brand new."

He pushed the last bottle into place, stood up with easy grace and dropped the rag in a bin.

"So, what brings a cleaning expert to my pitiful, abandoned outpost of a bar?" Without looking at her, he turned on the tap at the sink.

"I'm hunting the elusive grass-fed beef burger. Seen any around these parts?"

"Well now, Goldilocks, there might be one or two out back."

She smiled and watched him wash, mesmerized by the sight of his wrist bones and knuckles as he lathered his hands.

"I heard tell they're pretty darn good," she continued in her best Western drawl.

"You heard right, lady." Zach straightened and dried his hands on a fresh towel as he surveyed her, his expression relaxed and friendly. "Shall I wrassle one to the ground for you?"

"Sounds good. No chips, though."

"On a diet?" He lifted one brow. "Not you."

"Gotta start sometime."

"What can I get you to drink?"

"This is going to sound weird, Zach, but do you have any milk?"

"Milk?"

"My stomach's been off since I got back from Europe."

"Sorry to hear it." He reached into the undercounter fridge and pulled out two cartons, one whole milk, the other chocolate. He wiggled them in the air. "White or red?"

"White. Make it a double, please."

"You got it." Zach poured the foamy beverage into a tall glass and pushed it toward her.

"Where is everyone?" Sarah took a sip of the creamy drink.

"I expect they're at the Broadway Under the Stars thing. That's tonight. It always draws a big crowd."

"Oh, right. I forgot about that."

"And said crowd will be straggling in soon. So, I'd best put your burger on."

"Before you do," she put in, "Do you happen to know of a Roger Larue?"

"The dentist? Guy who hangs out at the plaza?"

"*Aye*. Do you know what happened to him?"

Zach shook his head and gazed down at the bar. "That's a real sad story."

"What is it? I tried to find something about him but could only read headlines."

"Well, Roger was a long-time dentist up in Kenwood. He took care of most of the bigwigs in the valley. Implants and crowns. A real specialist."

"But there was a fire?"

"Yes. The Kincaide Fire near Santa Rosa. He had a house in the hills up there. Huge place. A pool. Five car garage. Horses."

"Dentistry is that lucrative?"

"I take it you haven't been in a while."

"No, I haven't. Haven't had to." She ran her tongue over her teeth, thankful to have a healthy rack of pearly whites and not a single cavity. "So, what happened?"

"The fire jumped a line and caught his wife and kids in the car as they were evacuating."

The pit of Sarah's stomach went cold. She could guess what the rest of the story was, but she waited for Zach to continue.

"They tried to escape by running down the side of the mountain. They didn't make it."

"Jesus."

"Yeah. Two kids and a wife. Roger lost it. It's like he blamed himself. I heard stories that he went blank. You know, catatonic. He simply walked away from his practice. Walked to Sonoma in fact. That's a good ten miles. And now he just sits in the plaza."

"When was the fire?"

"Two years ago. Same year my dad died."

"How does Roger live?"

Zach shrugged. "I hear people feed him."

"But where does he sleep?"

"I don't know."

"Jesus."

"Yeah. Makes our troubles seem insignificant, doesn't it?" He held her gaze for a long moment, and she wondered if he knew about her and Matteo, or if he was relaying something about himself. Before she could decipher his meaning, he slapped the bar with both palms, breaking them out of the somber mood. "Enough of that. One burger coming up."

He disappeared into the tiny kitchen in the back while Sarah settled in with her phone. A constant stream of enological articles was fed to her each day, which she did her best to keep up with. Being a wine expert wasn't limited to wine-tastings and tours. Hours of research and reading were a major part as well. It was her job to find the most exciting up and coming winemaker, the underrated and soon to hit the market cuvée, the labels that had lost their cachet, and the ones expected to go gold.

She couldn't wait for the day Zach would unleash his cabernet sauvignon on the world. She expected his wine to be amazing, and she hoped to corner the market for every important client on her list.

Just as Sarah smelled the heady fragrance of onions sizzling on the grill, she heard the bell tinkle behind her. A small, squat woman in a jeans jacket, rust-colored leggings, white socks and black oxfords paused at the entry, looking around as if searching for someone. Sarah was just about to inform the woman that Zach was in the back, when he appeared at the opposite end of the bar, carrying a plate.

"Mr. Zachary," the older woman exclaimed. "Thank the Holy Virgin!"

"Maria?" He stopped his forward progress, the plate extended toward Sarah. "What's wrong?"

"Everything! *Todos*!"

Sarah studied the small woman. Until she had heard the woman's name, she hadn't recognized the Paradise Valley housekeeper out of uniform.

Maria fled to the bar and struggled onto a stool. Sarah could tell that she had been crying. "I don't know what to do. I don't know what to do!"

"Hold on," Zach said. He carried the hamburger to Sarah, slid utensils wrapped in a napkin next to the plate and plopped her usual condiments on the bar. Sarah didn't mind the brusque treatment. She was as worried about his customer as he was.

Maria didn't look to the side to see who sat in the vicinity. She was too intent on sniffling and fumbling for a tissue in her purse.

"So, what's wrong, Maria?" Zach filled a glass with water and slid it toward her. She grabbed it and took a large gulp. "What's going on?"

"I don't want to lose my job. I can't lose that job, Mr. Zachary."

"No one's losing a job."

"I've worked at Paradise Valley for forty years. All my life. You know how hard I work. And I need to work. For money to send to my family."

"You are a good daughter, Maria. Everyone says so."

"I work hard. For your father. For the Friskes. I need to work. I need my job." She blew her nose. "What am I to do? *Ay*!"

"But why do you think you will lose your job?"

"Because of the police. They will ask questions. I know this. What will I say to them?"

"No need to worry. Your papers are in order, Maria. We've seen to that. Together."

"I know, Mr. Zachary. It is not the papers. It is the questions they will ask."

"About what?"

"I lose my job, I lose everything! Like dominoes. Knocking everything down." She chopped the air with the side of one hand. "Eh, eh, eh. Everything!"

"Okay." Zach poured a small glass of red wine and gave it to Maria. He squeezed her free hand. "You aren't going to lose your job, Maria. Just get that into your head. Take a sip. Try to settle down a bit. We'll talk this out."

"I am a good woman, Mr. Zachary." She blinked as she took a drink. She clutched the stem of the glass with both hands. "An honest woman. But if I tell the truth to the police, I know she will fire me."

"Maeve Friske?"

"*Si.*"

"Why do you think the police will question you?"

"Because they took the trash. And they will find it."

"Find what?"

"The desk blotter."

Sarah came to complete attention—not that she wasn't avidly eavesdropping already. Her ears strained to hear each tear-choked word Maria uttered.

Confused, Zach cocked his head. "What's a desk blotter have to do with anything?"

"My fingerprints are on it. *Ay!*" She blinked again and gulped down the wine. "Now I am more worried. What if they think I killed him? What if she says I did it?"

"Killed who?"

"Mr. Friske."

Zach's expression went slack with shock. "Bill Friske is dead?"

"*Sí.*" She looked up at him and nodded vehemently, her troubled dark eyes searching his. She crossed herself.

"How?"

"Someone shot him in the head. Right here." She touched her right temple.

"Who would do that?"

Maria shrugged. She held out her glass for more. Zach poured another small one.

"All I did was clean up the mess," she continued. "It was supposed to be my day off, but she called me to serve him dinner and clean up the mess. That's all I did. Clean up the mess. But she will blame me. I know she will. She blames me for everything."

Sarah couldn't stand another moment of being a bystander. She leaned forward, her sandwich forgotten. "Was Mr. Friske sick? Is that what you cleaned up?"

At the question, Maria turned to glance at her. Her eyes lit up with recognition. "*Sí.* You saw it, Ms. McKee. You were there. Tell your police friends the truth. How could a little woman like me kill a big man like Mr. Friske?"

"He threw up before his death?"

"*Sí.* Mrs. Friske, she made me clean it up. She said she didn't want her husband in such a state."

"How did you clean around the blood?"

"I didn't. There was no blood. He was lying there. Across his desk."

"Dead?"

"No, breathing funny. Like having a heart attack."

Sarah exchanged a dark look with Zach. He broke it off to walk around the bar to Maria's side.

"I clean up the sick. I throw away the blotter and then I leave. She told me it was okay. That she would get his pills, and he would be okay." Maria lifted her wine glass with a trembling hand. "He would be okay, I told myself. Like always. So, I go to my apartment in the carriage house. I am tired." She gulped her wine. "And now he's dead. She will blame me. I know her. I know her, Mr. Zachary."

"She's not going to blame you." Zach put a hand on Maria's shoulder. "You were just doing your job."

Sarah was more interested in the Friskes than Maria's state of mind. "I thought I heard Mrs. Friske say she wasn't at the house last night."

Maria nodded. "She wasn't later on. She had a date in the city. The symphony. I heard her talking to her sister on the phone."

"She left her sick husband to go to the symphony?"

"He had a bad heart, but he had pills. I thought he would be okay. Maybe she did, too?" Maria took another sip. "If I talk to the police, she will fire me. I know she will."

"What would you tell them that's bad enough to get fired over?"

"Anything. Anything that went on last night. She is like that. Private." Maria shook her head. "And it was nasty, that sick. He had eaten curry. It was everywhere."

"So, Maeve Friske went to the symphony, and someone came by later and killed her husband," Sarah mused.

"Or she killed him after Maria left," Zach said.

"What about their manager, Chris Girard. He lives in the carriage house, too, right?"

"In the other apartment, *si*."

"Was he home last night?"

Maria thought a moment. "I think so. But I go to bed early. I am tired." She shook her head, considering Sarah's implications. "But not him. He would not do it. It would be Mrs. Friske. She could do it. She's that terrible. And she was really mad at Mr. Friske."

"Why?"

"He was going to divorce her to marry a younger woman. I heard them yelling at each other about it."

Sarah flushed. She wondered how she had sounded when she'd shouted at Matteo. Good thing she didn't have a housekeeper.

"She goes on and on." Maria waved a hand in the air. "How will it look? He will make a fool of her. She will not be able to hold her head up. How can he do this to her? It was a terrible fight. Terrible."

"Motive right there," Zach said.

"The sheriff thinks a Chinese triad killed Bill," Sarah put in.

"Triad?"

"Like a gang," Sarah explained. "But super corporate."

"Ah." Zach nodded. "Arthur's client, I take it."

"*Aye.*"

Maria's gaze flitted from Zach to Sarah and back to Zach, confused by their exchange. "But what do *I* do? What do I tell the police? I know they will question me."

"Tell them the truth, Maria," Zach replied. "That's all you can do."

"She will fire me."

"That's the least of your worries. If Mr. Friske is dead, who knows what will happen to Paradise Valley? Maeve hates the place. I doubt she'll keep it up."

"She will close the winery?"

"She might. Or sell."

"And close the house? *Ay!*"

"She might." Zach sighed. "And if she fires you, Maria, I will find another job for you. I promise."

"But Paradise Valley," Maria cried. "No! It is my life, Mr. Zachary. It is my home."

The kind expression on Zach's face turned grim. He could say the same thing about Paradise Valley, but his Sullivan pride would not allow a single word of anguish to pass his lips.

"This will all work out." Zach stroked her back in comforting circles. "Don't worry, Maria. It will all work out."

"How can you be so sure?"

"It's the only way I *can* be." Zach held the older woman's gaze. "I'm in this for the long haul, Maria. And I'm taking you with me."

"Promise?" She clasped his hand in hers.

"I promise."

"Ah, Mr. Zachary. You were always such a good boy. So good." She heaved a sigh and slipped off her stool.

"Don't worry," he said. "Just tell the truth."

"*Si. Gracias.*" She threw her arms around his waist and hugged him. He bent to the tiny woman and returned the embrace with a tenderness that struck Sarah to the core. No one had ever hugged her like that. Until this moment, she hadn't known such an embrace existed outside the movie industry. A streak of longing sliced through her.

Zach walked Maria to the door and opened it for her. "And if you need me to be there when the police question you, you call me. Tell them you require an interpreter."

"I will. *Si*, I will."

Zach closed the door after the tiny housekeeper and walked back to the bar. He grabbed Maria's empty glasses and nestled them into a dishwasher rack.

"The only mother I've ever known," he remarked.

"She raised you?"

"Yeah. She worked at the house ever since I can remember. And became my nanny when I was two. That's when my mother died."

"I didn't know."

"So that witch Hunny Friske better be good to her, or she will have to answer to me." Zach glared out the window, as if he could see up the road, all the way to the winery.

"My mother died when I was two, as well."

"Sorry to hear that, Sarah." Zach's solemn gaze came back to settle on her. "Sucks sometimes, doesn't it?"

"I don't remember her at all." Sarah shrugged. "And I wasn't lucky enough to have a Maria."

"Yeah, she's been good to me. I love her like my own."

"I can tell."

Just after Maria left the saloon, Kelley walked in. Sarah and Zach stared at her expectantly, ready to dump their latest information on law enforcement.

Kelley stopped at the threshold and held out both hands.

"What?" she demanded. "What did *I* do?"

"Nothing," Sarah patted the stool beside her. "But I hope you brought your notepad with you."

"Did you find out something?" Intrigued, Kelley sat beside her and hung her purse on the hook under the bar.

"I'll say," Zach put in. "Sarah can fill you in. I've got a mob arriving." He nodded at the front of the saloon, where a parade of patrons headed for the door. "Blue Moon?" He cocked an eyebrow at Kelley.

Kelley propped her chin on her shoulder to glance at her friend. "What do you always say, Sarah?"

"Is the pope Catholic."

Kelley looked back at Zach. "Is the pope Catholic, Zach?"

Zach shook his head and smiled as he filled a glass for her. A minute later, the noise level of the bar vaulted to a roar as every bench, stool and chair filled with chattering Broadway Under the Stars attendees. Sarah leaned closer to Kelley so she could tell her what the Paradise Valley housekeeper had confessed. Kelley took notes on her phone, her frown deepening.

"Man," she commented, scanning what she had written when Sarah had finished. "This doesn't look good for Hunny Friske."

"No, it doesn't."

"I'll let Steven know all this tomorrow."

Sarah nodded.

"But what I'm really curious about," Kelley nodded at her beverage. "Is why you're drinking milk. Yuck."

"My stomach is off. Has been for a while."

"Is that why you went to the doctor?"

"Partly." Sarah linked her fingers around the cold glass. "I'm just not myself lately. I'm tired. Bloated. I keep gaining weight. And now I'm nauseated all the time."

When Kelley didn't say anything, Sarah glanced at her. Kelley had tilted her head and was staring at her with an annoying smirk on her face. "Do tell, Sarah."

"What?"

Kelley cupped the air above her tummy with both hands and raised her brows.

"No. Impossible."

"Have you tested yourself?"

"No." She took a gulp of milk. "I can't be pregnant. It takes a man and a woman for that to happen."

"When was your last period?"

"Now you're sounding like Dr. Dena."

"I'm serious, Sarah."

"Oh, I don't know." Sarah sighed and lifted one shoulder. "I've never been regular, so I don't keep track."

"I'd get a test."

Sarah stared at her friend as the possibility of being pregnant washed over her. After all the years of trying—however sporadic her sexual encounters with Matteo had been—she would be ecstatic to bring a child into the world. A baby would be the best thing ever. But she couldn't get her hopes up.

"How ironic would that be?" Sarah muttered, setting down her glass.

"Right?" Kelley put her arm around Sarah's shoulders. "My friend, I think it's time to pee on a stick."

Chapter 14 | SS Wines

The next morning, as Sarah was settling into work, her cellphone buzzed. She picked it up.

"Houston," Zach's voice said, "We have a problem."

"What's going on?"

"A lot of Paradise Valley Zin just came into the warehouse. For the auction."

"And?"

"It's a 2016."

"But how's that possible? Isn't that the year you kept back?"

"It is."

Sarah stood up. "Who's the seller?"

"An outfit named SS Wines. Came in on a truck a few minutes ago."

Sarah's pulse quickened. SS Wines had something to do with the counterfeiter, she was sure of it. Maybe something to do with the murder of Bill Friske, too. "What's the address on the bill of lading?"

Zach paused and came back on the line. "A place in Bodega. Do you know where that is?"

"I'm guessing somewhere near Bodega Bay?"

"Yeah, a few miles inland from there."

"SS Wines lists PVZ on their website," Sarah mused. "But now we know they're brokering the most sought after PVZ. The missing year. And fakes at that."

"We need to shut them down."

"Yes, we do."

"Can you do me a huge favor?" Zach asked. "We're slammed here at the warehouse. Last minute stuff for the auction is pouring in."

"You really shouldn't allow that."

"It's Maeve Friske's doing. She wants as many vendors at the auction as possible."

"So, do you want me to check out SS Wines? See if they're legit?"

"Would you?"

"In a heartbeat. Text me a shot of that bill of lading."

"Sure thing. I'll owe you for this, Sarah. Big time."

"I only want one thing from you, pal."

"What's that?"

"A taste of your cab. It must be ready. And I want to be the first to sample it."

"You drive a hard bargain, Goldilocks." She heard the smile in his voice.

"I'm a hard woman." She smiled back.

"You'll have to come up to my place for a tasting. I'm not letting the public know about the cab. Not until I'm sure it's good enough for the Sullivan name. I don't even have a label yet. Or a name for my winery."

"I'd like to come up. I've never seen your property."

"It isn't much. Not like the old homestead."

"Well, what about later today? Say five-thirty? Before your shift at the Wolf House? I can let you know what I find in Bodega."

"Deal. See you then, Sarah."

****

Sarah convinced Kelley to accompany her to the town of Bodega and picked her up outside the police station. They walked out to the parking lot.

"Better to go in my car," Sarah explained. "So, nobody suspects anything."

"If two people can actually fit in this tin can of yours." Kelley stared down at the passenger seat, her forehead wrinkled with doubt.

"Just move the ballerina," Sarah said, donning her ball cap. "There'll be plenty of room."

Kelley picked up Wesley Leslie's puppet and eased into the small space. "I don't know how you stand this thing."

"I love this thing." Sarah turned the key and the engine purred to life. "I wanted a sportscar since I was a *wean*. A child."

She backed out and sped down the street. Kelley clamped her hands on the sides of her head. "My hair!" she shouted over the noise.

"Glovebox," Sarah shouted back. "Extra cap."

They shouted their way to Sebastopol and beyond, racing through the rounded hills dotted with cattle and scrub oaks and gashed by cloudbursts and quakes. Lonely farms ringed by eucalyptus clung to the sides of a small creek near the road. The old motorway must have been built following the path of the stream as it meandered to the sea.

For Sarah, the meandering road was fun to drive, but one glance at her companion and she realized she would have to take it easy on the curves. Kelley had turned white. Sarah slowed as they passed an ancient store with a statue of Alfred Hitchcock standing near the entrance.

"What the hell?" Sarah remarked.

"The Birds. The movie," Kelley yelled over the wind. "It was filmed here. The white building on the hill?" She pointed to the left. "That was the school in the movie."

"Ah." Sarah remembered the film with the flocks of birds that attacked residents of a small seaside village. The memory cast a pall over the place as the sun shifted behind a cloud, increasing the gloom. The schoolhouse turned an eerie green color, and the doors and windows seemed to stare at her as she drove closer. The entire village looked abandoned but still at attention, watching her. She'd toured haunted battlegrounds in Scotland that seemed like Disneyland compared to this place.

"Jesus," she muttered.

"Turn here," Kelley announced, pointing left again.

They were going to go right past the scary school. Sarah shifted down for the climb up the hill and tried not to shudder as they passed the rickety fence and dilapidated playground. A rag and a pair of sneakers tied together hung from the power line, twisting in the wind. On edge, Sarah focused her concentration on the road.

The dirt lane crested the hill and plunged into a small valley filled with skeletal trees and a slow-moving creek. Was everything in a state of decay here, or had the plants not put out leaves yet? If this was spring in Bodega, she wondered what fall or winter would look like. A graveyard, no doubt.

"Should be on the right," Kelley said, looking at her phone. "Damn the reception out here. Just lost the route."

"That's it over there," Sarah said, rolling onto a narrow drive. A mailbox tilted precariously toward the creek. The address painted on the side of the metal container was faded but still legible. They passed over a one lane wooden bridge and approached a shack so tiny, it looked as if it contained no more than one bedroom—if that. Judging by the tiny outbuilding in back, the shack lacked a bathroom as well.

"This is SS Wines?" Sarah braked in front of the house and turned off the engine.

"That's what the bill of lading says." Kelley held up the piece of paper Sarah had brought with her. "This is the right address."

"A front if I ever saw one."

"Yeah." Kelley struggled out of the Triumph and crunched through the dried weeds to the front door. She knocked while Sarah peeked through the dirty front window into the living room. All she could see were worn wooden floorboards, adobe walls and a couple of cardboard boxes stacked next to a table.

"Police!" Kelley announced. "Anyone home?" She pounded again.

No one answered the door. Sarah wasn't surprised.

"Looks like recent tire tracks," Sarah observed, wandering to the side of the house. The tracks led to an unpainted barn. She followed the tracks to the padlocked door, with Kelley close behind. Sarah pulled at the lock.

"Careful," Kelley warned. "We need a warrant to proceed much farther. And gloves."

"Any windows on your side?" Sarah asked, moving to the right. Kelley ambled to the left.

"Nope," she answered. "I'll look around back."

Sarah stood at the corner of the barn and surveyed the dilapidated farm. This was no legitimate operation. Kelley tromped up beside her.

"So, we know where SS Wines is," Sarah mused. "And now we know it's a front. But who in the hell owns it?"

"Oh, we know that," Kelley said.

Sarah turned to stare at her. "Who?"

"The same person that paid Joe Salgado's rent. Anya Sarnova."

"And who is she?"

"Still working on that. She doesn't seem to have a digital presence. Like she doesn't exist."

"It's all connected, Kelley." Sarah scowled at the house. "I feel it. I know it."

"And I agree with you, girlfriend. But so far, we don't have any suspects other than Arthur Chen."

"Arthur wouldn't kill anyone."

"Boss doesn't agree. He's arrested Chen."

"What?"

"Yeah. And Chen doesn't have an alibi. So, it doesn't look good."

"But Arthur doesn't have a motive."

"His client does. Bradley thinks Chen might have been pressured into killing Bill Friske."

Sarah shook her head in disbelief as her mind raced over the salient points from the conversation with the Friske housekeeper. "What about Hunny Friske? Have you talked to her?" Sarah walked back to her car. "Does she have an alibi?"

"You think Mrs. Friske might have killed her own husband?"

"Aren't most homicides perpetrated by a family member?"

"Yes, but Mrs. Friske?" Kelley rolled her eyes. "No way. That's crazy talk."

"Not as crazy as arresting Arthur Chen. You should question her as well."

"We can't. She's still in the city. As soon as she comes back, we'll talk to her, though."

"That might not be until the auction."

"I know," Kelley eased herself into the passenger seat. "But the boss isn't really interested in her. So, he has no reason to send anyone to San Francisco. Plus, it's out of our jurisdiction."

"What about Chris Girard, Friske's manager? He lives on the property. He might have seen something."

"He's also in the city." Kelley plopped the ballcap on her head. "The only people we've managed to interview are Chen and the housekeeper. Boy, was she a wreck."

"Anything?" Sarah didn't let on that she had already discussed the murder with Maria.

"Just that you were right about the vomit smell. Bill Friske did toss his cookies before he was killed. And, like you said, there was a desk blotter. We found it in the trash."

"Any prints on it?"

"Just the housekeeper's and Friske's."

"We also found a gun during the search. Possibly the weapon used to kill both men."

"Where?"

"In the bushes at the back of the house. We're running tests on it now."

"That's all you found?"

"Yeah."

Sarah frowned at the lack of evidence against Arthur Chen. This was a classic case of small-town racial bias. She planned to have words with Sheriff Bradley and demand that Arthur be released. She started her engine.

"And Sarah?" Kelley added.

Sarah broke off her dark thoughts and turned toward her friend.

Kelley had shoved the ballerina puppet onto one finger. She bobbed the puppet in front of Sarah's nose and spoke in a falsetto voice.

"If you go a hundred miles an hour on the way back, the nice police lady says she will have to arrest you."

****

At five-thirty that afternoon, Sarah motored up the gravel drive to Zach Sullivan's house on Moon Mountain. Like Zach had said, his house was not awe-inspiring. In fact, it appeared to be a prefab home, modern and modest, with a glass-fronted great room and deck overlooking his vineyard and the valley below. The house had been built at the pinnacle of the mountain, so high she could see the cars on Highway 12 down below, but she couldn't hear them. It was peaceful up here, with the late afternoon sun turning everything to gold.

Peaceful but windy.

She grabbed her jacket from the back of her car and crunched to the house. Zach must have heard her arrive. He ambled out to the deck. She waved.

"I thought you said your place wasn't much," she called up to him.

"It isn't. It's the bare minimum."

"But look at the view!" she swept her free hand through the air, indicating the vast expense of hills and valleys in every direction.

"Kind of the opposite of Paradise Valley," he said.

"I'll say. Paradise Valley is like an intimate secret. This..." She scanned the valley again, struggling to find the right words. "This is out and out *gob smacking.*"

"Whatever that is." Zach trotted down the steps. He seemed distracted. Upset. Maybe because of the fake Paradise Valley wine. "C'mon." He walked quickly around the back of the house. Maybe he seemed distracted because he was in a hurry. With two jobs to keep down, the man didn't have a moment to waste.

"Is Courtney around?" Sarah pulled on her jacket.

"Not right now."

Zack unlocked a set of double wooden doors set into the side of the hill, much like the earthen cellars of long-established wine country properties. To the left was a slope dotted with white grow tubes, meant to protect new stock from hungry animals and unpredictable Mother Nature.

"You've been busy," Sarah remarked.

Zach nodded at the new vineyard. "Cabernet Franc. The vines love it up here."

"You going to do blends?"

"That's what everybody wants these days. I've got to make a living."

He motioned her through the doors.

Wondering at his brusque behavior, Sarah walked into the cool darkness of the cave and allowed her eyes to adjust. The cellar extended far into the hill and was coated with stucco or sprayed concrete, she wasn't sure which. The floor was covered in sanded bricks. Terracotta amphorae set on blocks stood like soldiers along the left wall. A table with a decanter and glasses sat on the right. Beyond the table, far in the distance, she caught a glimpse of equipment glinting in the low light: sinks and hoses, a large press and tanks where Zach began the fermentation process.

"It's a small operation now. And old school," Zach said. "I keep the berries cool, from the moment they're picked. And picked by hand."

He brushed past her, enveloping her in the clean laundry scent she loved so much. She closed her eyes for a moment and breathed him in. When she opened them, she found Zach surveying her, hands on his hips, scowling at her—not his usual relaxed self.

"So, what did you find out about SS Wines?" he asked.

"Definitely a front." She described the property as Zach continued to scowl. Concerned about his expression, she kept her description brief.

"Not a warehouse, then?"

"Just a house and a small, locked garage."

"I'm going to refuse the PVZ shipment and force someone to come forward."

"Not sure if that's the best strategy." She buttoned her jacket. "If I were involved in counterfeiting, I wouldn't make a fuss about a refused shipment. I'd send a delivery van to pick up the lot and try selling it somewhere else."

"True."

"Obviously SS Wines has no idea you work at Oakville Wine Storage and that you have a personal interest in Paradise Valley Zinfandel."

"So, whoever's involved is an out of towner," Zach mused.

"Or a complete *bampot*." Sarah went silent for a moment, as she considered how to proceed.

"What are you thinking?" Zach asked.

"How to catch the seller."

"Think out loud."

"Okay. What if we use the auction to catch the seller?"

"What if the seller is dead? What if it was Bill Friske?"

"And his shipment came in after his death via SS Wines?"

"It could have been delayed because of the weekend."

"True. What if the seller isn't Friske, though? We might be able to flush out whoever it is."

"How?"

"You know how the highest sale gets that award at the auction gala?"

Zach nodded, his eyes intense. "The seller might be induced to come forward to claim the trophy."

"Right. If they didn't suspect we knew about the fakes, they probably would. That award is a big deal. A person gets media coverage. A lot of free publicity."

Zach looked at her and smiled for the first time that afternoon. "Sarah, you might be a genius."

He turned his attention to the decanter on the table, lifted it, and slowly poured rich, purple wine into each goblet, allowing air to mingle with it. Sarah watched in silence as she admired the color and depth of his new wine, giving it the respect she knew it would deserve. Then Jack held out a goblet for her. His smile had faded as quickly as it had appeared.

"But how do we make sure the PVZ gets the highest bid?" he asked.

"Because I'll make sure." She didn't want to talk about the fake wine anymore. She wanted to savor the cabernet in her glass. Without dropping her nose into the goblet, she could smell leather and tobacco floating on the air.

"The fakes will be a popular item," Zach continued. "Do you have enough collateral to back an offer of that size?"

"*Aye.*" Impatient, she swirled her wine, not appreciating being distracted by all the questions. "But, if the killer comes forward, I'll never have to make good on my bid. I'll talk to Sheriff Bradley. Make sure he's in on the sting."

"Sounds like you have it all worked out." He heaved a sigh and the darkness settled like a cloud around him.

She tilted her head and studied him. She would take no pleasure in this wine-tasting until she found out what was bothering him. "And now will you please tell me what's got your knickers in a twist?"

Chapter 15 | Apologies and Perfume

Zach set down his goblet. "I'll tell you what's eating me." He planted his fists on his hips. "You've been keeping me in the dark."

"About what?"

"You know damn well what. Were you going to wait until the whole town knew before I did?"

"Knew what?"

"That you've kicked Matteo out."

Sarah flushed.

"Sarah, what's going on?"

"It's complicated." Sarah turned her back so Zach couldn't see her face. She pretended to inspect the nearest clay amphora.

"I thought we were friends," Zach said behind her.

"We are," she shot back. "But I didn't come here to talk about personal stuff. I'm here on business."

"Is that how you want it to be with us? Just business?"

"I'm not ready to talk about it."

"Why?"

"I'm just not."

"So, the whole town knows you and Matteo are splitting up, but one of your best friends has no fricking idea."

"Sorry. I didn't know it was public knowledge. Who told you?"

"Does it matter?"

She shrugged and hugged her chest. "It's just that..."

"It's just what?"

"That I'm not ready to talk about it."

"Well, you've made me look like an idiot."

"I'm sorry, Zach. It wasn't my intention."

"That tells me you're afraid to be truthful with me. While I bare my soul to you with that cabernet in your hand."

"It's not the same thing," she countered.

"It damn well is. It's a matter of trust." He held out his hand for the goblet. "Give it back."

She looked down at the deep violet wine swimming in the goblet. She had so wanted to taste Zach's cabernet, but the opportunity had slipped away. Zach had dredged up all that she was striving to forget. And now her shortcomings stuck in her throat in a hot lump.

The tasting was over. In her present condition, she wouldn't be able to tell a Chianti from a Pagan Pink Ripple anyway. When she was upset, her nose didn't work. And when her nose didn't work, her palate went flat.

She relinquished the glass.

"You don't trust me," Zach said, his voice full of gravel.

"Yes, I do."

"If you did, you would have told me."

"I don't trust anyone all that much. With personal stuff."

"Well, maybe you should have a think about that." He walked away and placed the untouched wine glasses on the table. His shoulders sagged.

Sarah stared at his back, wanting to say something pithy to change his opinion of her—or at least lighten the mood. But for once, nothing came to mind.

Shellshocked by his withdrawal, she took a step backward. Where did he get permission to criticize her like that? She was what she was. She didn't have to answer to him or confide in him.

But Zach had dismissed her, and it stung. She felt like bursting into tears, which wasn't like her. What was going on with her damn hormones? She clenched her jaw, refusing to shed a single drop in front of him.

"Bye then, Zach."

"Bye." He didn't look back.

****

Sarah was still in a funk later that night as she sat on the deck in her robe, nursing something red and thin in a cloudy white wine glass. Who cared if it was the wrong type of glass? Who cared if she had used the same glass for the last two days? She didn't care. She couldn't taste what she drank. She could only feel it. And after three glasses, she thought maybe—just maybe—she would be able to fall sleep.

Her doorbell rang, rousing her from her warm buzz. She ignored the summons. There was no one she wanted to talk to tonight. Especially Matteo. Even more especially Zach. The chances were slim, however, that either man would visit her at this hour. They'd be at work. That was going to be her life from here on out. Every night alone.

The doorbell rang again.

"Go away," she muttered, sinking farther down in her chair. She wouldn't budge for anyone tonight. Not even for

Kelley. The person at the door couldn't be her friend, anyway. Kelley always worked the night shift on Tuesday.

"Not too drunk," Sarah mumbled to herself. "Know what day it is. Tuesday." She held up her dirty goblet and smiled at it. "Tuesday is booze day."

The doorbell went silent. Sarah listened for the sound of a vehicle leaving the drive but didn't expend all that much attention on the task. Relieved that the visitor had given up, she contemplated the bottle of red blend on the table near her chair. Should she drink the last glass or call it a night?

Or sit here until she went completely numb, both mentally and physically?

Just as she reached for the bottle, she heard footsteps crunching along the side of her house. She looked in the direction of the sound, the hairs prickling at the back of her neck, and struggled to her feet.

"Sarah," a male voice called. "You alright?"

A male figure came into view at the side of her deck, but his dark clothing and coloring concealed his identity. Sarah stumbled backward toward the sliding glass door to her kitchen, ready to make a run for it. Then she saw the flash of a badge as the man vaulted over the railing.

"Bradley?" she gasped.

"I called. Numerous times."

"I've been away from my phone."

"Why didn't you answer the door?"

"Didn't feel like entertaining."

"I was worried. With all the homicides." Sheriff Bradley clomped across the deck while his gaze took in the wine bottle on the table and the glass in her hand. Then his surveillance rose to her face.

"You drunk?"

"No."

"Sure?"

"Got a breathalyzer on you, pal?" She brushed the door behind her, trying to locate the handle of the slider.

"Let me get that."

He stepped closer and reached around her for the latch. She didn't move aside.

"You can't barge in here like this," she said.

"Yes, I can. People are being killed, Sarah. You shouldn't be sitting out here like this. You should be more careful."

"What's with everybody these days?" she retorted, waving her glass in the air. "Be more forgiving. Be more trusting. Be more careful. I am what I am!"

"What you are, is drunk." He pried the goblet out of her grasp.

"I am not," she made sure to punctuate each word with a jab to his chest, "inebriated."

He stared down at her, unmoving, his dark eyes glittering.

She gazed at his shiny badge. "Even Kelley has something to say. She doesn't approve of my driving. Or my car. She hates my car."

"No accounting for taste." He clutched her arm. "Let's get you some food."

"Don't have any. Don't want any." She let him guide her into the kitchen.

"You've got to have something." Bradley closed the slider.

"No kale. No pistachios. No lepidoptera."

"That's not a food. That's a butterfly."

She shot him a baleful stare. Did the man not possess a single ounce of humor inside that uniform of his?

Then again, maybe she didn't need funny. Maybe at this moment, what she needed was sexy. And Sheriff Bradley was sexy personified.

She needed to shut off her mind. She needed to let her body sing, to let it do whatever it wanted tonight. That was the kind of night it was. She might not be trusting of others. She might not connect that well on an emotional level, but she damn well knew how to enjoy a man's physical attributes.

She backed against the island and grabbed the corners with her hands, aware that her robe would fall open to reveal her cleavage.

Much to her annoyance, Bradley reached for something behind her, bypassing her breasts.

"What's this?" he held up the box of perfume she had purchased for him.

"It's Joe Malone Grapefruit."

"Isn't this a man's cologne?"

"*Aye, 'tis.*" She straightened and yanked her robe shut. "It's a light scent. Citrus, with a dirty, fruity undertone."

"Dirty?" He held the box closer, as if verifying the term "dirty."

"You know, earthy, finishing with a light floral note that perfectly balances the stronger elements. The grapefruit'll soften and linger on the skin for hours. Without being overwhelming."

Bradley frowned, unconvinced, as he examined the back of the box. "Sounds like one of your wine descriptions."

"Perfume is very much like wine." She pointed at the box. "Open it," she urged. "I got it for you."

"For me?" He turned in surprise.

"Steven, you are sexy as hell. I can't tell you how sexy." She pulled away from the counter. "But you smell like a locker room."

His long, curled eyelashes fluttered. "I beg your pardon?"

"A locker room full of sweaty, teenage boys."

"No one has ever complained." He put the box on the counter. "Maybe your nose is off."

"Trust me, it isn't."

He stared down at her, and she wondered if he was embarrassed, insulted or trying to figure out who else had made comments about his cologne.

"Do me a favor and try it," she added. "Find out how it reacts with your skin."

"Now?"

"No, after you take a shower and wash off the locker room." She nodded at the hallway.

"You mean now? Take a shower now?"

She picked up the box and pressed it to his chest. "And don't bother putting on your clothes. I want to smell it on you *au natural.*"

He blinked again and studied her expression, as if he were translating her words into a language he could understand. "I was going to make you something. An omelet."

"Don't have any eggs."

"Toast."

"Don't have any bread."

"What do you have?"

"Galactic cap condoms. Ever try 'em?"

****

The next morning, Sarah woke up to the heavenly smell of coffee brewing. She scampered to the bathroom, relieved herself, brushed her teeth and returned to the bed as Bradley ambled into the room carrying two mugs.

"You do have coffee," he announced. "I managed to find it. Nothing else, though, so it's black."

"I like it black." She smiled and accepted the steaming mug. Her inuendo was lost on him.

Bradley stood beside the bed, fully dressed and smelling like a new man. He sat on the edge of the mattress and looked down at her.

"I did have a legitimate reason for coming over here last night."

"Not just for the workout?"

The man could pummel. She felt thoroughly thrashed. But in a good way.

A grin flitted over Bradley's mouth. Even his lips were muscular—also in a good way.

"Not just for the workout." He sipped his coffee. "I wanted to apologize. For the other day. At the Friske place."

The memory came flooding back, cooling the closeness she had felt with him during the night.

"For treating me like a criminal, you mean?"

"When I'm working, I must play by the rules, Sarah. No favoritism."

"What about a little respect?"

"Yeah. That's what I wanted to apologize for. I was a little harsh."

"A little?"

"The news took me by surprise. That you and Arthur had spoken to the victim days before his death. Threatened him, even."

"We didn't threaten him." She put down her coffee, unwilling to take another sip of the brew he had made. "How many times do I have to say it?"

"But you have to understand that I have a certain position to uphold in this community."

"So do I."

"I can't let it get around that a civilian is working the investigation."

"Steven, I'm more than a civilian."

"People like Mrs. Friske might disagree. And when you start defending someone like Arthur Chen, I have to draw the line. You might be involved."

"Are you kidding me?"

"Arthur Chen is your friend. Right?"

"Colleague. I wouldn't go so far as to say he's a friend."

"Keep it that way. Because Chen is in big trouble."

"He shouldn't be. And he shouldn't be in jail. Where's the evidence against him?"

"How did you know he's in jail?"

"Kelley told me."

Sheriff Bradley rolled his eyes and stood up. "That's the trouble with small towns."

"You've got that right," she retorted. "Small town thinking. You're pinning a murder on the wrong guy. Just because he's Chinese."

"We've got the note with Xu written on it. That's proof enough. A dying man doesn't lie."

"If Friske wrote it."

"What are you saying?"

"That you're jumping to a lot of conclusions, sheriff."

They glared at each other. Sarah threw back the covers and stood buck naked in front of him. "And if you have such a stellar reputation to uphold, I suggest you park your police vehicle somewhere other than the front of my house."

"I did," he countered. "I left it up on the main road."

She flushed. Bradley must have assumed she would ask him in and maybe invite him to spend the night. But he didn't want the world to know what he was up to. She wasn't accustomed to being a backstreet kind of lass.

"Are you ashamed of me?" she asked. "Of this?" She wagged a finger between his fully dressed body and her naked one.

"No." His face went blank as he blinked furiously.

"Then why hide?"

"I was protecting you. Your reputation."

"Bullshit." She grabbed her robe from the end of the bed. "If you really wanted to protect me, you would bring your own condoms."

"I will next time."

"There's not going to be a next time, pal."

She breezed into the bathroom and slammed the door.

"I said I was sorry," he called on the other side of the door.

She turned on the tub full blast to drown him out.

Chapter 16 | Matteo Rescue

On Wednesday evening, as Sarah turned off the light by her bed, she heard her phone ring. She picked it up, expecting a spammer, and was surprised to see Zach Sullivan's name on her screen.

"Zach?" she sat up straight and brushed the hair out of her eyes.

"Sarah, sorry to call so late, but you need to come down to the Wolf House. Immediately."

"Why?" She slipped out of bed.

"Matteo's not fit to drive. He got into a fight, too. I think someone might have called the police. You should get him out of here."

"I'll be right there."

Sarah pulled on jeans, tee-shirt and a leather coat and trotted out to her car. In less than two minutes, she sped into the parking lot of the Wolf House, as a county sheriff vehicle, lights flashing, rushed in behind her. Sarah jumped out, hoping to get Matteo out the back door and out of the public eye, and didn't wait around to discover what law enforcement officer had arrived. Since Kelley had worked the night shift on Tuesday she wouldn't be on duty and able to help. Anyone else would be interference—especially if the officer was Sheriff Bradley.

She dashed to the rear door of the pub and pushed through, into the deafening noise of the crowd. In the corner near the restrooms, she saw a man sitting back in a booth and holding a bag of ice on his mouth, with a crowd of onlookers above him. Matteo was nowhere to be seen. Then a hand shot out of the noise behind her and enveloped her elbow.

"He's in the back," Zach's voice said near her ear. "I separated them."

"Right." Sarah followed Zach down a short hall to a room she'd never been in. It contained file cabinets, a messy desk, a small window and her husband sitting in a chair, holding an icepack to one eye.

"Matteo?"

His head rose at the sound of his name. He looked terrible. His black hair was a forest of spikes, his eyes were bloodshot, and his clothes reeked of spilled beer. He squinted her into focus.

"What's she doing here?" He waved the air and nearly lost his balance.

"Sarah's going to take you home."

"I don't have a home. She stole it!" He poked the air and lurched backward. "She's going to steal everything!"

"Let's go, Matteo." Zach reached down, shoved an arm behind his slighter friend and hoisted him to his feet.

"Where did you park?" Zach asked, glancing at Sarah.

"By the tree in back." She tried to catch his eye, to communicate that she wanted their friendship to get back to normal, but he ignored her.

"Get the door."

Sarah skittered to open the door as Zach guided a weaving, ranting Matteo out to the parking lot.

Before Sarah could shut the door, she saw a man shoulder through the doorway after them. The streetlight illuminated the shining outline of Sheriff Bradley's head—the last person Sarah wanted to see.

"Halt!" he demanded. "Stop right there!"

Zach paused, with Matteo's arm draped over his shoulder. He looked back at the law enforcement officer. "Just making sure a customer gets home safely."

"Someone called in a drunk and disorderly."

"Just a misunderstanding. Nothing to worry about, officer."

"It's sheriff." Bradley ran a probing glare over Zach, then to Sarah and on to Matteo, as if trying to sort out the relationship between the three of them.

"Is that man drunk?"

"He's had a few, but he's all right."

Sarah placed her hand on Matteo's forearm. "This is my husband, Matteo."

"Husband?" Bradley retorted. "I thought you told me you were separated."

"We are."

Sarah noticed Zach was doing the evaluating now, as if he were trying to sort out the relationship between the sheriff and Sarah. He didn't look happy with his findings. She bristled. Her personal choices were none of his business now that he'd cut off her friendship.

"I'm going to have to give him a breathalyzer test." Bradley held up the device. "Sir, blow into the tube."

"But he's not going to be driving," Sarah took Matteo's other arm, hoping to make him appear less inebriated. "I'm taking him home."

"If he started a fight, and his alcohol level is above the legal limit, he will face a drunk and disorderly charge."

"Matteo DiSanti?" Zach struggled to support the entire bulk of his now limp friend. "You're going to charge Matteo DiSanti? He's the best chef in Sonoma."

"So? I'd charge Santa Claus if he started a fight."

"Oh, c'mon," Sarah said. "Matteo didn't hurt anyone."

"There's a guy in there that might disagree." Bradley nodded toward the bar behind him.

"It's only a bloody lip," Zach said. "Come on, sheriff, altercations happen all the time."

"Not in my town, they don't," Bradley snapped.

"And for your information, the other guy started it."

Bradley raked Zach with a cold stare. "I don't like your attitude. What's your name?" He swiped an app on his phone. "And what's your relationship to DiSanti?"

"Please. No harm has been done," Sarah interjected. "Please, sheriff. Can you let this go? Just this once?"

Bradley ignored her. "Are you going to answer the question, sir, or do I have to take you in as well?"

Zach rolled his eyes. "It's Sullivan. Zach Sullivan. Friend. Bartender at the Wolf House."

"Do you know it's against the law to overserve a customer, Mr. Sullivan?"

"The man had a couple of beers. Tops."

"Then why is he incoherent?"

"My guess is he must be taking something."

"You mean a narcotic?"

"I don't know, sheriff. I'm a bartender. Not a doctor."

The heat between the two men had escalated to a precarious level. Sarah moved to stand between them, shielding Zach. Bradley's lip twitched as he watched her take sides.

"Matteo might have taken painkillers," Sarah put in. "He's got a bad back."

"Prescription painkillers?" Bradley rolled *his* eyes. "And he's drinking alcohol? He'll destroy his liver doing that. More reason to take him in. Instill some fear in him."

"Please, Steven. We're all family here in Sonoma. We work together. And sometimes we cut each other some slack."

He looked down his nose at her. "You expect me to break the rules."

"No, bend them a little. The town will talk if you take him in. It's my husband's career that's on the line here."

"He should have thought about his career before he mixed alcohol and pills." Bradley turned back to Matteo. "Sir, I'm asking you one last time." Bradley held the breathalyzer in front of Matteo's face. "Blow into the tube. If you refuse to submit to the test, I will be forced to take you in, where you will have to wait until a blood test can be arranged."

"*Ficcatelo su per il culo*," Matteo spat on the ground.

"What did he just say?" Bradley demanded.

Sarah shrugged, playing dumb. If Bradley found out Matteo had told him where to stick the breathalyzer, the sheriff would lock him up for sure.

"Oh, for Pete's sake." Zach heaved an exasperated sigh and dragged Matteo toward Sarah's sportscar.

"What do you think you're doing?" Bradley shouted, trailing after him.

"I'm putting Matteo in Sarah's car."

Sarah hurried to the passenger side and yanked open the door.

"Sir," Bradley thundered.

Zach ignored the officer and settled Matteo into the seat. Matteo leaned back with his mouth hanging open. He started to snore.

Zach brushed his hands together. "And now I'm returning to my customers."

"Sir!"

"If you can get Matteo to complete a breathalyzer test, have at it."

"You'll never wake him up." Sarah gazed down at her unconscious husband. "Once he's asleep. He's *asleep*."

"This is unacceptable." Bradley fumed. "Unacceptable. All of this."

"Maybe where you come from, it's everything by the book," Sarah said. "But around here, we take a more humane approach."

"And Sarah will need help getting Matteo out of that car." Zach waved and strode back to the bar through a handful of patrons who had come out to investigate the flashing lights.

"Does the man think he owns the place?" Bradley grumbled, his nostrils still flared with anger.

"Well, his family did own a good deal of this valley at one time."

"And he works at a bar?"

"It's a long story."

Bradley shook his head, glared up at the moon, and then sighed. "Okay, it was pills. Accidental contraindication. I'll put that in the report."

"You're a saint, Steven."

"I'll follow you to the house."

He stomped past the crowd. "All right, people, go back inside. There's nothing to see here. Just a medical incident."

Sarah collapsed in her car and looked over at her gorgeous ex-partner, snoring away. Why he wasn't at the restaurant was a mystery. Why he was drunk was a bigger mystery. He never let himself go this far when he drank. Was he that torn up about their failed relationship? Or was his condition, like Zach had proposed, drug induced and a mistake?

She scowled and backed out of the parking space, and then sped across the bridge toward home, with Bradley following close behind. Once at the house, the sheriff half-dragged, half-carried Matteo into the living room.

"This way," Sarah said, leading him to the guest bedroom. Bradley dropped Matteo on the mattress and reached for his dangling right foot, which he tossed on the bed as well.

Sarah scooped off Matteo's expensive loafers and grabbed a throw to drape over him. Bradley stood at the end of the bed, hands on his hips, recovering his breath.

"You weren't kidding," he commented. "The man sleeps like the dead."

"He does."

Sarah walked out of the room and down the hall to the kitchen. Bradley padded after her.

"Cup of tea?" she asked, keeping to her best Scottish manners, even though their last conversation had been contentious. "Soda? Glass of wine?"

"Still on duty." He stood at the end of the island. "Do you have any sparkling water?"

"I do." She retrieved a bottle from the fridge and held it out. "I went grocery shopping today. It's a miracle."

He unscrewed the cap.

"And sheriff," she held out her hand. "I appreciate what you did for Matteo."

He crushed her hand in his large, warm one. "Don't expect me to look the other way the next time."

"I won't."

"Just because, you know..." He broke off and released his grip on her, but his probing stare kept her prisoner. "Sarah, I..."

"I should go back to bed," she said. "I've got an early meeting tomorrow with the UK."

"Of course." He gave the island a pat and barreled toward the front door. On the threshold, he turned.

"So, what's the story with you and Matteo? Just separated? Getting a divorce?"

"He'll be served papers on Thursday."

Bradley nodded as he studied her. "I've been thinking," he said. "About what you said."

"In what regard?"

"Us."

The word scalded her in a flood of heat and apprehension. "Oh?"

"About not being on the up and up." He took a deep breath. "You know. Screwing around."

"I'm not sure I'm—"

"It's not how I usually conduct myself."

"Me neither."

"I wanted to put it out there. Just so you know."

Sarah could only nod and hope that she could close the door soon. She reached for the knob and tipped her head onto the wooden edge of the door, praying he would get the hint that she was exhausted. He didn't seem to notice.

"I don't know what got into me those times," he said.

"Me neither."

"I've been single for a few years now, and it's been difficult to find the right partner. I lost control."

"That makes two of us, Steven."

"So, I wanted to apologize."

"There's no need. I wanted it as much as you. Maybe more."

"Really?"

"*Aye*. My marriage has been...tough...for a while now."

He nodded, eager for more information. She eased the door forward.

"I really have to get to bed."

"I understand. I need to get back to work, too."

"I do want to talk to you about the wine auction, though. Maybe tomorrow?"

"Come and see me in the morning," he said. "I'll be in the office by ten." He pulled a card out of a chest pocket. "Give me a call to let me know you're coming."

"All right."

"Goodnight, Sarah."

"Goodnight."

She watched him walk to his vehicle. She closed the door. As she turned the lock, she realized she had been holding her breath. She was still of two minds about the sheriff, and she didn't like the limbo. That's not how she lived her life, waffling about things. She would have to make up her mind about their relationship. *And better the noo.*

****

The next morning, Sarah had finished her conference call and was stirring milk into her second cup of tea when Matteo trudged into the kitchen, scratching his chest.

"'Morning," he mumbled. "Any coffee?"

"There's instant." She pointed at the electric kettle. "Help yourself."

"*Che buono!*" He looked up at the ceiling and smiled. "It's good to be home."

"This is not your home. And you're not staying long."

"*Amoré*, you can't mean it. I am a wreck. Look at me." He touched his black eye gingerly and then spread his arms wide. His tee shirt stretched over his muscular chest. "I am injured. And I haven't slept for a week."

"Not my problem."

"The couch in my office is killing my back." He grabbed the jar of instant out of the cupboard and winced. "I couldn't work last night. I couldn't even walk."

"So, you decided to take some pills and go to the Wolf House."

"I wanted to talk to Zach. I had to talk to someone."

"Not about us, I hope."

He flushed. "Why not?"

"It's personal, that's why not. Why air our dirty laundry in front of the whole town?"

"Everyone knows anyway."

"How? I didn't tell anyone. Only Kelley."

"Well, there you go."

"Don't go blaming Kelley. It was probably an employee at the restaurant, who has seen you sleeping in your office. Or your boyfriend."

He plopped onto a stool and stirred his coffee. "One of my employees wanted to know if we had out of town visitors. Because there was a black pickup parked out front all night. What's up with that?"

It was Sarah's turn to blush. "That's none of your concern. And no one else's, either."

"You're seeing someone." He glared at her. "I knew it."

"That is not the reason for our...trouble."

"Really?"

"And you know it."

He shrugged a shoulder. "How am I supposed to believe that? You're not the kind of person to jump in bed with a stranger."

How little he knew her. Then again, she barely knew herself anymore. She gulped her tea.

"So, I have to think you have been seeing someone behind my back. And that's what this is all about."

"Well, you would be wrong." She tapped her phone and looked at the time. Nine-forty-five. "And however much I'm enjoying the sight of your sorry *arse* sitting in my kitchen, I have somewhere I have to be."

"It's my kitchen, too. I'll sit here if I want."

"You'd better not be sitting here when I get back. And I want your stuff out of the garage, too."

"I'm sick, *amoré*. Have a heart."

"I don't have a heart, Matteo. Remember? You broke it."

"I can fix it. Fix everything. Let me stay, *cara*. Just until my back is better. Just a few days. In the guest room. I'm begging you."

"No way, pal."

His expression sagged. When she called him pal, they both knew the argument was over.

Sarah grabbed her purse from the rack in the foyer and slung the strap over one shoulder. "I'm not joking, Matteo. I don't want you here when I get back."

"Why? I miss you, *amoré*. I miss you. Please!"

"And don't use my toothbrush!"

"I'm sick! How will I cater the auction if I'm sick? *Amoré*!"

She slammed the door, cutting him off. Then she stormed out to the driveway and called Steven to tell him she was on her way.

Chapter 17 | Bradley's Office

Sheriff Bradley met Sarah in the lobby of the Sonoma County Sheriff's Office in Santa Rosa and led her to his office at the end of the bullpen of investigators. The space was tidy, bereft of paper piles and file folder stacks. A row of binders on a shelf and a framed photo of Bradley winning a race was the only indication that someone occupied the desk.

The man was new to the position. Maybe he hadn't had the opportunity to accumulate a mess. Then again, Sheriff Bradley, with his shining bald head, glowing skin and neatly creased uniform, didn't seem like the kind of person to tolerate untidiness. And now, wearing the cologne she had bought for him, he even smelled tidy.

She sat down in a chair on the other side of his desk. They got down to business without wasting much time, in the same way they'd jumped into the kip without much foreplay. The memory of their reckless romps made the tips of her ears burn.

Trying not to think about sex with Sheriff Bradley, Sarah leaned forward and outlined her plan for the sting operation at the auction. She was surprised that Bradley had no objections, other than the fact that he thought she was wasting her time. He was convinced the Chinese triad had killed Bill Friske.

"Maybe," Sarah said, "But not Joe Salgado. He didn't sell fakes. As far as we know, he only made them. Why kill him?"

"But the same person who paid his rent also owns SS Wines. That's a connection right there. Maybe Joe Salgado *was* SS Wines."

"But he's dead. How could he send a shipment to a wine warehouse *postmortem*?"

"Maybe it was a scheduled delivery."

"I doubt it. You don't leave expensive wine out in the middle of nowhere unrefrigerated."

"How do you know SS Wines is out in the middle of nowhere?"

"I went there."

"On whose authority?"

His imperious tone riled her. She got to her feet. "I don't need police permission to go to a place of business."

"But you do need permission to investigate a crime."

"I don't believe that's true," she retorted, staring him down.

"Tell me you didn't break into the place." He rose, using his physical presence to dominate the argument. "Did you?"

"Of course not."

"Small favors," he muttered. He yanked open a desk drawer. "And for your information, we have discovered there *is* a connection." He slapped a piece of paper on the desk.

Sarah hovered close enough to examine the paper. She recognized the strange list of numbers and checkmarks that Kelley had showed her on her phone. As far as Sarah could tell, the list on the desk was the same list that had been found on Joe Salgado's body. Or maybe it *was* the list that had been in Salgado's pocket. Were there two lists or one? She wanted to be sure.

"Where did you find this?" she asked.

"On the victim, Bill Friske."

Sarah studied it, trying not to show too much interest.

"We found an exact duplicate on Joe Salgado."

"What is it? What am I looking at?"

"We don't know yet. That's what we have to figure out. This list is the key." Bradley stabbed the paper with a long, muscular finger. "I know it is. This is the connection, and I'm going to get the truth out of Arthur Chen, one way or another."

"Are you holding him without bail?"

"No, we had to release him yesterday. Some hotshot lawyer from San Francisco showed up. But that doesn't mean he can't be taken in for more questioning."

"What about the autopsy?"

"What about it?"

"Bill Friske was sick the night he died."

"That was a coincidence."

"How do you know for sure?"

"We know what killed him, Sarah. It's obvious. A bullet." His challenging stare burned across her face. "But what I want to know is how did you know he was sick that night?"

"His housekeeper came into the Wolf House Bar the other night when I was there and talked to Zach."

"Why?"

"She was frightened about being interviewed by you and your staff."

"Why would she talk to a bartender about it?"

"Because she used to be his nanny. She wanted his advice."

Bradley's lip curled. "Who is this Zach character, anyway?"

"Like I told you, he's the scion of a longtime Sonoma Valley family. The Sullivans used to own Paradise Valley as well the land from the winery to the sea, but Zach's father gambled the place away. Zach is determined to re-establish the family reputation, while Bill Friske was destroying everything the Sullivans were known for." Sarah propped both hands on the desk, "And that's the thing. The person passing fake Paradise Valley Zinfandel doesn't know that much about the area. Or that Zach works at Oakville Wine Storage. Otherwise, they would never have submitted the PVZ for inspection for the auction."

"I thought he was a bartender."

"He has two jobs."

"So, he's busting his ass while someone is passing fake PVZ and about to make a fortune. As well as possibly besmirching the family name." Bradley's eyes gleamed with inspiration. "There's motive right there."

"Not Zach." Sarah shook her head. "Never."

"It's always the one you don't suspect, Sarah. Always."

"Zach would never kill anyone."

"How can you be so sure?"

"Because I know him."

"Maybe you don't. Maybe you're not impartial." He jabbed a finger to his chest. "But I am. It's my job."

"To suspect innocent people?"

"To keep an open mind. Zach Sullivan might be at the bottom of this entire thing."

"Don't be ridiculous!"

"Think about it. If he gets rid of Bill Friske and his counterfeiter, maybe he can get back Paradise Valley. Or at least get revenge. And that's motive."

"A highly unlikely motive."

"I didn't get to be sheriff without thinking outside the box."

"I thought sheriffs were elected."

He ignored her comment. "Well, we'll find out something at the auction, won't we?"

Sarah straightened. "We?"

"I intend to be at that gala."

"I don't think that's a good idea, Steven. If the killer sees law enforcement hanging around, they might think twice about coming forward."

"They won't know I'm law enforcement if I'm there in plain clothes. As an attendee."

"That won't work." Sarah shook her head. "You're not part of the wine industry. Believe me, everyone knows everyone. People will be suspicious. In particular, SS Wines."

"Not if I go as your date."

"My what?"

"Your date." He smiled and sat down. "It'll be a good way to go public, too. Let people know. About us."

She gaped at him. "Are you serious?"

"Always am." He smiled again and opened the calendar on his phone. "The auction gala's on Friday night, right? What time should I pick you up?"

****

Desperate to talk to someone after her chat with Bradley, Sarah called Kelley to meet her at the Sunflower Café for a quick cup of coffee. They carried their lattes to the front patio and sat down.

"What's going on, Sarah?" Kelley asked, pulling out her chair. "You sounded kind of strained on the phone."

"Bradley thinks he's taking me to the gala."

"Is that a bad thing?" Kelley set her keys on the table and sat down. "Everyone knows you and Matteo are on the outs."

"Do they? *Gawd.*"

"It's a small town. News travels fast."

"It's just that..." Sarah sighed. "I'm not ready to go public yet. With Bradley."

"Are you saying that you and he...he and you, you know..." She twirled a finger in the air.

"*Aye.*" Sarah stared down at the creamy heart design floating in her cup. The frothy heart mocked her, reminding her that there was no romance in her life and hadn't been for a very long time.

"You didn't!"

"We did. I couldn't help myself. He's a walking sex machine."

"And?" Kelley leaned forward, eager for details.

"Kelley, do you honestly think I would kiss and tell?"

"Okay, a hint then. What was he like?"

"He's built. That's all I'm going to say."

Kelley grinned and sat back in her chair. "Oh, this is classic, Sarah. Really classic."

"I know," Sarah glared at her. "And that's what everyone else is going to think, too. I'll look like a *slag* and Matteo will look like an *eejit*."

"Then don't go through with it. Make up an excuse."

"But I need Bradley there, for the showdown."

"What showdown?"

Sarah explained her plan while Kelley nodded and sipped her drink.

"So, you see," Sarah continued, "He can't go to the gala by himself. That would be a massive red flag."

"Hmm."

"There has to be another way," Sarah thought for a moment. "I know," she put down her cup. "Why doesn't he go with you? I can get you a ticket. It'll be an acting job. I'll even pay you."

"Oh, no." Kelley held up both hands. "No. No way."

"C'mon, *hen*. Please."

"No. This is your plan, girlfriend. And he's your date. End of story."

"I thought we were friends."

"Friends don't make friends fake-date cops."

"That's a fine thing to say, you being a cop yourself."

"Well, it's a fact." Her phone rang. She picked it up and listened. Then she jumped to her feet and grabbed her keys. "Sorry, Sarah, gotta go. They've found something in that shed at SS Wines."

"What?"

"Didn't say. I'll catch you later."

****

Sarah sat at the café, not in the mood for working or for going back to the house to discover Matteo was still there. She ordered a sandwich, sat back to watch the world go by, and tried to come up with a way to get out of the gala date with Bradley. Other than illness or making up with Matteo, she couldn't think of any other excuses. Maybe she would have to be honest with Bradley and confess that the relationship was nothing but a sexual fling to her, and that it would be best to stop playing around.

Such a confession wouldn't be easy. Bradley would be greatly offended. The last thing she wanted was to make an enemy of the man. She glared at the plaza, knowing she had to extricate herself from the situation but not sure how. She should never have told him that he didn't need to apologize for jumping her bones, that she had wanted it as much as he had, maybe more. Her and her big *gob*.

The sun climbed higher, dappling the shaded plaza across the street but failing to lighten her mood.

Just as she finished her duck and arugula sandwich, she saw Roger Larue shuffle across the street and head for the fountain where he passed his days. He still wore the lavender polo shirt and faded jeans, and he walked as if a dark force pulled each step downward, sucking him toward the sidewalk.

"*Peer soul*," Sarah muttered, watching his forlorn rambling. He looked as if any second now, he might break into pieces and blow away—and he wouldn't care if that happened.

Sarah paid for her brunch and ordered two of the largest lattes on the menu to go. Then she carried them across the park.

Roger stood alone, gazing down at the water, with his hands in his pockets. Bits of leaves stuck to the back of his shirt and wiry hair. Where did the man sleep?

"Hi, Roger. Like lattes?"

He gazed over his shoulder at her, his eyes dull. He looked at the coffee cup and then into her eyes, not warming to her. "I'm not a charity case, you know."

"I know that. They messed up my order. Thought I'd ask if you wanted it." She held out the tall paper cup in her left hand. "No sense dumping it. Go on." She wiggled the cup. "It's yours."

"Well, okay," he accepted the drink. "Appreciate it." He sat down.

"I heard about your family. I'm really sorry, Roger."

"Don't want to talk about it."

"Suit yourself." She sat on the edge of the fountain and didn't say anything more. She sipped her coffee and gazed out at the park. Ducks chased each other in the pond. Turtles bulldozed through reeds to find the best patches of sun. Light filtered through the trees that ringed the plaza, warming the lush grass. If a person had to spend their days in one place, this was the perfect spot.

Roger sighed and sat down a few feet away. She smiled at him but didn't make additional conversation. She had found not talking was the easiest way to get someone else to chatter. He took measured sips of the latte and watched the ducks, his shoulders slumped.

Sarah said nothing.

"You're from Scotland," he finally remarked. "They have a lot of ghosts in Scotland, don't they?"

"So, I'm told."

"They say the theater here is haunted."

"The one behind us?"

"Yeah. There is supposedly a female ghost in the women's restroom."

"Ever see it?"

"No. Never go in the women's."

"Do you believe in ghosts?" she asked.

"Not really. I want to, though."

"*Aye*. I do as well." Sarah gazed at the sidewalk in front of her. "I'd like to talk to my dad. Hear his voice again. You know?"

His gaze flitted over the side of her face and away.

She said nothing more. She could feel his need to talk to someone sizzling like an entity between them.

"There's another ghost that hangs around the courthouse." He pointed his drink in the direction of the square stone building at the center of the plaza. "A ghost named Michael."

"Really?"

"A little boy. Deaf kid. Got trampled by the horses pulling the fire wagon. Way back when."

"That's terrible."

He nodded and set the coffee cup beside him. "I often wonder, when you see a ghost, do you see them in the condition they were in when they died? Or the way they looked when they were...you know...at their best?"

"I think they would appear the way they *want* you to see them."

"Yeah." He dropped his head in his hands and his entire body collapsed in on itself. "God."

"But I'm no expert, Roger." She reached over to touch his back, to comfort him, but he got to his feet.

"And ghosts haunt the place where they died," he said. "Not just anywhere. That's what I figure."

"If you believe the stories. *Aye*." She watched him pace the pavement in front of the fountain. "But I've also heard that you can talk to spirits, Roger. Tell them to leave you alone."

He stopped pacing to gape at her. "You can?"

"If that's what you want. *Aye*."

He heaved a sigh and continued his pacing.

"With my dad," Sarah stared down at the lid of her cup. "It was hard. I missed him so much that sometimes I felt as if I couldn't breathe. It was worse at night. I thought I would die of grief sometimes."

She felt him listening.

"And it got to the point where I knew I had to do something."

"What did you do?"

"I decided to spin that feeling. Turn it around."

"In what way?"

"When that thing came at night to press down on my chest, I decided to talk to it. I decided the feeling I was experiencing wasn't grief. It was my dad, trying to get my attention. Visiting me, *ye ken*?"

"And you talked to him?"

"*Aye*. Like he had come for a chat." The memory of those nights warmed her now, instead of crushing the soul out of her. "It helped me." She took a deep steadying breath. "And now when I feel that wave coming, I say, 'Hi, dad. How is it going up there? How's the choir?' He liked to sing, *ye ken*."

She looked up to find Roger staring down at her, listening with his entire being. She gave him a quiet smile and got to her feet.

"I should go, though." She brushed wrinkles from the back of her pants. "I have things to do. Like kicking my husband out of the house."

"I heard you and Matteo were separating."

"Apparently the whole town knows."

"Word gets around." He nodded at her. "Thanks for the coffee."

"Anytime."

She headed down the sidewalk toward her car and had taken only a few steps when his voice stopped her.

"I also heard Bill Friske's been killed. Know anything about it? Since your friend's a cop?"

She hoped he referred to Kelley and not Steven Bradley, and that news of her liaisons with Bradley hadn't made the gossip circuit yet. She turned around. "Who told you?"

He shrugged. "One of the skateboard guys. His aunt works at the Friske place."

"This town," she muttered, shaking her head. She would have to be doubly careful about personal activities in the future.

"Who do you think killed him?" Roger asked.

"I have no idea."

"I think the wife did it."

"Maeve Friske?" Sarah turned to face him. "I rather doubt it."

"Then what was she doing with the oleander?"

Sarah completely forgot about her liaisons with the sheriff. "What oleander?"

"The oleander in the park."

Sarah studied his grizzled face, wondering if she could believe him. "Go on."

"So, I go up to the park to relieve myself the other day."

"What park?"

"Depot. The one with the train cars." He pointed north. "Up there a couple of blocks. It's out of the way. Not too many people use the restrooms up there. So, I have some privacy."

"And?"

"Nobody's in the park except her, way in the back, cutting oleander branches. Gloves and everything."

"Why is that strange?" Sarah asked.

"What does Maeve Friske want with oleander?"

"Maybe she was making a floral arrangement."

"Not for *her* house. Oleander's considered a weed around here. It grows everywhere. Maeve Friske strikes me as an orchid type of person. Or silk."

"And why the gloves?"

"Because oleander is poisonous." Roger's expression changed from a dull flicker to a flame. "I had to get rid of the stuff on our property in Santa Rosa so the horses wouldn't accidentally eat it. A single bite can kill a large animal. You can't even touch the plant for any amount of time."

"It's that poisonous?"

"Yes. And Maeve must have known it. Because she was wearing those gloves."

"Why pick a poisonous plant?"

"Exactly." Roger nodded, thoughtfully.

"When was this, Roger? Can you remember?"

He looked up, thinking hard. "Saturday?" He squinted one eye. "No, Sunday. Sunday afternoon, I think." He scratched the back of his head. "It's hard for me to keep track these days."

"Would you be willing to talk to the police about this?"

"Not really. The police have been hassling me a lot. Mostly that sheriff."

"About spending time here?"

"Yes. And he's way out of line. This is a public park. It's also a free country."

"It's supposed to be," Sarah retorted wryly. "I tell you what, Roger. I'll ask the police to go easy on you if you agree to talk with them."

"I don't know..."

"It might be worth it." She gave him a meaningful stare. "For a Friske-free town."

He smiled for the first time, albeit wanly. "You drive a hard bargain, lady."

"That's what they say."

"Well, you know where to find me. Just don't send that sheriff."

"I'll do my best, Roger. You've been a huge help."

Even though Sheriff Bradley was the reason for her midday indigestion—she had to return to his office and face him again.

Chapter 18 | Oleander in the Park

"Sarah?" Sheriff Bradley greeted in surprise as he trotted across the entry plaza of the station. "You're back?"

"I have new information." She waited at the curb.

"About Zach Sullivan? Because I'm on my way to talk to him."

"No." She swept him with a scathing look meant to convey her utter disbelief in his choice of suspect. "And I never will have info on Zach."

"See? You're not impartial," he retorted. "Like I told you."

She ignored him. "You need to have your forensic team check for oleander in Bill Friske's stomach."

"The autopsy has already been performed."

"Well, can they do another test?"

"Toxicology takes days. Sometimes weeks."

"Even if they know what to test for?"

"Sarah, I'm not going to waste taxpayer money on some wild goose chase."

"It isn't a wild goose chase. Roger Larue saw Maeve Friske cutting oleander in Depot Park on Sunday."

"Larue. The homeless guy in the park?"

"Yes. And Maeve Friske was wearing gloves. She knew what she was doing."

"I hardly think that bum is credible. Besides, there's a good chance Bill Friske's organs have been disposed of already."

He brushed past her toward the parking lot. She followed him, frustrated that he didn't seem to grasp the implication of what she was telling him.

"Oleander is poisonous, Steven. Deadly poisonous. And Bill Friske was sick the night of his death."

"But that doesn't mean Maeve killed him. It's just coincidence." He kept walking toward his SUV. "She had no motive."

"She did, though. Bill was going to divorce her."

"And you know this how?"

"The housekeeper said so. At the Wolf House."

Bradley yanked open the door of his vehicle and glared over his shoulder at her. "Is there anything else you've failed to divulge?"

"I thought you knew. You questioned Maria, right?"

His lip twitched as he looked down at her. "She didn't mention a divorce."

"Well, now you know. And I think the oleander merits getting an official statement from Roger Larue. And questioning Maria again. And a toxicology screen."

"I have a better idea, Sarah."

"What?"

"Why don't I do my job the way I see fit, and you stick to yours?"

"Because you're arresting my friends!" She glared at him. Heat roared up her neck. She could feel blotches of outrage on her cheeks and ears.

"I *should* have arrested your husband." He shook a finger at her. "Remember that."

"He wasn't drunk."

"We'll never know, will we?" He reached for the door. "I'm going to be late. Please step away from my vehicle."

She glared at him. "You're making a mistake with Zach."

"That is yet to be seen."

"If you arrest Zach, the whole town is going to hate you."

"I'm not afraid of that." He started the engine. His eyes were like flint when he looked back at her. "I'm an officer of the law. Whether people love me or hate me doesn't keep me up at night."

"Well, I won't either," she shot back. When she saw that her comment confused him, she added, "Keep you up at night, pal. And don't expect to take me to the gala. I don't wish to be seen with you."

The confusion in his eyes switched to indignation. "Because I'm brown."

"No. Because you're an *arse.*"

She flung the door shut and stomped away, as Kelley pulled into the parking lot next to him. Bradley roared backward in his SUV, barely missing a squad car behind him.

Kelley jumped out of her vehicle and into his path. "Boss!" she called, waving her arms to stop him from leaving. He screeched to a halt and rolled down his window. Sarah followed her friend, curious as to what Kelley had found during the official search of SS Wines.

"This better be good," Bradley snapped, his face florid.

"It is. We found a car in that shed at SS Wines."

"Any registration?"

"No. No paperwork."

"Make? Model?"

Kelley flipped to a page in her little tablet. "A 2009 Miata. A dark green one."

"Get the VIN number?"

"I did."

"Good. Run a check."

Sarah nodded at her tablet. "Didn't Woody drive a little green car? I remember Wesley Leslie mentioning that."

"You mean Joe Salgado," Bradley corrected. "And yes. Which is another reason to link Salgado to SS Wines."

"Yeah," Kelley put in. "And Salgado begins with an 'S,' too. I wonder who the other 'S' is."

"What about that Anya person?" Sarah said. "The person who paid Woody's rent? Anya Sarnova? Her name starts with an 'S', too."

"Way ahead of you, McKee." Bradley glared at her. "I'm on my way to arrest the real 'S' right now."

Kelley turned to Sarah. "Who's the real 'S'?"

"Zach," Sarah said. "Zach Sullivan. According to your boss."

"That's right. Your friendly bartender isn't all you think he is, Sarah. Word came in about the gun used in both murders. It belonged to Zach's father." Bradley jerked his SUV into gear and roared away.

Stunned, Sarah stood in the middle of the parking lot, unable to move.

"There must be some mistake," Kelley muttered, surprised as well. "Some explanation."

"Zach would never kill anyone, Kelley. He just wouldn't."

"You and I know that, but Bradley doesn't."

"He has a really bad habit, that man." Sarah planted her hands on her hips. "And it's starting to annoy me."

"Jumping to conclusions?" Kelley offered.

"*Aye*. And this time he's gone too far." She scowled. "He's refusing to request a toxicology report."

"For what?"

"Oleander. I have reason to believe Maeve Friske poisoned Bill. That's why he threw up."

"It would be hard to prove," Kelley replied. "The CSI team found tincture of oleander in Bill's medicine cabinet."

"They did? What would a person use that for?"

"Lots of things. I looked it up. Cardiac issues. Asthma. Erectile dysfunction. Even leprosy."

"The housekeeper did mention Bill had heart trouble."

"And maybe ED, too. A man his age." Kelley wiggled her tablet in the air. "Listen, I have to run this VIN ASAP. Want to catch up tonight?"

"Don't you have rehearsal?"

"Night off."

"Sounds good."

"Your house?" Kelley raised her brows. "Or the Wolf House?"

"Wolf House." She wasn't about to admit to Kelley that Matteo might still be at the Glen Ellen house, and that she had failed to throw him out a second time. In addition, no matter how Zach felt about her right now, she needed to ensure that he was safe and sound, pulling beers and serving popcorn at the bar. "See you around seven."

Kelley waved and strode away. Sarah pulled out her phone and punched in the number for Oakville Wine Storage.

After being connected to two different employees at the warehouse, she heard Zach came on the line.

"Yes?" The chilliness of his voice took her aback.

"I'm calling to warn you." She kept her tone businesslike.

"About what?"

"The Sonoma County sheriff is coming to arrest you."

"What for?"

"The murder of Bill Friske."

"Friske? I had nothing to do with his death."

"Bradley thinks you did. He thinks you had a motive and owned the weapon."

"You have to be joking. The only weapon I have is a Swiss Army knife."

"He's means it, Zach. The gun used to kill Friske and someone else belonged to your dad."

"Jesus."

"You need a rock-solid alibi for Sunday night. Courtney can vouch for your whereabouts, right?"

There was a pause on the line. Then she heard Zach heave a heavy sigh. "I appreciate the heads up, Sarah."

"And Zach, about Matteo and me—"

The call ended. The dead air rang in her ear, final and infinite, reminding her that she had offended Zach by withholding the truth from him. She had to find a way to explain herself so he would understand where she was coming from. Because she did trust him. She trusted Zach more than anyone she knew.

The disconnect with Zach added to Bradley's accusation of him made her feel untethered and anxious. She hated the feeling.

Sarah stuffed her phone in her back pocket and walked to her car, as the duck and arugula roiled in her stomach. Great. Her nausea had returned full force, exacerbated by the contention with Zach and her drama with Steven.

Off to the grocery store for antacid tablets. And a pregnancy test. Something was definitely wrong. She called her doctor's office, but Dr. Dena was unavailable. She left a voicemail with her assistant.

****

In the health and wellness aisle of Sonoma Market, Sarah noticed a familiar figure bending down to inspect the analgesics on the bottom row.

"Arthur?" she called.

He looked up and smiled. "Sarah. Hello."

"How is it going?"

He walked forward and bowed. "Thank you for the excellent lawyer. It seems the focus is no longer on me."

"Good to hear. How do you know it's not, though?"

"This is the first day I have spent away from the police station. I take that as a good sign." He held up a bottle of ibuprofen. "But I have been living on these. I am finding the murder inquiry very stressful."

She touched his arm. "Well, maybe you will be able relax soon. I'm sure they will catch the real killer shortly."

"One can hope."

"Are you still coming to the Flight of Fancy tomorrow night?"

"The auction is the only reason I am staying. Yes. But I may never come back."

"I wouldn't blame you, Arthur."

"I'll see you tomorrow." He bowed again and ducked around the end of the aisle.

Sarah finished her shopping and returned to her car. Standing next to her Triumph and looking down at something near the gear shift was Wesley Leslie, holding his bike with one hand. The pink and white streamers wafted in the warm breeze.

At the sound of her boots on the pavement, he looked up.

"Hi, Wesley," she greeted.

"I saw your car."

"I was shopping."

"You still have my ballerina." He pointed at the cubby in front of the gearshift.

"*Aye*. She's my good luck charm. For driving."

He evaluated her, his jaw slack, as if trying to decide if she was telling the truth or making fun of his handiwork. She opened the door, hoping he would step back so she could leave.

"Have the police found out who killed Woody?" he asked.

"Not yet, but they're working on it."

"If it helps, I saw the man and the lady just now."

"What man and lady?"

"That visited Woody sometimes. And were mean to me. Maybe they were mean to Woody, too."

"Did you call the police?"

"Don't have a phone. I was going there on my bike. Then I saw your car."

"Where did you see them?"

He jabbed the air behind him. "At the hotel back there. The one with the giant fountain. They were having a fight in the parking lot."

"Just now?"

"Duh."

"I'll try to catch them." Sarah got into her car more quickly than she had ever managed. "Good work, Wesley!"

She tore out of the parking lot and down the few blocks to the hotel. As she turned into the drive, she surveyed the two-story hotel with its turquoise doors and second-floor balcony. The spray from the large stone fountain caught in the wind and strafed her car as she drove past.

Sarah stopped to wipe the drops from her face, in time to spot a male figure stomping toward a door at the end of the balcony. She grabbed her phone and took a photo, hoping an enlarged image might provide more details than the naked eye. Then she scanned the parking lot, in search of an irate female, but didn't see anything but parked cars. She snapped a few shots of the parking lot, for examining later.

A sedan honked behind her. Sarah put her car in gear and rolled out of the way. As the sedan motored past, the passenger flipped her the bird. Sarah waved and smiled.

The interaction was typical for the kind of week she was having. Might as accept it. Big old Jupiter must be in retrograde, not just hot little Mercury. If that was at all possible. She'd have to ask Kelley.

Sarah parked and looked at the photos she had taken. None of the images showed enough detail to identify the man. Damn. She'd have to knock on his door and confront the guy. And make up an excuse for doing so.

She extricated herself from the car, hurried up the stairs to the second floor of the hotel and—fighting for breath—knocked on the door at the end.

Chapter 19 | Denials

The man Sarah had followed yanked open the hotel door. She could tell from the expression on his florid face that he assumed she would be someone else—someone who had upset him. At the sight of Sarah, his anger cooled to surprise.

"Sarah?" He stammered, struggling to regain his composure. He looked around and then down at the parking lot.

"Chris?" She exclaimed, also surprised. What was he doing here? Had he been involved in the argument that Wesley had witnessed? If so, whom had he been talking to? And if Wesley had identified Chris correctly, that meant Chris had been at Joe Salgado's apartment. Was he linked to SS Wines? Possible connections to Woody's death fanned out before her, scrambling her thoughts. Were the two homicides related, as Sheriff Bradley suspected? How did Chris Girard fit in the puzzle?

Chris wasn't capable of planning a murder. Even if he did try to kill someone, he would most likely bungle it. Zach Sullivan, on the other hand, with his vineyard-honed broad shoulders, muscular torso and vast determination, could easily end a person's life with his bare hands if he chose to. The image scalded her.

No. Just no. She took a deep breath and shut out the thought.

"What are you doing here?" Chris pulled out a Pall Mall and a Sullivan lighter with a blue stone this time. The habit of lighting a cigarette seemed to quiet his initial shock, enough to allow his smirk to creep forward.

"I saw you go into this room," Sarah explained. "I mean, I saw a man go in. I didn't realize it was you. I came up to let you know that you left your lights on."

She pointed at her Triumph.

"That's not my car."

"Oh, I thought someone told me you had a sportscar." She watched his face for a reaction.

"Nope," he answered, without so much as a blink. He took a deep draw on his cigarette and held it in. "I drive a BMW sedan."

"Oh well, looks like somebody's going to be sorry when their car fails to start."

"Why don't you inform the manager?" He blew smoke in an arc that ended in front of her face. "And quit bothering the guests?"

"Right." Sarah peered around his spare body, hoping to catch a glimpse of the woman he'd been arguing with, but saw nothing but a queen bed and a desk. His female companion might be Anya Sarnova, the second possible link between the two deaths. But that would be jumping to conclusions—which was Sheriff Bradley's specialty, not hers.

Girard shifted his body to block her line of sight. She got the hint and turned her attention back to him.

"You aren't staying at the winery, Chris?"

"Don't want to drink and drive tomorrow. And I don't want to be out in Glen Ellen either." His dark eyes settled on her face. "Dead people give me the creeps."

"The body is no longer there."

"Still." He poked the cigarette into his slit of a mouth. "Any other questions, McKee?"

"As a matter of fact, yes. Did you notice anything out of the ordinary the night Bill Friske was killed?"

"Wasn't there."

"Oh? Where were you?"

"With a lady friend." He planted the edge of one hand on the doorjamb near his head and slouched in the doorway, as if to block further inspection of his room. "As if that's any of your business."

"Do you know a person named Joe Salgado?"

"Who?"

"Salgado. Young guy. Red hair."

"Doesn't sound familiar."

She studied his face, hoping to discern a hint of evasiveness, but saw nothing unusual in his expression. Chris was telling the truth or was a master at keeping his face a blank mask.

"Why the twenty questions?" He tapped ashes off the end of his cigarette.

"Just asking. I'm concerned about Maeve. She was so torn up about Bill."

"Yeah, right." Chris snorted. Then he broke off and regarded her with narrowed eyes. "I didn't know you and her were close."

"We're not. Passing acquaintances. I was there the morning Bill's body was discovered."

"Oh, were you?" He shifted again, straightening to attention.

"And I heard Maeve and Bill were having marital problems. Do you think that's true?"

"Wouldn't know." He blew smoke through both nostrils. "And what's this have to do with the Joe guy?"

"Probably nothing."

"Do you think Hunny and this Joe guy were involved?"

"They might have been."

"Come to think of it," Chris said, "she does like the younger types. I saw her with a guy at the pool once. Doing the nasty."

"Maeve Friske."

"Yeah. And the pool boy kind of looked like the bartender at the Wolf House."

"Zach? You've seen Zach at the winery?"

"He comes to visit the old lady that works there. Don't know why. And only when the Friskes are gone. Usually. There was that one time, though..."

"Zach would never fool around with Maeve Friske."

"I could be wrong," Chris said. "But not about good ol' Hunny. I could see her wanting to bump off the old man. Take his money. Run off to Italy with one of her boy toys. I could see it." He flicked his cigarette butt over the balcony.

Sarah wondered how many wildfires he would start during his stay in Sonoma County. If she had anything to do with it, Chris would be kicked back to San Francisco as soon as possible.

"Are you staying on, then, Chris? With Bill being dead?"

"At Paradise Valley?" He grimaced. "No. Bitch isn't keeping me."

"Sorry to hear it." Not.

"Don't worry about me, Sarah. I'm going to be all right. I always land on my feet." He winked and made claws with his fingers. "Just like a cat."

Right. An alley cat. With worms.

He reached for the doorknob. "Catch you at the auction, McKee."

"Really? Are you still going? What with Bill being dead?"

"Gotta hustle business while it's here. Rub shoulders."

"I'll see you there, then." Sarah turned to leave.

"If you want a real deal, McKee," Chris called after her, "Now's the time. Hunny'll be liquidating Bill's cellar. Call me if you want the latest inventory. I'm the only one who knows what he really had. I can work your clients a deal."

She waved him off. The only way she would ever call Chris Girard would be a butt dial.

Sarah hurried toward the stairs, knowing she had a big problem if Chris remained at his window to watch her leave. She couldn't retrieve her car. He'd see it was the one with the lights on, and that she was playing a game. He would suspect that she knew something about his part in Salgado's murder.

She trotted down the steps and across the parking lot as Wesley Leslie III pushed his bicycle through the hotel's port cochere, out of view from Chris Girard's room.

He waved when he saw her.

"Did you see them?" he asked.

"One of them. And I recognized the guy. Good going, Wesley."

He nodded. "You'll tell the police who it was?"

"I will."

"They were the ones who hurt Woody, I'll bet."

"Or at least robbed him."

"Yeah." Wesley clenched the handles of his bike and looked away. The streamers trembled. "I miss Woody. I really miss him."

"It's tough, I know." She gave him an understanding smile and decided it would be best to change the subject before he broke into tears. "I watched your show, by the way. It was funny. Hilarious even."

His curly head pivoted in her direction. "For real?"

"*Aye.*"

"But without Woody, it's over." He sighed and looked down. "I'll have to get a stupid, boring job. My mom's coming next week, and she's going to make me."

"That's too bad. Do you have enough money to last until then?"

"Yeah." He sighed again. "I guess."

"When your mom comes, will you have her call me?"

"Sure, but I don't have your phone number."

Sarah retrieved a business card from her purse and held it out. "Here, that's my number there." She pointed at the last line.

"Okay." He inspected the card. "Wait a sec. It says here that you're a wine consultant." He gazed up at her. "I thought you were a sheriff."

"No, I'm a wine expert."

"That's a cool job." He smiled at her but then curled his lip. "Except that wine tastes like poop."

"Some people would disagree with you there."

Sarah surveyed Wesley's diaphanous green wrap, lavender and yellow plaid shorts and red cowboy boots and wondered if she could take a chance on him. At this point, she really didn't have a choice.

"Tell me, Wesley, do you know how to drive?"

His brows drew together, which seemed to release his jaw. His mouth went slack. "Sure. I learned in high school."

"A stick?"

"Duh."

"Want to earn a quick twenty bucks?" She held out her car key.

Chapter 20 | Confessions

When Sarah arrived at her Glen Ellen house late that afternoon, she spotted an unfamiliar car parked next to Matteo's Land Rover.

Not again. Not another tryst. Bad back, her arse.

She tramped up the sidewalk, her anger rising with each stride, and threw open the door. She expected to find Matteo in the shower again, getting his rocks off with Surfer Dude, or maybe defiling her brand-new bed linens. She was surprised to find him sprawled on the couch, clutching a manilla envelope to his chest. A woman stood over him, hands on her hips.

Woman? Perplexed, Sarah paused in the doorway as the female pivoted to glimpse who had come in the door.

"Sarah," the woman exclaimed. "Thank goodness. Maybe you can talk some sense into him."

All became clear the instant Sarah recognized Av Burnham, the pixie-haired, petite sous chef at Olive Restaurant. The fragrance of bacon and sauteed onions wafted off her white chef jacket.

"We're catering the auction gala tomorrow," Av said. "And we have a full house tonight. Matteo needs to get off his duff and come to work." She stabbed the air in the direction of Matteo's reclining figure. He had one arm flung over his face. A moan emanated from under the elbow.

Sarah slung her purse on the hooks behind the door and marched forward.

"Matteo, come on. You have to get up."

"I can't, *amoré*. My back..."

"Take some pills. Your restaurant needs you."

"No, *cara*. I have lost all reason to live." He flung the manilla envelope into the air. The packet landed near Sarah's boot. She picked it up and noticed the name of her attorney in the return address. Her friend's lawyer had made quick work of filing the initial divorce papers. She wondered if someone had been hired to drop the packet off at the door to make sure Matteo received them. Her lawyer had told her that sometimes a sheriff would serve such papers. *Gawd*. Had Sheriff Bradley chatted with her soon-to-be-ex-husband?

Matteo was now swooning on the couch like the leading lady in a melodrama.

"You couldn't wait," he wailed. "You couldn't give me a single chance."

"It's not like we're getting divorced tomorrow. There's a built-in cooling off period. Months."

"But what about the black pickup guy?"

"He's none of your concern. Where's your pride, Matteo? It's not like you to lie there and let your restaurant go to hell."

"I have lost my dream. My world."

"Oh, have *ye* now?"

"My entire reason for living. You."

"Don't be daft. Your dream is a Michelin star." She grabbed his free hand. "Now grow some balls and get up." She tried to yank him to a sitting position.

"Ow!" he shrieked.

Sarah released him and straightened, frustrated, but concerned that she might have hurt him.

"Think it's for real?" Av asked, shaking her bottle-blonde head while she surveyed her moaning boss. "If it is, we're screwed."

"He's always been a wee dramatic."

"Tell me about it." Av sighed. "But this time, I don't know what to do."

"Hmm." Sarah's gaze fell on Matteo's leather jacket hanging near the door. She walked across the floor, shoved a hand in the right pocket of his coat and pulled out a bottle of his pain killers. He didn't take them often. Only when his sciatica flared up. He needed them now, though. She walked back to Matteo, shaking two pills onto her palm, and looked down at him.

For the second time, she was struck by the sight of Matteo as a totally different person. How could she have fallen in love with such a cute little man-boy? That's what he was. Still a boy. And still so very cute.

Her initial anger at his infidelity had subsided over the past few days because she knew his cheating on her was only a symptom of their crumbling marriage, not the reason for it. Matteo wasn't completely to blame for their faded relationship. When she'd married him, she'd been a child herself, incapable of selecting a partner who would suit her for life. She had just turned twenty years old when they met. A baby.

She smiled to herself at the vision of the two of them back in the day. She had thought she was so mature, moving to America on her own, finishing her degree at Berkeley, getting an evening job at the café where she had been introduced to the young chef, Matteo DiSanti, fresh from Milan. They explored San Francisco together. They explored their bodies. A few months later, they moved in together. They had been little more than children. And they had grown so much since then.

Apart, mostly.

If she let him, Matteo could still charm her into doing anything he wanted. She had to remain strong and focused. The divorce had been a long time coming, but now that she had taken the first step, she knew it was the right path to be on. That didn't mean Matteo had to become an enemy.

Sarah held the pills out to her soon-to-be ex-husband. "These will help," she said. Memories of the past softened her tone. "Your restaurant needs you, Matteo. Your staff is depending on you. The town, too."

"I can't, *amoré*. I can't."

"What would your mother think, looking down from heaven right now?"

Matteo's eyelids fluttered open. "Eh?"

"I can hear her." Sarah looked skyward, channeling the sound of his mother's constant stream of Italian. "Matteo, you are such a good boy. So handsome. So talented. You make your mamma so proud." She gestured with one hand, tugging at the air with her fingers, like his mother used to do.

Matteo stared at her as if he had seen a ghost.

"What would she think if she saw you like this?" Sarah held out the pills again. "Make your mamma proud, Matteo. Do what you do best. Cook."

"Yeah," Av added, shoving a glass at him. "Here's some water to wash those down."

****

A few minutes later, as Sarah stood on the front step watching Av and Matteo's vehicles climb up to the main road, she spotted Sheriff Bradley's SUV speeding down it. Sarah took a deep, fortifying breath and remained where she was. She wasn't about to let Bradley take a single step inside her home.

He jumped out and reached for the car door to close it.

"Have a warrant?" she barked.

"Pardon?" His hand remained on the window frame.

"I'm not talking to you, sheriff. Or letting you into my home."

"Because of Zach Sullivan?"

"Damn right."

"It's my job, Sarah."

"Did you question him?"

"I did. And he didn't have an alibi for Sunday night. He claimed he was sleeping. At home. Alone."

"What about his wife? She'd vouch for him."

"He didn't mention a wife. All he would say was that he was sleeping."

"So, you took him in?"

"You bet. And locked him up. A few hours in a bare room, and he'll be more reasonable."

"It's the Flight of Fancy Auction tomorrow," Sarah said, incredulous. "You can't keep Zach Sullivan in jail! He has a ton of work to do for the auction."

"I guess he'll have to miss it."

"Did he get to call a lawyer?"

"Not yet. I'm letting him worry. It's an effective way to encourage cooperation."

"You prick." She turned for the door and grabbed the knob. She heard him stride up behind her.

"There are two homicides still unsolved, Sarah. I can't turn a blind eye this time."

"You don't know how blind you are."

She stormed into the house and was about to shut the door in his face, but Bradley's hand shot out and flattened against the door panel, preventing it from moving another inch.

"Step back," she growled between her teeth, incensed.

"Sure, but just so you know, Mrs. Friske is coming in."

Sarah paused, shocked. "What?"

"Claims she's being blackmailed. Wants to make a statement." He let his arm fall to his side. "I thought you might like to hear what she says, since you're so involved in the two cases."

"You'd let me listen in? Isn't that bending your precious rules?"

"It's not an official interrogation. It's just a statement. You'd have to stand behind a one-way glass, so she can't see you."

"Okay..." She kept a firm grip on the door handle. "When? Where?"

"At the substation on Grove Street in Sonoma. She'll be there in a half hour. I'm on my way now." He walked down the stairs and turned to gaze back at her. "So, for the record, I'm not a complete asshole."

"Jury's out," Sarah called after him. She couldn't help but watch the rise and fall of his muscular buttocks as he strode away. She closed the door as a familiar tingling fanned out in her chest.

Her breasts had already forgiven him. They ached and tightened, longing for his touch. Traitors. *Hormones*. Maybe she *was* pregnant. There was only one way to find out.

Sarah grabbed the pregnancy test and headed for the bathroom.

****

A half hour later, Maeve Friske swept into the interrogation room, chin held high, and breasts thrust forward. She wore fawn-colored slacks and a print blouse, with multiple gold chains glinting at her chest, probably genuine. Sarah wasn't sure about the boobs.

Sheriff Bradley and Kelley filed in and sat across from her. Kelley hit the recorder and stated the date and time and the names of those present.

"I don't have much time," Maeve said, folding her hands on the table. "What with the auction. But I don't want anything to happen tomorrow, either. To spoil the festivities. It's such an important charity event."

"What do you think might happen?" Bradley asked, his expression bland.

"I think the blackmailer will try to humiliate me in public, and I won't stand for it. I want you to arrest him."

"Okay, back up." Bradley held up a hand. "Who is blackmailing you? And why?"

"Chris Girard." She grimaced, which accentuated the fine wrinkles around her lips. "The creep my husband hired a couple of years ago."

"Why would he be blackmailing you?"

Maeve clenched her hands together. Her multiple rings glinted in the light of the bare room. "Because I told him to clear out."

"You have every right to fire him day of," Kelley put in. "It's legal in California."

"I know that," Maeve retorted, shooting an angry glare at her.

Kelley sat back in her chair, chastised but undaunted.

"But there must be something he knows about you," Bradley ventured. "Something he's holding over you."

Maeve looked at her hands and clenched them again. Then she peered to the side and took a deep breath.

"Okay. All right. I'll tell you. Because this is getting out of hand." She considered the far wall as she spoke. "A year ago, I asked Chris Girard to make some inquiries for me. For a little trick. Just a party trick."

"What kind of inquiries?"

"For someone who could make fake wine."

"A counterfeiter?" Kelley leaned forward.

"Yes, a counterfeiter. Not for commercial use, of course. For personal reasons. Personal reasons only."

"What kind of personal reasons could there be for fake wine?" the sheriff asked.

Sarah would have questioned Maeve about the counterfeiter instead, but she wasn't leading the investigation. She was only observing. She shifted her weight and shoved her hands in the pockets of her trousers.

Maeve pursed her lips, considering the question. Then she skewered Bradley with her cool blue eyes. "For one, my husband was an asshole."

At the familiar remark, Bradley glanced in Sarah's direction. She flipped him the finger, even though she knew he couldn't see her.

"My husband knew everything about everything, and he never let me forget it. Whenever I tried to impress him with something I had learned about a specific wine we were drinking, he would mock me. He told me I had the palate of a teenager. With mono. That's the kind of treatment I had to put up with. Day in and day out. In front of guests. Untenable."

Sarah nodded to herself, knowing how it felt. She'd been treated the same way as Bill's employee.

"Sounds rough," Kelley put in.

"It was, but I made him pay. Believe me."

"How did you make him pay?" Bradley asked.

"Treated myself to the best of everything." She sat back and crossed one slender leg over the other. "Jewelry, travel, clothes." She swept the air in front of her designer shirt. "If he wouldn't treat me like a queen, I made damn sure I did. I spent his money. Each time he made me look like a fool, I spent as much as I could the next day. He didn't say a word.

He liked the way I looked. He liked that I had expensive taste. I was part of his public persona. His collection."

"But what has all of that to do with counterfeit wine?" Bradley said.

"So, I planned a birthday party for him last year. His birthday is—was—on April Fool's Day. And I decided to play the best trick ever—to get back at him for all the humiliations I had endured. Everyone was there. All his hotshot friends." She tapped one high heeled toe in the air as she thought back. "I served the wine he'd been trying to buy for years. I told him that I'd finally procured a bottle for his sixty-fifth birthday. And that he deserved it."

"A Domaine St. Emile Pinot Noir," Sarah murmured.

"A Domaine St. Emile Pinot Noir," Maeve said. "A '73. He couldn't believe I had found a bottle. He savored that wine. He poured small samples for each of his friends. They did backflips trying to outdo each other with their descriptions of it. The nose, the high notes, the fingers, the finish. Sickening. My god, what a show." She shook her head and smiled. "I could barely keep from laughing."

"Because it was fake," Kelley put in.

"Oh, it was. And when I peeled off the fake label and showed Bill and his cronies that they'd been drinking a cheap red blend made in somebody's kitchen, you should have seen his face." Maeve put her manicured fingers to her cheekbones and smiled even wider. "It was the perfect April Fool's joke. My finest hour."

"I'm surprised he didn't divorce you on the spot," Sarah mumbled.

"But it was war after that," Maeve played with the bangles at her wrist. "We stopped doing anything together. I think he started seeing someone."

"And he sold the DSE," Sarah mused.

"Soon after, he sold the pinot noir to that collector in China. He never wanted to look at that pinot again."

"So, the entire case was comprised of fakes?"

"I don't know. I had only one bottle made. As a trick. Plus, it was a different vintage than the ones in his collection."

"So how did fakes end up in China?"

"I don't know! Maybe he had bought fakes and didn't know it." She jumped to her feet. "But Chris Girard told me if I didn't pay him 500,000 dollars, he would reveal me as the leader of a counterfeit ring. At the gala tomorrow. In front of everybody. When I am no such thing!" She paced the floor behind her chair.

"Okay, okay." Bradley held up both palms. "Settle down, Mrs. Friske. And please sit down."

She huffed a huge sigh and perched on the edge of the chair. "I want you to arrest Girard." She stabbed the table with her index finger, accentuating every word. "Today. For attempted blackmail."

"Do you have any proof?" Bradley asked.

"What do you mean?"

"Of the blackmail. Something in writing?"

Maeve jumped to her feet again. "No, I don't have any proof. Do you think he would write me a letter on personalized stationery? Don't be ridiculous."

"We can't arrest a person without proof."

"Oh, really?" Sarah planted her hands on her hips, almost as upset at Bradley's comment as Maeve Friske was. Why, then, was Zach languishing in a cell down the hall?

"You don't seem to understand, sheriff," Maeve countered. "I can't be humiliated at the gala. I'm the chairperson. My credibility will be destroyed. Do you have any idea how many donations we'll lose if that happens?" Maeve glowered down at Bradley. "Sick children are depending on me. Something must be done."

"Unless Mr. Girard extorts money from you, or someone heard him threaten you, I'm afraid my hands are tied."

"Ask about approaching Joe Salgado," Sarah texted Kelley. "See how she behaves."

Kelley read the message on her phone. Then she leaned forward.

"What if we talk to the counterfeiter?" Kelley said to Bradley. "If he corroborates Mrs. Friske's story, we will know Mr. Girard is lying."

Maeve shot Kelley a dark glance, full of worry or anger, Sarah couldn't tell which from her position behind the glass. "I don't think you can," Maeve said. "That is, I don't think it's possible."

"Why not?" Bradley demanded.

Maeve shrugged a bony shoulder. "Because I don't know the man's name. He's a *counterfeiter*. He doesn't exactly come to my parties."

"So, you never met the man?" Kelley said. "In fact, how do you know the counterfeiter is a man?"

"Well, I simply assumed..." Maeve's coiffed head swiveled from Kelley to Bradley.

"How did you pay the guy?" Bradley asked.

"Chris Girard took care of that. In return, I paid Girard."

"It appears we will have to question Mr. Girard for details, then. About the counterfeiter."

"Yes, but don't be surprised if he denies everything. He would throw his own mother under the bus if he had to."

Bradley nodded. He contemplated the surface of the table, as if thinking something through. Then he looked up.

"One more thing, Mrs. Friske. Do you often take cuttings of a plant called oleander?"

Sarah was surprised at the subject change. Maybe Bradley hadn't discounted her suspicions after all. Maybe he had actually listened to her. Maybe she'd have to rethink her opinion of the guy.

Maeve paused for a second, as if considering who could have seen her in the park, but she instantly composed herself. Sarah sidled closer to the glass, intent on gauging the woman's expressions and body language.

Maeve sat back in her chair, ramrod straight. "Pardon?"

"You were seen cutting oleander in Depot Park on Sunday."

"By whom?"

"That's not important right now," Bradley retorted. "What I want to know is *why* you were picking oleander."

"What has that got to do with blackmail?"

"Please, Mrs. Friske, answer the question."

"Well, if you must know, I like oleander."

"Even though it's poisonous."

"'Yes, but I take precautions."

"What did you do with the oleander you picked?"

"I..." Maeve fiddled with her right earring. "...I made a floral arrangement."

"For your home?"

"Yes."

"Why did we find the oleander in the trash then?"

Maeve's head tipped back as she paused to consider her answer. She took a breath, as if filling her body with ammunition. Then she turned to skewer Bradley with her eyes again. "Inferring what, exactly?"

"I'm not inferring anything. I'm asking what you did with the oleander."

"I see no connection whatsoever with Chris Girard and his blackmailing of me and a floral arrangement."

"There might not be a connection. I just want to hear about the oleander. Humor me."

"If you must know—the flowers were full of bugs."

"So, you chopped the plant up?"

"Yes."

"Into tiny pieces?"

"Yes."

"Why?" Kelley asked.

"I was angry." Maeve shrugged one shoulder again. "Sometimes I get angry. I'm human."

"And you took it out on the oleander," Kelley added.

"There's no law against chopping up plants." She stood and grabbed her handbag off the back of the chair. "It's obvious that I've wasted valuable time coming here."

Bradley rose. "We are doing our jobs, ma'am, to the letter of the law. And to the best of our ability."

"Well, your best isn't good enough, is it?" She marched to the door, her heels clicking on the terrazzo floor. She turned. "You'll be hearing from the commissioner about this. He's a close friend of mine."

"We'll speak to Mr. Girard. That's the most we can do."

Maeve curled her lip at him and huffed down the hall.

Sarah watched her disappear and then reached for her phone to turn the ringer back on. A notification from her doctor had come in during the Maeve Friske interview. She played the voicemail while she walked down the hall to the conference room of the substation. Doctor Dena's voice came on the line, urging Sarah to make an appointment as soon as possible to get her test results.

"*Aye*, in my spare time," Sarah muttered under her breath. She hadn't had any personal downtime since getting back from Germany. She stuffed the phone in her pocket and tried not to think the worst about the state of her health: an ulcer, stomach cancer, or IBS. She didn't know for certain what IBS was—only that women her age seemed to be plagued with it, and it had something to do with the digestive tract.

She wasn't pregnant. The test had shown a BFN. Big Fat Negative. Unless the test was faulty. She should have purchased two of them. Or maybe three. Best two out of three was always more accurate.

No sense worrying over the unknown. Sarah turned her thoughts toward the homicides instead. She strode into the conference room, anxious to discuss Maeve's visit with Kelley and the sheriff. Plus, if they chose to interrogate Chris

Girard, they would need her help. Of the three, she was the only one who knew where to find the man.

Chapter 21 | The Interview

Bradley lowered his lean frame into the chair at the head of the long conference room table while Kelley plopped into a chair at his right. Sarah stood near the whiteboard on the wall, hands propped on the back of a chair.

"So, what did you think?" she asked. "Did you believe her?"

"I did," Kelley said.

"No reason not to," Bradley added.

"Did you notice how she touched her earring when you asked about the oleander?"

"I didn't," Bradley leaned back. "No."

"I think she's lying about it."

"You think she used the oleander to poison her husband?"

"Or at least make him sick."

"That isn't a crime, Sarah." Bradley ran a muscular hand over his shining head.

"Plus, he was taking oleander anyway," Kelley put in.

"Right." Bradley tipped back in his chair. "All we know at this point is that Chris Girard hired the counterfeiter."

"No, we don't," Sarah paced the floor in front of the whiteboard. "All we have is Maeve's *claim* that he hired the counterfeiter."

Bradley chewed his lip and stared at the wall, upset at her contradiction but considering it all the same.

"Maeve also claimed that Chris Girard might throw her under the bus. Well, if you ask me, she did that to him just now."

"As far as I'm concerned," Bradley shot back. "This deal with Friske and Girard is a dead end that I'm not going to waste any time on. Not when I have the real murderer in a cell right here."

"No, you don't," Sarah snapped.

"Zach Sullivan lost his family estate to the Friskes." Bradley counted off the motives on the fingers of his left hand. "They are letting the place go. They fired longstanding employees. They represent everything his family is not. And someone—probably the Friskes—are selling his prized wine under his nose at the auction. Plus, don't forget the weapon."

"Are his prints on the gun?"

"All over it."

Sarah sank into the nearest chair. "Jesus."

"So, unless anyone has any other bright ideas, I'm calling it a day."

"But letting Zach call a lawyer first."

"Have to. It's the law."

"Can I at least talk to him?"

"No."

Sarah slumped in her chair, unwilling to let a single lead slip through her hands while Zach remained in jail.

"What about Girard?" she asked. "We should question him."

"Why? Think he's going to admit to blackmailing Maeve Friske? That's not going to happen."

"We could play them against each other."

Kelley nodded. "Yeah, Maeve throws Girard under the bus, and he throws her. We might learn something."

"He already did throw her under the bus," Sarah said.

Bradley tipped forward in his chair. "What do you mean?"

"I talked to him this afternoon."

"Why?"

"To find out who he was with."

"Why?"

"Because he and a woman were spotted at Joe Salgado's apartment, taking stuff. Remember?"

"Not Girard specifically."

"Well, he was identified by a witness this afternoon as someone who had visited Salgado."

"What witness?"

"Wesley Leslie."

"The guy with the puppets?" Kelley sputtered, trying not to laugh.

"He saw Girard and a woman arguing in a hotel parking lot."

"And told you?" Bradley cocked his head. "Why?"

"He thought I was a detective. He saw me at the market."

"Why didn't you call me?"

"I didn't have time." Sarah grabbed the arms of her chair to prevent herself from lunging at the sheriff. "I raced to the hotel as soon as I could, but only saw Girard."

"Tell me you didn't speak to him," Bradley began, his jaw clenched.

"There's no law against talking to someone."

"So how did he throw Maeve Friske under the bus?" Kelley inquired, clearly not as worried about interference of an investigation as her boss.

"He claimed she liked young men and that she might have had a relationship with the counterfeiter. That she was the type to get rid of her husband and run off with someone."

"Far-fetched," Bradley countered. "Pure conjecture."

"He claimed he didn't know Joe Salgado."

"He would." Bradley sat back in his chair, his expression dark.

"But Wesley said that he saw Chris at Salgado's apartment, and that he was mean."

"And you believe that nutcase?"

"I do." Sarah straightened. "Yes, I do." She leveled her stare on Bradley. "And I think we should inform Girard that we know he was involved with the counterfeiter. Either directly or indirectly. Put the pressure on him. He's not a critical thinker. He might slip up. He's lost his job."

"So?"

"I know him. If he is involved in the homicides, maybe he'll slip up and tell us. Stress will make him careless."

Bradley studied her face, deep in thought.

"Plus, Steven, what about those lists?"

"The ones found on the bodies?" Kelley asked.

"*Aye*. What do those lists have to do with Zach Sullivan?"

"Plenty," Bradley replied. "They're connected to the counterfeiting."

"Exactly. And why would Zach be involved in counterfeiting?"

"To ruin Bill Friske." Bradley rolled his eyes. "Isn't it obvious?"

Sarah jumped to her feet, frustrated. "Everything comes back to Zach with you, doesn't it?"

"Because he's guilty." Bradley stood as well. "Take off the blinders, Sarah. Who else knew about the Chinese triad guy? You, Arthur Chen and Zach Sullivan."

"Impossible," Sarah fumed, pacing again.

"I've thought about this." Bradley picked up a pen and rolled it between his fingers. "A lot. Apparently, you haven't. This is how it went down. Sullivan hires a counterfeiter, fills Bill Friske's cellar with fakes." He punctuated each statement by tapping the air with the pen. "Maybe sells the real stuff for a massive profit, and then tells Friske to get out of town—maybe even hand over the estate—or else he'll expose him for passing fakes."

Sarah stared at the sheriff, incredulous.

"Then," he tapped the air at her again, "Friske refuses to comply, and Zach kills him. Or Friske kills himself because he knows he's ruined. And for some reason someone ditches the gun afterward."

"Why?"

"Haven't figured that out yet. I have checked the Friske accounts, though. The man has absolutely no liquid assets." Bradley's eyes drilled holes into Sarah. "We also checked Zach Sullivan's accounts. And guess what? He recently made a huge deposit—and I mean huge."

"How would Zach get fakes into Friske's cellar?" Sarah countered. "Girard would never let anyone near it without him."

"That housekeeper woman, that's who. Talk about sketchy."

"But then who sent the Paradise Valley Zinfandel through SS Wines?"

"Salgado, evidently. He left his car out there, too."

"The car in the barn was registered to him?"

"Yep." He tapped the pen on the top of his desk.

"And then he came back to his apartment and got shot. How did he get back?"

"Maybe Sullivan gave him a ride. Then killed him."

"Or Girard."

"Girard didn't have a motive. Zach did. Think of it. Zach must have been incensed to discover Salgado had made counterfeits of the Sullivan family's pride and joy."

"If Salgado and Zach were partners," Sarah retorted. "He wouldn't have dared make fakes of PVZ."

"And Zach and a woman," Bradley continued, talking over her. "Probably that wife you mentioned—cleared out the incriminating evidence from the apartment."

"Or Girard and his girlfriend."

"No motive," Bradley warned again.

"And didn't think to look in the refrigerator. That's more Girard's speed."

"Again, no motive, Sarah."

"Why don't you ask Wesley if he ever saw Zach at Woody's apartment?"

"Wouldn't prove anything. And besides, picture that fruitcake on the stand. Do you think for one minute anyone would believe him?"

Bradley walked to the door. "So, that's where this is going, but I'm out of here for the night. Big day tomorrow." He held open the door and motioned the two women out. "Pick you up at six, Sarah? I was told there's wine-tasting before the auction."

"You were also told that I prefer to go solo."

"Not possible. Certainly not with this Girard and Friske blackmail threat. I need to be there. This case is going to crack wide open. I can feel it."

"But according to you, you've cracked it." She brushed past him, her voice chilled. "You have the blood-thirsty killer in jail."

"But not the rest of SS Wines. Like you said, how could Salgado be the other half of SS Wines and make fake PVZ? So," he pointed the pen at her, "it looks like a date."

****

"I'm not going on a date with Bradley," Sarah vowed at the Wolf House later that night. She bit into the hamburger she'd ordered for dinner. The meat crumbled in her mouth, too dry to hold together. Zach would never make such a terrible sandwich. Sarah swallowed the cardboard beef, regarded the hamburger with disdain and plopped it back on the plate.

Kelley picked at a salad. "Just be honest with the guy. You're only there for the sex."

"That sounds so shallow."

"It's the truth, though, isn't it?"

Sarah pulled her glass of wine toward her but thought better of it. One look at the alcohol and her stomach roiled in protest. The antiacids must have worn off. She set her jaw and searched the contents of her purse for the packet of pills. "Do *you* think I'm shallow, Kelley?"

"No, you're having a midlife crisis a little early. It can happen to anyone."

"I don't want a relationship right now."

"He shouldn't either. He should know better, too—you being on the rebound and all."

"*Aye*, but it's like when we're around each other—alone—our clothes fall off."

"More reason to tell it like it is."

Sarah chewed two chalky tablets and surveyed Kelley's garden salad, dressing on the side. "Are you on a diet?"

"Yeah, I want to lose a few pounds. Come June, I don't want to be the fat cat on the stage, know what I mean?"

Sarah smiled and nodded and then surveyed the length of the bar. She sighed. "It's not the same here tonight. It's way too quiet."

"Because Zach isn't here," Kelley mumbled around a forkful of lettuce.

"*Aye*. That's it."

"He kind of makes the place."

Sarah picked up the hamburger for another try but put it back down. "We can't let him sit in jail, Kelley, not without doing something. We're his friends."

"He probably won't be there much longer. I expect he'll get out on bail."

"Really?"

"Bradley's the only one in town who thinks he's guilty."

"That's a relief. Still," Sarah ran her gaze over the ornate framed mirror behind the bar. "There must be something we can do. All I can think about is Zach, trapped in a cell, innocent. He must be so frustrated. He's been given the short stick all his life. And now this."

"Yeah." Kelley chewed thoughtfully.

Sarah thought back to the chaos of the last few days and how Kelley usually attributed events of the day to planetary configurations. There had to be *some* reason for the mayhem.

"Is there such a thing as Jupiter in retrograde?"

"Not that I know of," Kelley replied, one cheek full of greens. "Just Mercury. Why?"

"It seems like everything that could go wrong...is. Big things, I mean. Like Jupiter."

"I know." Kelley kept chewing. "And things come in threes."

"You mean like three murders?"

"Yeah. It's weird. It happens."

"What about that list." Sarah held out her hand. "Can I see that photo you took again?"

"Sure." Kelley slipped her phone out of her purse.

"Bradley's got one thing right. The key to the homicides is that list. Why did both dead men have the same list on them?"

"Did they?" Kelley flipped through photos on her phone until she found the puzzling image of numbers and circles and checkmarks. She slid her phone over to Sarah. "I'm not sure they were *exactly* the same."

"Didn't anyone compare them?"

"We looked at them," she shrugged. "At first glance, they seemed to be the same. But you're the detail expert."

"Can you send me that image?" Sarah pointed at the photo. "And then get me a photo of the list that was found on Bill Friske?"

"Okay." Kelley tapped her phone. "I don't think Bradley would have an objection. Now that he's kind of looped you in on this case."

"Can you get it tonight?"

****

Late that night, Sarah sat at her desk with a cup of tea, a packet of antacid tablets and a printout of each list found on the dead men. As far as she could tell, the lists were identical.

"Think, McKee," she said to herself. "Focus."

She chewed two more tablets and studied the papers. Without taking her gaze off the lists, she brought the teacup to her lips to wash down the chalky bits.

She let her mind ease. She relaxed the muscles in her face and took a deep, steadying breath, much like she did during a wine inspection. Her mind was the most powerful tool she possessed, and she knew she needed to step out of the way and let it do its thing.

She stared down at the list on the right, allowing her gaze to slip out of focus. White paper. Black numbers. Black circles. Black checkmarks.

Now the list on the left. White paper. Black numbers. Black circles. Black checkmarks. Everything the same. Same numbers, same pattern.

But something was different. She concentrated on the right list again. Same groups of numbers. Left list, same. Her brain told her something was different. What? She sat back, perplexed by the niggling sensation that all was not what it seemed.

Then she lurched forward, as the details of the list suddenly coalesced into a glaring, obvious and tangible clue.

The writing on the left list was hurried and tilted slightly downward at the ends of each line. The figures on the right list were deliberate and the lines straight. Sarah nodded to herself, knowing she had found the detail her brain knew was there.

When a person made a copy of something by hand, the copy was always neater. The pen was always pressed harder into the paper, as the writer was confident of what to put down. Someone had made a handwritten copy of the first list. Why? Why not scan it or take a picture of it with a phone?

Because they didn't want a digital trail that might come back to implicate them in a crime—a crime they intended to commit or were already involved in.

Salgado had the original list in his pocket. Bill Friske had been found with the copy. What did it *mean*?

Look harder, a voice inside her urged. There's more.

Sarah put herself in the Zen state again. This was her specialty. Details. Connections. Something not quite right. She had to let her brain slip and slide over the nuances in front of her. She had to hang loose and consider every spark that fired on the periphery of thought.

Then it hit her. The groups of numbers, some of them circled, represented cases of wine. Four across, three down.

This list was a map of a wine cellar or collection.

But whose? And had Salgado penned the original list? Had he given the list to Bill Friske?

Sarah sat back in her chair. She could think of one place to look for such a collection, but she would have to wait until tomorrow when the coast was clear.

That and find a way to break in.

Chapter 22 | The Cellar

"Are you sure she is gone?" Maria asked the next afternoon as she fumbled with the keys to a side door of the Paradise Valley mansion, now owned by the Friskes.

"*Aye*. Her blond hair is unmistakable. She drove right past me." Sarah watched the housekeeper's hands shake as she unlocked the door. "*Dinnae fret*, Maria. Mrs. Friske won't be back until the gala is over."

"I'm only doing this for Zachary."

"I am as well."

Sarah followed the short woman as she hobbled through the mudroom, the utility room, and then through the largest kitchen Sarah had ever seen. The ceiling had to be twelve feet high, with cabinets that reached almost that far up. A hallway connected the kitchen to the gracious rooms at the front of the house. Halfway down the hallway was an ornate portal set deep into elaborate layers of moldings. Wide columns, rosettes, and an architrave that boasted a running horse bordered the paneled door. Maria flipped on the light switch at one side.

"Mr. Friske's private wine cellar is down here." She unlocked the ancient door and pushed it open. Then she motioned Sarah through.

Sarah surveyed the stairs, which were illuminated only by a low yellow light near the top. The stairs took a turn that concealed the room below from view. She'd never been fond of basements, in particular the ones in older homes, where the lowest floor was often unimproved. The combination of earthen floors, stone walls and seeping ground water gave her the willies.

"You aren't coming?" Sarah's voice caught in her throat. She pulled on the latex gloves she had brought with her for the search.

"I am not allowed. Only to clean, and then under supervision."

"They don't trust you enough to clean on your own?"

"No. It is not like the old days here. Then, I was part of the family."

Sarah shook her head, knowing her old days were slipping through her hands as well.

"There is another light switch at the bottom of the stairs," Maria instructed. "Call me when you are finished, and I will come back and lock up."

"All right." Sarah descended the creaking wooden stairs, glad for the handrail. When Maria shut the door behind her, the sound made Sarah's heart skip a beat. She didn't like descending into the gloom under this massive old house, alone. But she had to. For Zach.

Once at the bottom of the stairs, she switched on the lights, and the sight before her made her suck in a breath. She had imagined a musty room lined in stone and wine boxes, with a bare lightbulb hanging from a wire.

Instead, an enormous rustic chandelier and numerous horse-head sconces illuminated a grand chamber covered in gleaming walnut woodwork, with wine cubbies on top, an angled platform to display prized bottles at counter height and shelves below for wine boxes. A library ladder, rolled to one side, reached to the highest section of cubbies. In the center of the room sat a round table with lion-footed legs and a mosaic stone top, surrounded by six upholstered wine barrels that served as chairs.

Sarah drifted forward, awestruck. She had been in some luxurious wine cellars over the years, but this one at Paradise Valley rivaled the very best. She could picture Zach's grandfather and great grandfather here, toasting friends and fellow vintners.

Zach had been raised in this grand home, and now he was forced to live in a modest prefab on the side of a mountain. What must he think of the downward spiral of his life? He didn't seem bitter, but maybe she didn't know the man as well as she thought she did. Come to think of it, he didn't talk about his past.

Sarah slipped the list of numbers from her back pocket and studied it. Then she checked the layout of the room, hoping to spot a corresponding pattern. The cubbies weren't grouped like the numbers on the list, and the crates on the shelves had no apparent arrangement, from what she could tell.

She frowned, perplexed and disappointed. She'd been so sure she had cracked the code of the list.

"Think, McKee," she muttered. "Think."

Undaunted, she turned a three-sixty and examined the entire room for the four-by-four pattern. Nothing stuck out. The only element that held any promise was a set of narrow doors on the right. She padded across the tiled floor, past the library ladder, all the while worrying that the doors might lead to the dreaded earthen part of the cellar. She steeled herself as she opened one of the paneled doors and slipped through.

Sarah ran her hand over the wall until she located an old round light switch with a flat knob. She turned it, and a series of lights along the barrel ceiling blinked on to reveal a large chamber with a flagstone floor and plastered walls. To the left, reaching into the vast darkness, were stacks of wardrobes, dining sets and chests, and other furniture no longer in use. Maeve had probably cleared out all the antiques in the house and stashed them in this space.

Wide plank doors, like the gate of a castle, took up most of the wall on the right. And like a castle, the doors were secured by a massive wooden drop bar. She guessed the doors opened onto an exterior loading bay at the side of the house where wine was delivered or shipped out. In the center of the room sat a pallet of wine crates, stacked in neat rows, waiting to be transported.

Transported out or in? That was the question.

Sarah counted the boxes stacked on top of each other. Four across, four down, four deep. Bill Friske had either purchased or was going to sell 800 bottles of wine. Depending upon the age and worth of the bottles, this cache in front of her might be valued—at the very minimum—at one-hundred-thousand dollars. Knowing Bill's taste in wine, however, the shipment was likely worth ten times that. And knowing the state of the Friske finances, she assumed this shipment was going out the door to be sold.

She scanned the paper she still held in her hand. On the list were four groups of numbered clusters, four across, four down. And each cluster was comprised of twelve numbers, which were sometimes circled. Some of the clusters had checkmarks next to them and no circles around their numbers.

Sarah studied the pallet as a chill raced down her back.

Just as she had guessed, the list in her hand was a record of the wine shipment in front of her. Each level of the stack was represented by one of the groups on the paper. Each box of wine was represented by a cluster. And each bottle was represented by a number, some circled and some left unmarked.

The circled numbers must indicate counterfeit bottles of wine.

All she had to do to prove her theory was identify the fakes in one of the crates.

Sarah walked around the pallet, studying the wooden boxes. The easiest fake to spot would be the Domaine St. Emile pinot noir with the incorrect number of chimneys on the label. She searched the stack, hoping DSE was part of the shipment.

And there it was—on the second level of boxes at one corner.

She reached for the crate of cabernet sauvignon sitting on top of the DSE. The weight of the box and the bottles inside was almost too much for her to lift, but she managed to wrangle the lot to the ground. Then she straightened and approached the box of the very old and very valuable DSE.

Carefully, she opened the box by sliding the front panel out of the wooden track and setting it on top of the pallet. Then she consulted the dead man's wine list, matching circles to the bottles of wine sitting in the first tier. According to her theory, the third and fourth bottles on the top layer should be the same—both real or both fake. She studied the labels, comparing the second and third bottles without touching them. The single chimney labels seemed to be genuine. Minutes ticked by. She concentrated on taking deep steadying breaths as she let her subconscious work without interference.

She saw nothing. Not a single anomaly. Slightly disappointed, she rotated the bottles in their wooden racks and scrutinized the back labels. The second bottle on the list was not circled. Was it real or fake? What was different about it from the third and fourth bottles? She rotated the third bottle and then the fourth.

"Think, McKee," she said. "See it."

A snippet of song from a childhood television program floated through her mind.

One of these things is not like the other...

She let her vision shift to just shy of blurriness. What was different?

Then she saw it. A very subtle signature—so subtle, most people wouldn't notice.

"*Ye cheeky bastard*," she murmured in admiration.

She pulled out the wooden rack to look at the bottles in the second tier. The circled items bore the same signature. The third and final tier aligned with the circles as well.

So, her theory was correct. Each circled item in the dead man's wine list indicated a fake. The boxes with checkmarks indicated a lot free of fakes.

Chuffed with herself, she restored the box of DSE to its original condition and slipped on the lid. Just as she hoisted the box of cabernet sauvignon to replace it on the pallet, she heard the cellar door above creak open.

Sarah sucked in a breath and stared at the wine cellar across the way, momentarily frozen. Had Maria come back? Why? Had Maeve? Then more than one set of footsteps clattered on the stairs. Sarah scanned her surrounds for a hiding place, desperate to remain undiscovered. She was too far from the narrow door to shut it and turn off the lights. All she could do was scurry into the shadows at the back of the chamber and hide behind the furniture.

"Did you leave the lights on yesterday?" a familiar male voice asked.

"No," a female said.

"That slacker of a housekeeper must have."

Footsteps approached the storeroom. Sarah peeked through a crack between two wardrobes and spotted Chris Girard and a blond woman walk through the doorway. They were dressed as if they were attending two separate events. The blonde wore jeans, athletic shoes and a polo shirt, as if prepared for hard work, while Chris Girard wore a gray suit and blue tie, as if expecting to spend the evening in salubrious company: the gala.

Sarah turned her regard back to his partner, curious as to her identity. The woman carried a leather briefcase and wore a ball cap, with her long tresses tied at the nape of her neck. Her champagne-colored hair was styled much like Maeve's and her height and figure were similar.

The blonde placed the briefcase on the pallet and pressed the latches at the corners. The lid popped open. Girard slipped out of his suit jacket and set it on an old chair, dangerously close to where Sarah crouched. If he'd possessed a keen sense of smell, he might have realized a human being was hiding nearby. That was Girard's shortcoming as a wine consultant, though. His nose wasn't sensitive enough. Sarah held her breath anyway, praying that his sixth sense was just as undeveloped.

"I can't believe Hunny Friske is letting me go and is still keeping that old hag on the payroll." Girard walked back to the pallet. Sarah let out her breath, careful not to make a sound.

"She can't afford you."

Sarah detected a slight accent in the woman's voice. Was it Russian? She would bet the blonde was Anya Sarnova.

"*And* she doesn't deserve me." Girard patted a crate. "What do you think that old bitty Maria's been doing down here, anyway? Stealing wine?"

"Of course. You know what they say. When the cat's away," the blonde marched to the wide doors at the end of the room. "The mice will play. Help me with this?"

She placed one gloved hand on the drop bar. Girard ambled to the other end. With a grunt, he lifted the heavy wooden beam, and then the two of them walked it to the side of the room. Blondie swung open the doors to reveal a truck backed up to the bay. They must have turned off the engine and rolled down the slope to the cellar, because Sarah hadn't heard a single sound of the vehicle's approach.

Chris rolled a dolly out of the truck.

"You load while I check the documentation," the woman said. "To make sure you got all the files. We can't sell the wine without the paperwork. Or get it across the border." The blonde lifted file folders out of the briefcase.

"Stealing." Girard shook his head. "Jesus. I've been reduced to stealing."

"Quit complaining. What do you think counterfeiting is?"

"And it's all your fault," Girard grumbled. "The Salgado thing was the dumbest move ever made. I had something good going here."

"Yeah, well, Salgado got greedy. Stupid little man thought he could do it without me."

"Well, because of your stupid little *partner*, we have to hide in Mexico now."

"Not forever."

"It'll seem like forever. I hate the place."

"Then don't go with me." She stared back down at the papers. "It won't break my heart."

"You need me, though. My contacts. My experience. Plus, wine boxes are heavy." Girard slid a box toward his chest. "You couldn't possibly carry one."

"Just get to work, Girard."

He shifted the box against his chest, called out the name of the vintner, and then lowered the wooden box to the dolly. Blondie riffled through the paperwork and set a file to one side. They repeated the process until a mere four boxes remained.

That's when Sarah's phone rang.

For a second, Sarah paused, horrified, as the sound ballooned around her, echoing in the vaulted space. She knew the ring was her death knell. Two people were dead because of this wine shipment. What was one more?

She snatched the phone out of her back pocket and jabbed the button to answer the call as Girard came around the pile of furniture.

"Paradise Valley," Sarah blurted before he wrested the phone from her hand. He clutched her wrist and dragged her into the light.

"Who's that?" Blondie asked, raking her up and down. Her dark eyes and golden skin didn't match her hair color. Unlike Maeve, she was not a natural blond.

"Sarah McKee, the nosiest bitch in the west." Girard threw the phone on the floor and stomped on it with his heel. The screen went dark. "And the stupidest."

Sarah yanked at her arm. "Let go of me, Girard."

"No way."

"You're stealing Bill's wine."

"I'm relocating it," Girard growled. "Besides, The Friskes owe me."

"Did you kill him?"

Blondie tilted her head, cautioning him. "You don't have to answer her, Chris."

He brushed off the warning. "Kill who?"

"Bill."

"*She* did. Hunny. I merely finished him off. She told me to."

"How?"

"With a gun."

"No, I mean, how did *Maeve* kill Bill?"

"Chris," Blondie set her jaw and glared at him. "Stop talking. I mean it."

"People need to know," Girard retorted. "I was just doing my job. I'm not a murderer."

"So how did Maeve kill her husband?" Sarah urged Girard on, hoping her poisonous plant theory would be validated. "With oleander?"

"Not sure how, but he wasn't going easy. You should have seen him. Tongue hanging out. Gasping. Hunny was beside herself. I put him out of his misery. That's all." Girard's eyes clouded. "I thought she'd be grateful. Me, thinking how to cover it up and all for her. I thought we had an understanding. You know? But the bitch is letting me go. With no severance. Claims she can't raise the funds. And after all I've done for her."

"And now you are blackmailing her? Even though she has no money. That makes no sense."

"Bill owned half the world. He couldn't have been broke."

"Apparently, he was." Sarah leveled her gaze on Girard's face. "Tell me, was he alive when you shot him?"

"Who wants to know?"

"Why were you wearing gloves that night?"

Blondie grabbed Girard's arm. "Chris, stop talking. Now."

"Your prints weren't on the gun," Sarah added. "That means you put on gloves and took a gun to your last meeting with Bill Friske," Sarah continued, baiting him. "His death was premeditated. By you."

"No. I just wanted the list back. That's all. Just the list."
He squeezed her wrist, hurting her. "What are you? Some
kind of cop now, McKee?"

"Just a wine detective doing her best for a friend."

Girard leaned close to her face. "Well, you've stuck that
big, fat nose of yours into it way too far this time."

She lifted her chin but kept her stare aimed on his face,
worried that desperation might induce him to make more
poor decisions—like silencing her. "What are you going to
do to me?"

"Lock her up, until we have a good head start," the
blonde suggested. She dragged the rubber band from her
hair and held it out. "Put her in one of those wardrobes, and
I'll loop this around the knobs."

"Good thinking," Girard said.

"And get her car key, just in case."

Girard held out his hand. Sarah sighed, knowing she
had to submit to them, and dropped the fob onto his
outstretched palm.

"They're going to catch you," she said.

"Not if you can't go blabbing to the cops," Girard
snapped. "Now go." He shoved her toward the nearest
wardrobe. She stumbled forward, her mind racing. She had
no way to call anyone. The only person who knew where she
was, was Maria. She prayed the elderly woman would come
looking for her at some point.

"What about her car?" Blondie asked. "It will look
suspicious."

"What car?" Girard shoved Sarah's shoulder.

"It's got to be around here." Blondie's cold regard landed on Sarah. "Where is it?"

Sarah's worry intensified. If Maria saw a blonde get into her little car and drive away, she might assume that Sarah had concluded her search and had left the winery. If that happened, Maria might not bother to come back to the main house until morning—if then.

"I'll ask you one more time." Blondie's voice grated between her prominent teeth. "Where is your car?"

"I took the bus," Sarah retorted.

"Hilarious." The blond woman clutched Sarah's face and squeezed her cheeks against her teeth. Pain flared to Sarah's ears. "Stop wasting my time."

"You better tell her where it is, McKee. She can get kinda mean."

Sarah sighed. "Behind the carriage house."

"That's better," Blondie replied. She nodded at the nearest wardrobe. "Get her in there."

"I'm going to ruin this shirt."

"Do it."

Girard scowled and pushed Sarah forward again. Sarah stumbled toward the tall cabinet. She didn't like confined spaces, but it wouldn't kill her to do their bidding. A hair tie wouldn't hold her for long. She would do what they asked and kick herself free once they left.

Blondie flung open the doors and nodded at the dark interior. Sarah clambered into the wardrobe and pivoted to face them.

"Hope you don't get too thirsty in there, McKee," Girard smirked. He slammed the doors.

"Drag that other one over here," Blondie instructed. She was obviously the brains of the outfit. "And put it in front of the doors so she can't push at them with her feet."

All hope of an easy escape vanished. Sarah would never be able to kick herself free if a second wardrobe was wedged against hers. Sarah heard the scrape of wood on flagstone as Girard shifted a second wardrobe against her doors. Complete darkness enveloped her, as well as the overpowering smell of cedar, old paint and varnish. Nausea mixed with claustrophobia swirled in a sickening cloud, choking her.

She pressed against the back of the wardrobe, refusing to surrender to panic. She had to believe that someone would find her. If she didn't show up at the gala, someone would realize something was amiss. She should have told Kelley what she was up to, but she hadn't wanted to get her friend in trouble should anything go wrong.

Like this.

Fortunately, the wardrobe was tall enough for her to stand upright. She could also sit down if she needed to. She might have to. There was no telling how long she would be stuffed in this box.

"At least let someone know where I am," Sarah called. The words sounded muffled in the closed space. That meant her screams would be hard to hear as well.

"Someone will find you. Eventually."

Girard rolled the last four boxes into the truck. Then, without shutting the bay, he and Blondie secured the truck doors and drove off.

Soon afterward, she heard her little sportscar being driven up the hill. Someone grated the gears to get up the incline, struggling with the clutch, apparently unaccustomed to driving a stick.

"Zach, you'd better appreciate this," Sarah muttered. "They're taking my baby."

Chapter 23 | The Wardrobe

Time dragged in the wardrobe. Sarah might have been trapped for mere minutes or might have been there for hours. Without her phone, she had no idea how much time had passed. When her feet started aching from stomping on the doors, she slid down the side of the wardrobe to sit on the bottom for a while. Hope of rescue descended with her. She slumped back and gave a final desultory push on the doors, though she knew the effort was useless.

Then she heard a faint but familiar male voice.

"What was that?" the man asked.

Sarah came to attention. Zach? She sat up straight. She was sure the voice belonged to Zach. His twenty-four hours must be up, and Bradley had been forced to release him.

"Zach!" she shouted. Her words came back to her as if she had yelled into a pillow.

"Did you hear that?" the man asked.

"No. I heard nothing," a woman answered. Her speech was laced with an accent. Maria?

"Zach!" Sarah screamed at the top of her lungs and scrambled to her feet. She pounded as hard as she could, until her fist ached.

"There it is again." Silence. Then, "It's coming from in here."

"Zach!" She screamed.

"Sarah?"

The screech of furniture on flagstone rent the air as the blocking wardrobe was shoved aside. Determined to be found, Sarah crammed herself in the bottom of her prison and pummeled the doors with both feet.

"Hang on," Zach warned. "Looks like the doors are fastened together."

"It's a hair tie."

"Got it."

She went still as the silhouettes of his hands flashed in the tiny crack between the doors.

The doors opened to reveal a worried Zach bending close to peer inside at her. She'd never been happier to see a human being in her entire life. Or more *gob smacked*.

Zach was dressed in a dark blue suit, white shirt and red tie that set off his black hair and eyes. For a moment, she stared at him, not sure it was really Zach who had come to her rescue. She'd never seen him in formal attire before. He looked incredibly handsome—so much so that she had to force herself to stop gaping at him.

"Thank *gawd* you found me," Sarah exclaimed, struggling to catch her breath.

He reached inside, and she grabbed his hand. He pulled her out but didn't release her. She was glad for the warmth of his fingers and the genuine concern in his eyes.

"You okay?"

"I am now, but I wouldn't have been if you hadn't looked for me."

"When you didn't show up at the tasting, I was worried. And then when Kelley called you, she heard you shout 'Paradise Valley.' And then your phone went dead. So, I came up here."

"Why you, though? Why didn't Kelley or Bradley come to look for me?"

"They're under orders to apprehend a guy named Chris Girard when he shows up at the gala."

"He's probably there by now."

"Who is he?"

"One of the murderers, I'm guessing."

"One?"

"It's a long story. I'll tell you on the way."

"I'm sorry, miss," Maria hobbled to stand beside Zach. "I didn't think to check on you. I thought I saw you leave."

"That wasn't me." Sarah replied. "That was someone stealing my car. Girard's girlfriend. Or accomplice. Not sure which."

"Did Girard put you in there?" Zach pointed at the wardrobe.

"*Aye*. And stole a fortune of Bill Friske's wine. His girlfriend is probably halfway to Mexico with it by now." She picked up her ruined phone, scowled at it and stuffed it in her back pocket. "I need to call Bradley." She held out a hand for Zach's mobile phone.

"Sorry, they still have my phone at the station."

Sarah turned to Maria, who shrugged. "And I do not own one."

"Where's the nearest land line?"

"Upstairs."

"Show me."

Zach led the way. She followed, shaking and perspiring with relief. She hadn't known she was claustrophobic until being locked in the wardrobe.

"What were you doing here, anyway?" Zach said over his shoulder.

"Testing a theory. I think the counterfeiter made a list of the wine Friske was going to sell. And mapped all the fakes." She climbed the stairs behind him. "And my theory is that he gave Friske a copy, hoping to get money for decoding the list or for revenge. Not sure which."

"Why not let the police investigate?"

"Because they weren't interested. Bradley is so sure you killed Friske, I had to do something."

At the top of the stairs, Zach held the door open for her and Maria. She felt his regard on her as she brushed past him.

"I appreciate it, Sarah. You sticking up for me. Endangering your life like this."

"Someone had to. You're not a killer." She paused to look back at him. Gratefulness glinted in his eyes.

Without saying anything more about his innocence or guilt or their fractured relationship, Zach closed the door and turned off the cellar light. "There's the phone." He pointed to a side table below a large oil painting of a racetrack and then stood in the hallway, silent and aloof.

Sarah felt the dizzying distance between them still lingering on the air. She hated the sensation of being off kilter with Zach. She had to do something to restore balance and reestablish their easy friendship.

"Besides," she said, lifting a brow, "I had an ulterior motive in doing all this."

"Oh?"

"If you went to prison, I'd have to buy my own drinks at the Wolf House."

"Couldn't have that," Zach drawled. He slipped a hand in one pocket. A sapphire cufflink glinted at his wrist. "But just so you know, the free wine is going to end."

"How?"

"I'm going to stump you. I've got one that will have you guessing."

"Oh, really?"

He nodded and his familiar lop-sided grin pulled at his generous mouth, warming his expression. Relief poured over her. "Just you wait, McKee."

"Sounds like a challenge, Sullivan."

"Oh, it is."

More *chuffed* at repairing her connection to Zach than solving the dead man's wine list mystery, Sarah grinned and picked up the landline receiver.

"*Bollocks*," she said. Still holding the phone in the air, she turned to glance back at Zach and Maria. Her smile morphed into a grimace. "I can't call. I don't know anyone's number."

****

Instead of calling information and getting the number for Steven Bradley or Kelley, Sarah decided to show up at the Flight of Fancy auction unannounced. Only Maeve Friske would care that her dead husband's wine collection had been stolen. And Sarah didn't care all that much about Maeve Friske. Plus, Bill had probably insured his collection, which would reimburse Maeve Friske for the loss—and that, considering the collection was dotted with fakes, would be in her favor.

Since Sarah no longer had a vehicle, Zach drove her to the house in Glen Ellen so she could change into more formal attire for the gala. He pulled into the drive and stopped.

"Shall I wait?" he asked, resting one capable hand on top of the wheel. The cufflink glinted again. The sapphire looked real.

"No, come on in. You can have a glass while I take a quick shower." She reached for the door handle. "I *have* to have a shower. I smell like an old closet."

He chuckled and got out of his truck. She slipped out and hurried to the front door. It was an odd feeling, letting Zach into her home, but at the same time seemed natural. He and Courtney had never visited the house. They'd always come into the restaurant, or she saw them at the Wolf House. Zach drifted into the front room and looked around.

"Huh," he commented. "I like your taste. Simple. No knickknacks."

"I call it the TBD style."

"TBD?"

"*Aye*. Too busy to decorate."

"Ah." He chuckled again.

Sarah motioned toward the kitchen. "There's a wine fridge in the kitchen in there. Opener in the top drawer of the island. Help yourself to anything you like."

"Have any Romanée-Conti on the go?"

"In your dreams, pal." She grinned at his reference to one of the most expensive wines on the planet—and his inference that she'd ever let a bottle of DRC sit half-consumed after opening. "I'll be really quick."

"Take your time. The auction'll be going for a good hour still."

"Won't Courtney wonder where you are?"

"She's not there."

"She isn't?" Sarah paused and looked at his face.

"Nope."

"Is she working? On a Friday night?"

"Nope."

Sarah cocked one brow, challenging him to tell her more, but Zach turned away and headed for the kitchen. She followed, curious. Zach opened the wine fridge, perused the contents while he continued to ignore her, and pulled out a bottle. He seemed right at home. Or maybe she felt that way because he was on one side of the island and about to serve her a glass of wine, like he did at the Wolf House.

He looked gorgeous, standing there in her kitchen, all dressed up and concentrating on serving her. Gorgeous and dangerous. She had to stop thinking that way about him. Her mid-life crisis was tumultuous enough without adding Zach to the mix. Plus, she would never cross that particular line and jeopardize their friendship.

Damn her raging hormones.

Zach opened the bottle with easy expertise while she slipped two goblets out of the hutch and set them on the counter. He poured Buena Vista Sheriff—one of her favorites. Out of habit, they swirled the rich purple wine in the bowls of their goblets and studied the red blend as in warmed and opened in their hands, quietly evaluating the fingers and bouquet.

"Here's to rescuing damsels in distress," Sarah finally said, raising her glass.

"Here's to keeping me out of prison." He clinked the fragile curve of her goblet and took a sip.

"You've got that right. Because in that suit, you'd be targeted for sure in prison."

"Really?" Still holding his glass, he clasped the fronts of his suit jacket to display his trim figure. "Do I look like a San Francisco type in this outfit?"

"You look..." She swallowed another gulp of wine, struggling to come up with a politically correct term for his appearance without betraying her private thoughts. "You look great, Zach. I mean it."

His eyes twinkled as he took a sip without breaking his gaze.

She cut off the connection to rake an appreciative path down his dress shirt and trousers. "All that rugged charm."

"You make me sound like a piece of real estate."

"No, I mean you could be a model," she added. "You really could."

"Probably make more than working at the bar," he mused. "But then I'd miss your smirking Scottish mug."

"You wouldn't."

"*Aye. I would.*" He mimicked her Scottish accent but did it surprisingly well. His baritone burr rumbled across the island, all the way to her bones. She sucked in a breath and commanded her body to behave. No way. Never Zach.

She put an end to the nonsense flaring between them by setting her glass down with a clank.

"I have to take that shower," she said. If she had any sense, she'd make it a cold one. She hurried down the hall to the safety of the master bathroom.

Sarah was an expert wardrobe changer. She could get off a plane, shower, freshen her make-up and slip into business attire before her first cup of hotel coffee brewed. She went through her usual routine and minutes later emerged from the master suite dressed in the blue Kate Spade dress and her nude slings, with her hair pulled into a messy roll, a vermillion silk wrap around her shoulders and pearl earrings dangling at her jaw. She plopped the beaded clutch on the island and loaded it with her extra car key, lipstick and cards while Zach placed the goblets in the sink.

She snapped the clutch and slid it toward her.

"Ready?" Zach asked, raising both brows as he took in the change in her appearance.

"*Aye*. Let's catch a crook."

She led the way to the front door and was surprised when he reached around her to open it.

"By the way," he said, stepping back to allow her to exit the house. "I've never seen you in a dress."

"Good or bad?"

"Nice. Even better," he wiggled his eyebrows. "We match."

To her dismay, she realized he was right. Her blue dress and red accessories were the same hue as his navy suit and red tie. "Oh, *gawd*. We'd better go in through separate doors then."

"Right. What will people think?" He smiled, obviously not worried about it.

She stepped onto the porch, and a breeze ruffled her silk wrap. While she caught the ends of the fabric, Zach locked up. Then he trotted to the passenger side of his truck to open the door for her again. She wasn't accustomed to such gentlemanly manners.

She had to admit, she liked it.

Sarah settled into her seat and pulled the seatbelt across her chest. Her left breast protested when she brushed it with the side of her hand. Hormones. She was a walking hormone lately. More reason to return Doctor Dena's voice mail because she didn't think hormones played a part in IBS or stomach cancer. Maybe it was breast cancer. She would phone her on Monday. First thing.

That is, she would if she had a phone. *Bollocks.*

Zach drove up to the main road and headed for Sonoma where the auction was being held at the old Sebastiani tasting room.

"So, you never said where Courtney was," Sarah remarked, fishing for information.

"That's right. I didn't."

Zach turned onto Highway 12. He fell silent, concentrating on the road, with both hands gripping the wheel. A gold signet ring glinted on his right hand.

"Don't want to talk about it?" Sarah asked.

"Nope."

She sat back. He was loyal to a fault or hiding something. Either way, it was none of her business.

"Can you go any faster, Zach?" she asked. "I'm hoping to be able to bid on that PVZ."

"Already going five over."

"Floor it. We need to find out who's selling your Zinfandel."

Chapter 24 | Auction Antics

Regardless of their matching outfits, Sarah walked into the event space with Zach, who carried a felt bag that contained a bottle of wine.

"You brought your own tonight?" she teased. "Sharing?"

"Nope. Just the real thing in case we need it later."

"Good thinking."

Theyx checked in to get their bidder cards and wove through the crowd toward the auction hall. The fragrance of food wafted around them, teasing her, as Matteo and his crew finished dinner for the upcoming gala. Arthur Chen, who was enjoying a tasting at a side table with a colleague, nodded at them as they walked by. People greeted her and Zach as they passed, and no one seemed to question that they were attending without their partners. In fact, many of them waylaid Zach to comment on the last-minute lot of Paradise Valley Zinfandel that had been donated anonymously (wink, wink), and how determined they were to be the highest bidder. That suited Sarah's plan just fine.

Sarah could hear the drone of the auctioneer's voice rising and falling in the room ahead. She turned the corner and spotted Sheriff Bradley, dressed in a black suit and standing in the auction hall doorway with Kelley, monitoring the proceedings and scanning the participants.

Sarah waved at Kelley, who wore a bright green dress that complimented her auburn hair, a black gaucho hat and black, sparkling heels.

"Hey, Sarah," Kelley greeted.

At the name, Bradley pivoted. "Where have you been?" he demanded, glancing from her to Zach and back again.

"You found her, Zach," Kelley interjected, deflecting her boss's rude question.

"I did."

"Thank goodness."

Annoyed by the inane niceties, Bradley stomped up to Sarah—so close, she could smell his irritation as it flared to the surface and clashed with his Joe Malone cologne. Someone should have informed him that wearing a fragrance to a tasting was frowned upon. Fortunately for Bradley, the Joe Malone was subtle enough to get by without eliciting too many sniffs of disdain.

"I went to pick you up at six, like we agreed," he said, his nostrils flaring. "And you weren't there."

"I had business," she retorted. "And FYI, I didn't agree to being picked up."

"I told you that I needed to go undercover to this." His eyes glittered down at her. "And here I am with Detective Miller. It's like the whole damn crime unit is on duty."

"I doubt anyone cares."

"Your little business escapade—or whatever you've been up to—" he shot a second glance at Zach and back to her, "—could have ruined everything."

"But it didn't." Sarah kept her attention fastened on his face. He was jealous. Of Zach. For no good reason. She felt no need to assuage him. He had ignored her preference to attend the event alone. That he had showed up at her house despite her refusal to go with him was his problem, not hers.

And a red flag as to his character. "From what I can tell, no one suspects a thing."

"How can you be so sure?" Bradley rolled his eyes. His muscular jaw worked as he fought to maintain his temper. "I don't see Girard around—do you?" He held out both arms, frustrated and fuming at her. "And I don't want to have to tell the commissioner that I couldn't apprehend Girard tonight—because my civilian girlfriend botched it."

"I am not your girlfriend."

"Then what in the hell would you call it?"

"Wait a minute." Zach shouldered closer to the sheriff. "There's no call to go talking to Sarah like that."

"You stay out of this, buddy." Bradley shook a finger at him. "This is between me and Ms. McKee."

"Not anymore, Bradley. Step outside."

Bradley clamped his jaw shut and glared at Zach. He blinked rapidly. Sarah hoped he was reviewing the last few minutes and seeing how much of an arse he appeared to everyone but himself.

Before Bradley could answer Zach's challenge, Kelley reached out and touched Sarah's arm. "Are you okay, though, Sarah?" Kelley squeezed her forearm. "We were worried when you didn't show up. What happened?"

"I got waylaid by Girard. He and his girlfriend stole a pallet of wine from the Friskes."

"They did what?" Bradley boomed, more upset and louder than ever.

The sound of his voice made heads turn in the last few rows of the auction hall.

"Let's move," Sarah suggested. She backed around the corner, out of earshot of the crowd. Steven and Kelley followed, anxious to hear what had happened regarding the case. Zach remained at her elbow. She was glad to have him as her ally.

"They stole a bunch of wine. Loaded it into a truck."

"Did you get the license plate?" Bradley asked.

"No, couldn't see it. It was a small white truck, though. Like a U-Haul one. I only saw it from the back."

"They locked her in a wardrobe," Zach explained, impatient.

"But from what I could glean of their conversation, they did something stupid to or with Salgado. Maybe killed him. Chris also shot Bill to make it look like a triad killing."

Bradley pursed his lips, doubtful. "Why would he do that?"

"He thought he was doing Maeve a favor. Covering for her. Because Maeve poisoned Bill earlier that night."

"So, who actually killed the victim?"

"That's the million-dollar question, isn't it?"

Bradley frowned. "The only real evidence we have is the gun."

"But it wasn't Zach doing the shooting. By Girard's own admittance."

Bradley's frown deepened. He cast a dark glance at the man standing at Sarah's elbow, but he didn't apologize for having accused him of murder.

"Nice work, Sarah," Kelley remarked.

At least Kelley appreciated the trouble Sarah had gone to. Bradley said nothing. It was clear that he was still nursing the broken date wound and her refusal to submit to his demands.

She leveled her gaze on his, as upset with him as he was with her. "I suspect that Girard will show up after the auction. He looked like he was dressed for the gala."

Bradley shifted his weight and frowned, as if he resented having the case solved by his civilian "girlfriend" and having his evening plans hijacked.

"And the lists, I believe you will find," Sarah went on, "once you apprehend the stolen goods, will show the fakes that are contained in the lot."

He heaved a resigned sigh. "I'd better call this in. Get the highway patrol involved." Bradley reached for his phone.

"I assume the girlfriend and the truck are waiting for Girard somewhere. They're headed for Mexico eventually."

Bradley nodded, punched in a number and held the phone to one ear.

"Plus, they stole my car. Red Triumph."

Bradley called in the details of both crimes and then slipped his phone into the chest pocket of his suit. "You'll be needing a ride home then. Afterward."

"I can take her," Kelley put in.

"I will." Zach's hand gently cupped her elbow. "It's on the way for me."

"As well as for me," Bradley countered. "I go right up the highway to Santa Rosa."

"But you'll be busy," Zach said, "Processing criminals."

"If I catch the bastard."

"Then I'd better keep out of the way. I'll stay in the back." Sarah slipped out of Zach's grasp and stepped forward, unencumbered by male attention. "Zach?" He followed, ready to accompany her, but Bradley blocked their path.

"You're *my* cover, McKee. Not his." He held out his elbow. "Don't mess this up."

Sarah ignored his outstretched arm and detoured around him. She felt the heat of his exasperation on her back.

"Wait. Put this on." Kelley lifted her hat and settled the black felt hat on Sarah's hair. "You won't be so recognizable with a hat. In case Girard comes early."

"Good point," Sarah replied. She adjusted the hat to tip over one eye. "How do I look?"

"Great," Zach said before Bradley could respond. "All that rustic charm..."

Sarah tried not to smile. She didn't want to have to explain the private joke to the other two standing in the hall. To cut off any more questions, she headed through the doorway to the farthest corner of the room, while the auctioneer introduced the final item of the night. A frisson of anticipation shot down Sarah's spine.

It was showtime.

"And now, ladies and gentlemen, a real treat from one of our own. A rare—and I do say rare—case of Paradise Valley Zinfandel."

Zach and Kelley found chairs near the front. Much to Sarah's dismay, Bradley lowered his lean frame into the chair next to hers in the back.

"This vintage is the lost year, ladies and gentlemen. 2016. We all know what happened that year. So many harvests were ruined. But Zach Sullivan managed to salvage enough grapes to produce one of the greatest Zins I've ever had the pleasure to taste. Who will start the bid on this exceptional lot of Sonoma's finest? Do I have nine hundred?"

Sarah fingered the edge of her bidding card, ready to raise it, but she didn't have to. Scores of white cards appeared above the heads of the crowd. She smiled, pleased that her plan to catch the counterfeiter was still on track, but even more pleased that Zach's expert winemaking skill was being recognized. After all he'd been through, he deserved it.

Bradley, though, must have misinterpreted her smile.

"We still good?" he had the nerve to ask—and an even greater nerve to place a hand on her knee.

She didn't look at him. "Not by a long shot, pal." She lifted his hand and returned it to his thigh as the auctioneer droned on.

His confused stare drilled into her.

"I thought you wanted to protect your reputation," she said, keeping her voice low.

"I'm not ashamed to be seen with you." He scanned the crowd. "We're in a relationship. People should know."

"I'm not ready to announce that, Steven. I thought I made that clear."

"When will you be ready?" He looked down his nose at her. His eyes were hard.

"*Dinnae ken*. And when I do, I'll tell you."

"Well, I'm not the type of man to sit around and wait."

"Your choice, pal." She cut off the conversation by raising her card.

"One thousand to the lady in the hat," the auctioneer pointed the gavel at her.

Sarah could feel Bradley sulking in his chair beside her, but she didn't look at him again. She refused to let his pouting spoil the evening.

Her stomach growled. She hadn't eaten all day. Or the night before. She looked forward to the banquet and a meal cooked by her favorite chef. She hadn't consumed a decent dinner since the curry on Sunday night.

Curry. Sarah thought back to her meal at Delhi Garden and how crowded the place had been. She remembered how Maeve Friske had berated the waiter for taking so long to fulfill her take-out order. Bill had eaten curry the night of his death, according to Maria. So, the oleander might have been put in the spicy food to mask the taste. If the forensic team checked the curry and found enough poison to kill a man, they would have the evidence they needed.

She barely registered the bidding all around her, but she did notice Kelley walking toward them. The auburn-haired officer knelt beside Bradley's chair.

"Just got a call from CSI," she said. "They found something in Salgado's car."

"What?" Bradley asked.

"A cigarette lighter."

"Prints?"

"Running them."

Sarah bent forward to look past Bradley's shoulder to her friend. "Anything specific about the lighter? Does it have a gem on the side?"

Kelley repeated the question into her phone. She peered up at Sarah. "Matter of fact, it does. A ruby, looks like."

Sarah nodded and sat back. "Evidence right there."

"Pointing to whom?" Bradley demanded.

"Girard. He had a lighter like that the other day. I'll bet he drove that car to Bodega and stashed it after killing poor old Woody. And the lighter must have fallen out of his pocket."

"Why keep the car, though?" Bradley asked. "Why not drive it over an embankment or something?"

"Like I said before," Sarah replied. "He's not the greatest critical thinker."

"Unfortunately, the lighter is only circumstantial evidence if we can't link Girard to the prints."

"And his prints have to be in your database."

"Correct."

"Or you can get them later."

"Correct."

"But if the prints do match, that means Girard is somehow connected to SS Wines," Kelley mused. "For sure, if he stashed the car there."

"Or he could be framing somebody," Sarah put in.

"What if he is SS Wines?" Kelley continued. "What if we've been wrong all along, thinking there are two people involved?"

"We'll find out soon enough," Bradley remarked. "There he is."

Sarah pivoted in her chair to see Chris Girard saunter into the auction hall. Bradley shifted in his seat and was about to stand up, but Sarah clutched his forearm to stop him.

"No," she warned. "Not yet."

"Commissioner's orders," Bradley shot back.

"We have to wait for the gala, Steven. Let this play out. Please."

Bradley's hard glance skewered hers. "If Girard embarrasses Maeve Friske, my career will be on the line."

"If she's the killer, then she deserves to get embarrassed."

"But what if you're wrong?"

Still clutching Bradley's arm, Sarah leaned forward again. "Kelley, can you ask your colleagues if they still have the trash from the Friske residence? See if there's a container of curry in it? Or test that blotter again? For oleander this time. And right now?"

"Sarah," Bradley protested, shaking his head and glaring at the ceiling.

Kelley paused, the phone clamped to her ear, unsure how to proceed.

"Humor me," Sarah said. "It's not going to cost you."

"I have a feeling it will." Bradley sighed. "All right. Go ahead, Kelley." Then he looked down at Sarah. "You owe me for this."

Sarah sat back and watched the auctioneer pound the gavel to announce the highest bid on the PVZ—more money than Sarah had ever known a Zinfandel to garner, and the highest-ranking auction item of the night—as she had hoped it would be.

"The way I look at it, sheriff," she quipped without looking at him. "It's you who owe me."

Chapter 25 | Gala Collapse

When the last dessert had been delivered and devoured at the Flight of Fancy charity dinner, the auctioneer marched up to the podium and leaned close to the microphone. Proud of herself, Sarah put down her fork. She'd limited herself to a single bite of Matteo's delicious chocolate cake.

"Ladies and gentlemen, may I have your attention?" The auctioneer waited for the buzz of voices and clink of silverware to subside. "Thank you for another spectacular Flight of Fancy, made more spectacular by being held in public this year."

The audience erupted in vigorous clapping.

"Our hearts go out to all those who lost loved ones to the pandemic. Truly, it has been a challenging two years. And I, for one, appreciated the opportunity to see all of you in person at this marvelous event. It was wonderful. Absolutely wonderful."

The audience erupted in another burst of clapping.

"But someone made this event exceptionally special."

He consulted a notecard in his hand. Sarah wondered if Maeve Friske had written the speech for him.

"This someone rose above personal tragedy to help the young patients at St. Francis Children's Hospital. She knew those sick kids were important. And she put her own loss aside to ensure that this charity event would go on as planned. And not simply go on. Be spectacular. That person, ladies and gentlemen, is here tonight. Please welcome your chairperson and our newest favorite resident of Sonoma Valley, Maeve "Hunny" Friske!"

He ducked back and waved her across the stage while applause thundered through the dining hall.

Sarah watched, hands in her lap, while Maeve walked to the podium in her incredibly high heels. Her gait was amazingly natural, as if she wore athletic shoes. Sarah had to admire the woman.

Her perfect figure had been poured into a bronze-colored Saint Laurent laminated jersey dress and shoed in black Manolo Blahnik crystal-toed pumps. Her outfit had to have cost a fortune, certainly as much as the lot of PVZ.

Glittering in diamonds and glinting in metallic fabric, Maeve centered herself at the mic. Like a fawning lackey, the auctioneer skittered forward, elevated the mic for her and dropped back.

Maeve took a deep breath and threw back her shoulders.

"Thank you for coming," she began, surveying the audience below with a queenly demeanor that impressed Sarah—and she'd seen plenty of royals in her day. "As you know, I lost my dear husband, William Taft Friske, earlier this week. I knew he would have wanted me to see this charity event through. It was very important to him. So that is why I am here tonight with you. For my darling Bill and for the children." She bowed her head.

Her elegant pause was immediately filled with applause. After a moment, she lifted her head to cast a sightline over the audience, rotating her skull like the turret of a tank.

"Tonight, we did it together. You got through the pandemic and made it here this evening, and I put personal grief aside to join you. Because you and I know what's really important. The children of St. Francis."

She swept the air in front of her. Her wedding ring flashed in the spotlight, blinding Sarah, even though she sat near the back of the room.

"And tonight," Maeve continued, "I am thrilled to announce that we have raised four million dollars for those children. Four...million...dollars!"

She glowed in triumph, basking in the roar of applause and trying her hardest to project gratitude onto the crowd. Her proud beneficence didn't fool Sarah. She guessed Maeve loved being the center of attention. It was all about Maeve tonight. Above all, she loved being appreciated.

Then again, who didn't?

"Quite the chairperson," Bradley commented out of the side of his mouth.

"Quite the actress," Sarah replied.

The auctioneer strolled to the podium and readjusted the microphone to allow for his lesser height. "Thank you, Mrs. Friske," he announced. "Thank you." He smiled and clapped at her as she took a few steps to the right. "And now, the moment we've all been waiting for—the award for best in show!"

"Tonight's gold medal donor is..." He pulled an envelope from inside his tuxedo jacket and opened it. Then, with more dramatic flair, he slipped out a card and paused to read it. The audience fell silent. "Bud and Whitney Kovac!"

He shaded his eyes and searched the crowd while the audience clapped. "Bud?" he thundered into the mic. "Whitney?"

Chairs scooted backward as an elderly couple made their way to the stage. Event staff helped them up the stairs while another staff member strode onstage to give Maeve two silver trophies, one a round disc and one in the shape of a wine bottle.

After the prerequisite congratulations, Maeve presented the round trophy to the couple who had spent a fortune at the auction. While the audience applauded, the auctioneer took command again.

"And the highest grossing item of the night is...the mystery lot of 2016 Paradise Valley Zinfandel!"

Sarah thought she would go deaf from the roar that exploded. She wished she were sitting next to Zach at this moment. She would have put her hand on *his* knee. And squeezed it. Hard.

But she was here on business. She was here to help catch a murderer and clear Zach's name, not squeeze anyone's leg. She held her breath, expecting Chris Girard to make his move any moment.

"Will the owner of the lot please come forward and accept your award?"

No one stood up. Heads turned toward Zach. A buzz hummed in the crowd.

Then Sarah noticed Maeve flowing back to the microphone.

"Actually," Maeve began with a practiced chuckle. She bent down to the mic. "I have a confession to make. The lot of Zinfandel was part of the collection of my dear husband, Bill. He planned to donate it anonymously. So, I did it for him, after his untimely death." She held up the trophy. "Thank you for this award, Sonoma Valley Wine Association. He would have been so pleased to have accepted this great honor. Thank you."

"He must be rolling in his grave!" a man shouted from the back of the room.

Maeve stared in the direction of the man's voice.

"Pardon?" she quipped.

"I said, he must be rolling in his grave!"

Sarah turned in her chair to see Chris Girard storming down the center aisle in the direction of the podium. Bradley jumped to his feet. So did Zach.

The auctioneer rushed to the podium next to Maeve and put a protective hand on her forearm. He bent to the mic. "Sir, you are out of order."

"No, I'm not. I'm a truth teller. That lot of Zin is totally fake."

"What are you talking about!" Maeve gasped, clutching the trophy between her breasts.

"And you, *Hunny*, are the biggest fake of all." Girard jabbed a finger in her direction.

Maeve staggered to the microphone. "Officer!" she shouted. Feedback whined through the air. "Arrest that man!" Then she staggered backward—one hand to her temple. A second later, she wilted and collapsed onto the stage in a metallic heap. Someone screamed. The auctioneer dropped to his knees beside her. The crowd went crazy.

Bradley dashed to the center aisle while Zach ran to the stage and vaulted up the stairs. He grabbed the microphone.

"Okay, everybody, calm down. Calm down now." He held up a hand and stared at the audience in his steady, unflappable way, as if he were addressing a couple of surly drunks at the Wolf House Bar. The crowd hushed. He looked down at the jumble of jewels and jersey on the floor. The auctioneer nodded.

"Mrs. Friske is going to be all right. She's been under a lot of strain, but she's going to be all right."

Bradley grabbed Girard and yanked the man's arm behind his back, pinning him in place. "Sir, you are under arrest for the murder of William Friske."

Girard struggled against the sheriff. "Are you out of your fucking mind?"

"You have the right to remain silent. Anything you say can and will be used against you..."

"She's the murderer! Tell them, *Hunny*," he taunted, using her nickname. "Tell them what you did! Tell them who you really are!"

Like a monster in a movie, Maeve Friske revived. She lifted a hand to her brow. The auctioneer helped her to her feet. Complete silence fell over the room as Maeve collected herself. She tottered to the podium, her upswept hair tilting to one side. She shouldered Zach out of the way.

"I'll tell you who I am, you pitiful little toad." Her face contorted into a frightening mask that made her look as if a clown had applied her lipstick. "I'm a woman scorned. That's right. I'm a woman who is sick of being misjudged. Sick to death. I am not just a pretty face. I am not a trophy!"

She raised her arm to fling the wine bottle trophy at Girard, but Zach caught her wrist.

"Hey, now," he admonished gently. "Give me that. Should be mine anyway."

Maeve stared at him. "What are you talking about?"

"I'm the only person who owns a case of that particular PVZ."

"No, you aren't."

"With all due respect, ma'am, I am. Not a single bottle of my PVZ has ever been sold. Anyone in the valley could have told you that."

"You're wrong. My husband had a case of it in his collection!"

"That would be impossible."

"Yeah," Girard yelled. "You bitch. You don't know anything! And you think you can fire me? You boob!"

Bradley dragged Girard out of the room.

"What are you saying?" Maeve raked Zach with hot eyes. "That it's impossible?"

"I'm saying that whatever is in that lot of Zin is not the real thing."

"My husband was tricked?"

"Yes, ma'am, he was. Or didn't know about it."

Maeve studied Zach's face for a moment as she digested the possibility and the accompanying ramifications. She maintained her haughtiness and stood there, cool with disbelief. "No," she quipped. "Impossible. I don't believe you."

"There's one way to clear this up." Zach bent to the microphone. "Sarah?"

Sarah sat back, annoyed that Zach had called her out. She had no desire to put herself on display by walking up to a stage in view of hundreds of people. She was a wine detective, not a performing monkey.

"Sarah, you still out there?" Zach shaded his eyes and peered in her direction.

With a sigh, she took off the hat and rose from her chair.

"Can you please come to the stage?" Zach scanned the audience. "And Rick, can you get that case of PVZ up here? Kelley, can you fetch two glasses from out front? And a corkscrew? And bring my tote?"

A man exited a side door as Sarah made her way to the stage, feeling a hundred pounds overweight. She clattered up the stairs in her uncomfortable slings and joined Zach and Maeve at the podium. Maeve's cold stare swept over her. Sarah returned the inspection, all the while wondering how the woman could stand in front of so many people and act so superior after she'd killed her own husband. That kind of arrogance took a bucketload of sangfroid.

Zach shook Sarah's hand and guided her to the podium. She was surprised by the way he had taken control of the situation. She had never seen him in action in public like this. He was a natural born leader.

"For those of you who don't know Sarah," Zach continued. "She's our resident wine expert. She travels all over the world helping collectors verify potential investments. And testifying at trials. If there's anyone who can spot a fake, it's our own Sarah McKee. Sarah?"

Sarah was surprised when the crowd erupted in clapping again. She gave a small wave but held back from the microphone. She had never been a comfortable public speaker.

Then off to the left, Rick rolled a cart onstage, loaded with the box of PVZ.

"Can I open it?" Zach asked Bud and Whitney, who now owned the lot and might choose to gamble on its value by keeping their purchase intact.

"Go ahead." Bud clasped his hands in front of him and stared at the wooden box. "I'm as interested as you are in vetting this stuff."

Deftly, Zach pulled the cover out of its tracks and set it on the lower rack of the cart. Then he reached in and pulled out a bottle. For a moment, he inspected the label and capsule while the crowd hummed. Then Kelley ran up the steps and onto the stage, holding two goblets, his felt tote and the wine opener.

Zach put the bottle from the box onto the podium. Then he slipped the second bottle out of the tote. He flipped out the little knife nestled in the corkscrew.

"*Dinnae* need to do that," Sarah said.

Surprised, he lowered the knife. "You're not going to taste them? Make a comparison?"

"*Dinnae* have to." She held out her hand for the bottle taken from the wooden box.

"What's going on here?" Maeve demanded.

"Counterfeiting, Ms. Friske, that's what." Sarah rotated the bottle in her hands and inspected the label. Then she nodded and gave the bottle to Maeve.

"I'm afraid your husband was hoodwinked," Sarah remarked.

"Preposterous!"

"How can you be so sure?" The auctioneer peered around Maeve's shoulder to study the bottle.

"The counterfeiter who's been making fakes here in the valley was quite good at his craft. But he was also cheeky."

"What do you mean?" Zach pulled a second bottle from the box and studied it.

"He signed every fake label he made."

Kelley hovered at Zach's elbow. "He did what?"

"He put a little mark on the back label. You probably don't see it."

Four heads bent closer to their bottles of wine.

"Most people wouldn't bother to look at the back label of a wine bottle. Certainly not at the volume amount, because it's always the same on a standard bottle. Seven hundred and fifty milliliters."

Zach and Maeve rotated their bottles. Heads bent down.

"Look at the zero," Sarah instructed.

Maeve squinted and brought the bottle closer to her face. "There's a dot on mine, but isn't that a smudge?"

"Good printers don't produce smudges." Sarah said nothing more. Zach lifted a second bottle from the box and rotated it. Then a third.

"So, every fake the counterfeiter made has a dot in the zero," Zach mused. "That way, he could spot his own work."

"Exactly. And blackmail people, should he choose to." Sarah turned to Maeve. "Like your husband. Right, Ms. Friske?"

Maeve bristled. "I have no idea what you're talking about."

"And Bill suspected you were in on it because of your little April Fool's joke."

"I would never!" she shot back.

"Everyone in the valley knows Zach Sullivan is sitting on his 2016 PVZ. They all assumed he was the anonymous donor. But it was you. You offered that lot to charity, unaware that such a case couldn't exist in a collection. Because you're new here. You had no idea."

"That's right. I didn't."

"Who brought the Zinfandel to your attention?"

"My husband's property manager," she replied. "The man who's been arrested. Chris Girard."

"Well, Ms. Friske, looks like you've been punked." Sarah clasped her hands in front of her dress.

"And blackmailed twice," Kelley put in. "Right?"

"Yes," Maeve exclaimed. "And I must say, I'm outraged! Utterly outraged!"

"Do we get our money back?" Bud Kovac inquired.

"Of course, you do," Maeve replied. "We will straighten this all out."

"Okay. Here." Bud relinquished the trophy to the auctioneer.

"So, who gets the award?" The auctioneer looked to Zach for direction.

"The next highest bidder." Zach patted the smaller man on the back. "I'm sure you can take it from here. Ms. Friske needs to see a doctor. Make sure she's all right."

Maeve wrapped her hands around Zach's elbow. "Thank you," she said grandly, back to her normal regal self.

Zach had saved her from public ridicule. Sarah admired him for his gentlemanly treatment of her. But Zach didn't know about the curry.

She followed Zach and Maeve off the stage, with Kelley at her heels. The gala was over for them. It was time to handcuff Maeve "Hunny" Friske and throw her in the squad car with Chris Girard. Or, at the very least, take her to the station to play them against each other.

But they didn't get the chance.

Chapter 26 | Running for It

Sheriff Bradley met them in the pool of light at the main entrance. "Mrs. Friske, I'm going to have to ask you to come down to the station. Answer a few questions."

"Now?" Maeve drew to a halt. "It's eleven o'clock!"

"I'm well aware of the time, ma'am."

"I'm injured!"

"You can ride with me or Detective Miller." He nodded at Kelley. "Take your pick."

"But I have to go to the ER. I've had a fall."

"That's it. You're going with Detective Miller." He ushered her toward the parking lot, as a figure in a ball cap darted to Bradley's vehicle. He'd parked near the exit and had left his SUV running, intending to transport Chris Girard after he'd detained Maeve Friske.

"Hey!" Sarah yelled.

The female peered over her shoulder at Sarah and then yanked open the rear door of the SUV. Girard rolled out and dashed down the sidewalk to the vacant field at the edge of the Sebastiani property. If he made it very far into the gloom, they would never find him without a searchlight. He galloped into the oleander bushes, hands cuffed behind his back, and disappeared.

Bradley and Zach took off after him, but Girard had a good head start.

Maeve pivoted, taking advantage of the distraction to make a run for her car.

"Oh, no you don't!" Kelley grabbed her bangled arm. "You're staying with me."

Before Sarah could decide what to do and how much she *could* do in her tight dress and uncomfortable shoes, she saw the figure in the ball cap sprint back to the road, where a white truck idled, it's driver's door ajar.

"It's her!" Sarah exclaimed. "Blondie!"

She scampered as fast as she could after Girard's accomplice and was surprised to spot her little Spitfire parked a couple of cars down. Girard must have driven it to the event. Again, a stupid move. Or maybe he had planned to leave it there to be found. After all, they were—in the broadest definition of the word—colleagues.

Blondie hopped in the truck and pulled away from the curb, while Sarah scrabbled through her clutch for her spare key. Then, with an agility she never knew she possessed, she sailed over the side of her sports car, plopped into place and fired the engine. Just like a movie star.

For once.

Grinning, she sped after Blondie, barely noticing the chill of the April evening. Her grin soon faded to a grimace, however, when she considered her options. The lumbering truck would never outdistance her peppy little Triumph, but what would she do once she caught up with Blondie? She didn't have a weapon. She didn't have a cell phone. All she had with her was a purse and a ballerina puppet.

She had to believe that something would transpire to help her apprehend the woman. Maybe Blondie would make a wrong turn. Maybe Girard would break his ankle in an unseen gopher hole. Something had to stop their escape.

The truck rumbled up the road to the hilly acreage north of town, an area of narrow, winding lanes and dead ends. At least the topography was in Sarah's favor. But why was Blondie driving into the hills? To intercept Girard? They must have a rendezvous spot up there. Or was she counting on Girard being able to follow the white truck?

Sarah sped alongside the truck and crowded close, trying to force the vehicle off the road. Blondie lurched to the left to sideswipe her. Sarah braked, tires squealing, and narrowly avoided a collision. She let out a puff of relief and shifted down. She had to come up with a better strategy. Her little car could never stand up to the heavy-framed truck.

As soon as Blondie guided her vehicle back into position, Sarah sped around her and slowed, hoping to stall the truck's forward progress. Blondie pulled into the opposite lane, taking a blind curve with little regard of oncoming traffic. A pickup coming in the opposite direction blared a warning as it barreled toward them. The headlights blinded Sarah. Her heart surged into her throat, choking her with fear. She dropped back, and the white truck whipped around her to the correct lane without a moment to spare.

Sweating now, Sarah drove onward, wondering how she would ever stop Blondie. In her little car, she was like a bumblebee bothering a bear.

Then, off to the right, a careening figure struggled out of the ditch and onto the road. Sarah slammed on her brakes. She could see Sheriff Bradley and Zach in close pursuit. Kelley's squad car swept up beside her, lights flashing.

Blondie must have been looking in her rear-view mirror at her pursuers and not at the road ahead, because she plowed into Girard and knocked him off his feet. Horrified, Sarah yanked the wheel to avoid hitting him a second time. She skidded into the other lane and fishtailed into the ditch. Her car sailed headfirst in the weed-filled ravine and lurched to a stop.

Unhurt but shaken, Sarah scrambled out of the Triumph, still intent on stopping Blondie.

The truck screeched to a halt a few feet from Chris Girard's crumpled body. Sarah watched, expecting Blondie to leap out of the cab and check on Girard. To Sarah's utter disbelief, she saw the vehicle roll backward, alarm beeping. Blondie backed over Chris Girard, just as he raised his head from the pavement.

Sarah's mouth dropped open in shock. Blondie had deliberately run over her accomplice. She had killed a man in front of two law enforcement officers. She must be dumb or desperate or a complete loony.

A second later, the truck's gears ground their way from reverse to drive, but not quickly enough to outrun Sheriff Bradley. He jumped onto the running board of the passenger side and whipped out his concealed firearm.

"Halt!" he yelled. "Police!"

The truck lumbered to a stop. Zach knelt beside Girard's crumpled body.

Kelley hurried toward them, her gun drawn, her phone at her ear. She was probably calling for an ambulance. Sarah scrambled up the ditch and joined the others.

Blondie dropped out of the truck and held up her hands. "It was an accident!" she said. "I didn't see him."

"Tell that to a jury. Not me." Bradley kept his weapon trained on the woman as he gestured for Kelley to cuff her.

"What did I tell you?" Kelley said as she walked past Sarah. "They always come in threes."

Sarah's throat tightened. For once, she had nothing to say. There was no place for rejoinders when it came to critical injury and death. She looked up to find Blondie glowering at her. If looks could kill, she would be shot, beheaded, flayed and impaled upside down on a blunt pole.

Sarah broke off the stare and stumbled to Zach's side, where he knelt next to Chris Girard. She put a hand on his shoulder, more to support herself than to help. She forced herself not to look at the bloody mess on the road or the fuming killer. Instead, she stared down at Zach's glossy black hair. "Is he dead?"

"Pretty sure." Zach rose, his expression grim. "You all right?"

"Just a wee rattled. Not sure about my car, though."

Zach looped an arm around her shoulders and tucked her against his warm body. She let him hold her, glad for his strength while hers leaked out of her shoes.

"Anya Sarnova," Sheriff Bradley announced. "I'm arresting you for vehicular manslaughter."

"Go ahead." She curled her shapely lips and held out her wrists. "It'll never stick. I know people who know people. And you don't have a clue who I am."

"Sarnova isn't your real name?" Kelley cuffed one wrist.

"Do you think I'm an idiot?"

"So that's why we couldn't find anything on her, boss."

Bradley nodded, deep in thought, as he watched Kelley secure the woman's wrists.

Zach stuffed his hand in the pocket of his slacks and held out a small gold band. "Maybe this will help."

Sarah recognized the hair tie that had kept her prisoner in the wardrobe. Even in the dim beam from Kelley's squad car headlights, she could discern a few broken hairs wrapped around the braided elastic. Zach had possessed the forethought to save the hair tie. The man was a rock star.

Bradley held out a hand while he evaluated Zach and then Sarah, trying to make sense of their relationship as they stood side by side.

"It's hers." Zach nodded at the blonde. "She used it to trap Sarah back at the house. Maybe there's some DNA that will help identify her. And if you can't get her on homicide, you can nail her for wrongful imprisonment. I'll testify."

"Bastard," Anya muttered. "Stupid men." She surveyed Chris Girard's remains, her mouth contorted in a cruel line. "I'm so over fucking, greedy, stupid little men.

She and Maeve both.

Come to think of it, maybe Sarah was over men, too.

But not Zach. Never Zach.

Sarah felt the long, intense day sucking the final dregs of her energy. She slumped against her friend, grateful for his body heat and relieved that she had been able to prove his innocence at last.

As if from a great distance, she heard the sheriff reciting Anya's rights while he dragged her to Kelley's vehicle. The ambulance whined into view, red lights casting a glow across the tops of the oleander bushes along the road.

The gala had ended, but in a more deadly way than Sarah had expected. They still didn't know for certain who killed Bill Friske and Joe Salgado, but at least they had a better suspect in hand.

Zach looked down at her again. "You sure you're all right, Sarah?"

"*Aye*. I'm fine. I'm fine."

"You can get your car tomorrow. C'mon, I'll take you home."

Not a chance in hell. In her traumatized state, she knew she would have no defense against her raging hormones. She couldn't risk riding anywhere with Zach Sullivan or allow her traitorous breasts to come anywhere near his rustic charm. Reluctantly, she pulled out from under his arm.

"I'll be fine." She pasted a confident smile on her face. "I just need to get my baby out of the ditch and see if she's drivable. Can you lend a hand, Steven?"

"Sure." The sheriff padded over to her. "No problem."

While she put the car in neutral, Steven and Zach planted their palms on the hood of her little car and pushed it out of the weeds.

Within minutes and no worse for wear, she was on her way, driving past the old Sebastiani Winery, top down and heater blasting, safe and secure and alone. Just as she came abreast of the parking lot, however, a familiar figure in a white jacket flagged her down. She shifted to a stop.

"*Amoré*, are you okay?" Matteo jogged up to her side of the car. "We saw the ambulance go by. What happened?"

"Some woman ran over one of our chief suspects."

"Our?"

"I'm helping Kelley with a case."

"Oh. Who got run over?"

"Chris Girard. Manager of Paradise Valley. Former manager, that is."

Matteo shot a glance up the road. "Is he all right?"

"He's dead."

"*Cara*!" he exclaimed. "You must be traumatized."

"I'm fine."

"I will drive you home. I can leave. The staff can handle the clean-up." He pulled open her car door.

"No, Matteo." She grabbed the handle and closed it. "No need."

"For you, anything. You know that don't you, Sarah?" He reached for her hand, but she grabbed the wheel to avoid his false demonstrations of love. Even though he might have the best of intentions, his words no longer rang true.

She left Matteo standing in the road, watching her drive away. She motored past the plaza, which was lit up with late Friday nightlife and throbbing with music. She turned west and rolled out of town. Then she drove the few miles north to Glen Ellen.

Home.

Chapter 27 | The "P" Word

Five days later, Sarah walked into the Wolf House Bar to meet Kelley. Only a handful of patrons sat in the corner. It was Wednesday, after all. Not one of the busier days for the saloon, which meant more time to enjoy banter with Zach. At the sound of the bell tinkling, Kelley turned on her stool at the end of the bar.

"Speak of the devil," Kelley said.

Zach stopped polishing the wine goblet in his hand and looked up. "Goldilocks," he greeted.

"You two talking trash about me?" Sarah plopped her bag on the bar and sat next to Kelley.

"Where've you been?" Zach set the goblet down in front of her.

"Learning how to cook."

"Good." Kelley smiled and patted the top of her arm. "You need to take care of yourself, Sarah. It's important."

"Duly noted."

"Ready to be stumped?" Zach raised a brow.

"Always, pal. Just a wee sip, though."

Smiling, he bent for a bottle he'd stashed below the bar. All Sarah could see in the bag he'd twisted around the bottle was the glass opening, which reminded her of the mouth of a fish. As Zach poured the mystery wine, she watched the frothy, purple liquid rocking in her goblet. The wine settled into place to reveal a sumptuous robe glinting with ruby and garnet lights.

"Elegant," she murmured, sliding the goblet toward her. "Looks like velvet."

She swirled the wine without lifting the glass off the bar and watched the colors luminesce in the light from above. She could almost taste the richness—the lush, amazing, heartwarming thickness—of the wine in front of her.

Then she lifted the goblet and lowered her nose into the opening.

"Good *gawd*," she exclaimed.

Zach leaned closer. "What do you think?"

"I haven't smelled a cab this opulent in my entire life."

"Screaming Eagle," Kelley guessed, glancing at Zach. "It's Screaming Eagle. Am I right for once?"

"No, you are not." Zach smiled and crossed his arms over his chest, enjoying the game.

Sarah basked in his warm gaze but didn't search for clues in his expression. She didn't have to guess what wine this was. She knew, without tasting a drop.

"This is Figure." She tipped the glass to gaze at the wine again.

"Figure?" Kelley asked. "Never heard of it."

"You will." Sarah took a tiny sip and let the gorgeous cabernet sauvignon caress every taste bud in her mouth. Then she looked up to find Zach gazing at her intently.

"Figure," Zack's brows drew together. "I don't get it."

"Figure was the father of a new breed of horse. A uniquely American breed. The Morgan Horse. He could out-pull, outlast, outrun and outsmart any horse of his time. Just like you, Zach."

Zach flushed but never broke eye contact. She could tell by the patches of red blooming on his cheekbones that her praise had touched him.

"You calling me a horse, McKee?" he chided.

"Better than being called a horse's ass, right?" Kelley giggled. "But since when did you become a horse expert, Sarah?"

"Since forever. I was crazy about horses when I was a *wean*. You can put Figure's story on the back label."

"I could," Zach mused. "I like it."

"And people like a good story," Kelley added.

"Especially ones with good endings," Sarah took a second sip and closed her eyes. "And my *gawd*, Zach. This cabernet of yours has a finish I can't even begin to describe. And I'm the expert."

"This is your wine, Zach?" Kelley reached for the goblet. "Let me have a taste."

Reluctantly, Sarah released her hold on the glass and let Kelley slide it away from her.

"You shouldn't have any more anyway, Sarah."

"What, has she joined AA or something?" Zach inquired.

Kelley gave Sarah a loaded stare and nodded her head in Zach's direction. "Tell him."

"Tell him what?" Zach demanded, curious.

"There's nothing to tell." Sarah glared at her friend. "I'm just limiting certain foods."

"Because you're..."

"No, I'm not."

"You're not?" Kelley tilted her head, dismay plainly seen on her face.

"Sorry to disappoint you." Sarah covered her own disappointment with a sad smile. "But I've got PCOS."

"What's that?"

"Polycystic Ovary Syndrome. I finally had time to see my doctor."

"Ovaries?" Zach exclaimed. "Talk amongst yourselves, ladies. I'm out of here." He left to help a customer.

"It happens sometimes when you stop using the pill," Sarah explained.

Before Kelley could ask anything more about her condition, the door burst open and the bell tinkled so violently, it almost took flight. Sheriff Bradley tromped into the saloon. His gaze flitted over the three of them. For a moment he paused in the center of the saloon and studied them, as if perplexed to find everyone smiling at him. His stare landed on Sarah.

"Thought I'd find you here," he blurted. He marched forward, dressed in a uniform that looked as if he'd pressed it within the hour. He nodded at the others. "Miller. Sullivan."

"Boss." Kelley patted the bar next to her. "Join us?"

"Well, okay, but only for a moment." He sat next to Sarah, his back ramrod straight. "I'm off duty, but still in uniform." He adjusted the knot of his tie to tighten it, not loosen it.

Bradley appeared to be utterly uncomfortable. Sarah wondered what was making him more nervous—sitting in a saloon or sitting with a group of human beings.

The sheriff planted a sinewy hand on the bar. At the movement, the face of his Apple watch glinted. Or was it a FitBit?

"I stopped by to tell Sarah some news, but she wasn't at the house. So, I came here."

"Good guess, boss."

Sarah looked over at her friend. "Am I that predictable?"

Kelley shrugged and smiled. "You kinda are."

"But since you're all here," Bradley continued, still earnest. "I'll take the opportunity to inform you that the case is solved."

"That's good news," Zach said. "Very good news."

"Mainly for you." Bradley pointed at Zach. "It was touch and go, Sullivan. A real close call."

"I wasn't worried. Kelley always gets her man."

"Don't I wish," Kelley rolled her eyes.

"So, what did happen?" Sarah asked, after Zach took everyone's orders. "Who killed whom?"

"Well, turns out Anya Sarnova had a bunch of aliases. All of them criminal. She was recruited by Chris Girard for Maeve's April Fool joke. Sarnova, in turn, suggested Joe Salgado as the counterfeiter. Salgado was her client or partner or lover or all three. Still don't know."

"SS Wines," Sarah murmured.

"Yep. Girard had no connection."

"Nor did I," Zach put in, acidly.

"Just doing my job, Sullivan." Bradley took a sip of his soda without looking at the bartender.

"Zach is one of the good guys," Kelley said. "I tried to tell you."

"Yes, well, next time I'll know." His lips twitched into a fleeting smile.

Sarah studied the sheriff's stern profile. Was the man softening a wee bit? She couldn't believe it.

"So, what about Maeve?" Sarah asked, still curious about the details. "Did she crack under pressure?"

"Technically, she did not kill her husband. She thought she had, but there was no oleander in the curry."

"What?" Sarah leaned back in surprised. "How could that be?"

"I finally got the autopsy results. Apparently, Bill Friske had a massive heart attack. He didn't succumb to poison at all. He had a coronary that night. The gunshot finished him off, but he would have died regardless."

"There was no oleander in the food?"

"None. The housekeeper recognized the plant and didn't put it in. But she didn't tell anyone. She was afraid Maeve Friske would fire her for disobeying orders."

"Good for Maria," Zach said.

"We still don't know why Girard shot his boss, though. And why he missed the first time by such a wide margin."

"You found two bullets?" Zach asked.

"Yeah, one that went through Friske's head and one that hit a chair beside the window."

"Why shoot a chair?" Zach mused.

"That's easy," Sarah replied. "Girard probably fired the gun to scare Bill into giving up the list. Because the list was a link to the Salgado murder. We don't know if Girard intended to do more to his boss once he got the list back because Bill started having a second heart attack. That's when Hunny walked in."

"Why would that make him shoot Friske?" Kelley asked.

Sarah turned to her friend. "He freaked, I bet. He probably thought he had caused the heart attack and would be held responsible. And Hunny was freaking out that Girard had shown up during her poisoning attempt. She didn't want to be accused of murder. So, she goaded Girard into putting her husband out of his misery. He was going to take them all down. Including her. Girard never was much of a critical thinker."

"And just happened to have a gun on him?" Kelley asked. "Why was he even there that night?"

"According to Sarnova, Girard was called to the Friske residence." Bradley placed a hand over his muscular forearm. "Bill accused him of counterfeiting. Said he had a list to prove it. Said he was going to the police unless Girard told him who he was working for." Bradley shook his head. "Sarnova didn't tell us anything about her involvement in the crimes, but she told us plenty about Girard. According to her, he was the ringleader. Responsible for everything."

"I doubt that." Sarah raised the glass of Diet Sprite to her lips. "What about Joe Salgado? Who killed him?"

"We're pretty sure Sarnova did. He got too big for his britches and threatened to explain the list he'd sent to Bill Friske, if he didn't get a higher cut of the profits. Sarnova and Girard were selling tons of fake wine out of Friske's cellar, using Friske's documentation of the real stuff. They were making a fortune and Salgado wanted some of it. Good thing is, if we can't prove Sarnova killed Salgado, we have enough on her to keep her locked up for life."

"But where in the heck did Sarnova and Girard get my dad's gun?" Zach asked, crossing him arms.

"Girard found it stored in the basement. Along with your grandfather's collection of lighters. And helped himself."

"So, Maeve Friske is innocent," Sarah murmured. "I had it all wrong."

"Kind of innocent." Bradley shrugged. "It's a fuzzy line, though."

"But the case is closed," Sarah said.

"Yes. Thanks to you for figuring out what those lists were. And, okay, I admit it, thanks to Sullivan."

"Well then," Kelley held up her beer. "Damn! Here's to us. To quote Hillary Clinton, 'It takes a village.'"

"It certainly does," Sarah concurred, raising her soda.

The four of them clanked their glasses together.

"Welcome to Sonoma Valley, sheriff," Zach said.

"Okay." Bradley shook his head and bit back a begrudging smile. "Yeah. Here's to Sonoma Valley."

"Because," Sarah added. "To quote my dad and Dorothy Gale, 'There's *nae place like hame*.'"

Zach reared back, feigning shock. "Wait. Dorothy Gale was Scottish?"

They all laughed.

In that moment, Sarah knew that although her marriage was ending and she was struggling to redefine the future, she had all she needed.

Right here. Right now.

Author's Note

This book was inspired by an actual (and super mysterious) list that came in with a wine shipment from a collector who died soon after from mysterious circumstances. Thank you to Kyle Nichols for sharing the enigmatic list with me and propelling my writing into an exciting new genre.

The setting of this novel was inspired by my deep love for Sonoma Valley, a place I was fortunate to live for seven years. There's no place like it. And no better grapes than those grown along Sonoma's Highway 12. Pure sunshine and love in a glass.

Thank you to Benziger, Gloria Ferrer, Kunde, Lake Sonoma, Rams Gate, Roche, St. Francis, Valley of the Moon, Viansa, and Whitehall for many wonderful hours sharing excellent wine and conversation with friends, family and my beloved pooches.

Acknowledgements

My gratitude knows no bounds for my daughter, Jessica Cavoretto, who is always game to talk plot with me and offer insights into the human psyche, no matter how late in the day, no matter how often. Not many people are willing to indulge a writer like that! I appreciate her dedication to making every one of my books a better novel.

I would also like to thank The Bad Boys Book Group (unofficial title) for offering to read and review my works in progress. Ladies, I value your opinions so much and stand in awe of the number of books you manage to read each year! Donna Nichols, Martha DuHamel, Nole Ann Ulery-Horsey, Sidni Sobolik and Pat Lagerwey, I owe you each a bottle of 2016 Zinfandel—or maybe even a case!

Lastly, I would like to thank my critique partners, Beth Barany and Kay Keppler for their support and encouragement. It's hard to believe we've been "meeting like this" for twenty years. How time flies when you're immersed in the craft of writing.

Don't miss out!

Visit the website below and you can sign up to receive emails whenever Parker French publishes a new book. There's no charge and no obligation.

https://books2read.com/r/B-A-BYGY-SMSIC

BOOKS 2 READ

Connecting independent readers to independent writers.

About the Author

Parker French is a mystery writer from the Bay Area of California. She lives on a lagoon with her Scottish husband and two wee dugs.

* 9 7 8 1 7 3 5 0 8 2 8 4 4 *